NINE CROWS FOR A KISS

VERNON OICKLE

Cover design: Rebekah Wetmore
Editor: Andrew Wetmore

ISBN: 978-1-998149-81-0
First edition May, 2025

Moose House Publications
2475 Perotte Road
Annapolis County, NS B0S 1A0
moosehousepress.com
info@moosehousepress.com

Moose House Publications recognizes the support of the Province of Nova Scotia. We are pleased to work in partnership with the Department of Communities, Culture and Heritage to develop and promote our cultural resources for all Nova Scotians.

We live and work in Mi'kma'ki, the ancestral and unceded territory of the Mi'kmaw people. This territory is covered by the "Treaties of Peace and Friendship" which Mi'kmaw and Wolastoqiyik (Maliseet) people first signed with the British Crown in 1725. The treaties did not deal with surrender of lands and resources but in fact recognized Mi'kmaq and Wolastoqiyik (Maliseet) title and established the rules for what was to be an ongoing relationship between nations. We are all Treaty people.

Also by Vernon Oickle

One Crow Sorrow
Two Crows Joy
Three Crows a Letter
Four Crows a Boy
*Five Crows Silver**
*Six Crows Gold**
*Seven Crows a Secret Yet To Be Told**
*Eight Crows for a Wish**

Life and Death after Billy
Friends & Neighbours: a collection of stories from the Liverpool Advance
Busted: Nova Scotia's War on Drugs
Queens County
Ghost Stories of the Maritimes (volumes 1 and 2)
Dancing with the Dead
Great Canadian Ghost Stories Volume II (co-author)
Disasters of Atlantic Canada: stories of courage and chaos
Canada's Haunted Coast: true ghost stories of the Maritimes
The Editor's Diary: the first 13 years
Angels Here Among Us
Red Sky at Night
South Shore Facts and Folklore
I'm Movin' On: the life and legacy of Hank Snow

Beaches of Lunenburg-Queens
Nova Scotia Outstanding Outhouse Reader
Red Coat Brigade
Ghost Stories of Nova Scotia
Kiss the Cod!
Strange Nova Scotia
Newfoundland and Labrador Outrageous Outhouse Reader
Where Evil Dwells
How to talk Nova Scotian: the Bluenoser's book of slang
The Nova Scotia Book of Lists
My Nova Scotia Home
We Love Nova Scotia: a people's portrait
More Ghost Stories of Nova Scotia
Queens County: a history in pictures
The Second Movement: Nova Scotia's outrageous outhouse reader No. 2
So you think you KNOW Nova Scotia?
Forerunners: Harbingers of Death in Nova Scotia
Through Rain, Sleet or Snow: rural mailboxes of Nova Scotia
Grandma's Home Remedies

* available from Moose House Publications
moosehousepress.com

Thank you,
Brenda and Andrew

Nine Crows for a Kiss

Nine Crows for a Kiss

Prologue

The future. A constant state of flux. Nothing is certain. Nothing is carved in stone.

The nine crows know this all too well.

The world is quiet this morning. As are the crows. Ever vigilant, the large black birds watch over this territory, protecting it from evil forces while safeguarding those who call this place their home.

Perched atop the highest pine trees, they have a clear view of the entire town that hugs the Atlantic coast. They watch, their keen, pellet-like eyes in constant motion, searching for clues, piercing the veil of darkness, looking for anything that seems out of the ordinary. They remain especially alert for signs of trouble.

The nine can sense something sinister hovering on the horizon. There is a ripple in the universe. They feel it. They know it.

The majestic black birds are frozen in place. Snowflakes float effortlessly through the crisp early morning air, spreading a clean blanket of white over the town and masking the evil that lurks in the shadows.

The birds quickly turn to white as snow jackets their ebony feathers. Never to be fooled; never to be lulled into a false sense of security, they remain vigilant. There's a storm coming, a powerful tsunami of danger that promises to be unlike anything they've ever experienced.

They are keenly aware of a new threat festering below the surface. It is ready to burst like a pus-filled boil, unleashing unholy hell on the unsuspecting residents of Liverpool, Nova Scotia, the epicentre of death and mayhem throughout centuries.

As they huddle together for warmth on the branches of a stately pine that towers high above the other trees in the forest, they have no idea what's coming. But their collective senses tingle. They are on high alert, and the nine black sentinels stand ready to spring into action, knowing that the time will be soon.

Waiting. Watching. Willing to do whatever it takes to fend off anyone or anything that threatens their turf. The crows must defend those they are destined to protect.

That is the pact, their inherited duty. That is their reason for being—their *raison d'etre.*

Like their brethren before them over the centuries, no matter what is coming, the crows know what is expected of them and they are always in attack mode—ready to face the onslaught of evil.

1: Abandoned

It's the kind of cold that takes your breath away and causes your eyes to water; the kind of cold that freezes the tiny hairs in your nose in a second.

He hates the cold, always has, and these frigid mornings are getting the best of him. He needs a break. It's only December 31, but it has already been a long winter. Spring seems so far away. He's sure he'll never make it.

He doesn't like the early shift, especially in the winter when the morning weather is frigid and bitter, and the cars are covered in thick layers of ice and snow. Yes, he hates it. He despises having to clean off the vehicle before he can start his early patrol, but he understands it comes with the territory.

Besides, Constable Warren Hamilton thinks as he navigates his fully-equipped RCMP Ford Explorer along Highway 103 from Liverpool to the Lunenburg-Queens County line, the defroster blasting out the heat that provides a respite from the cold, *this is what I signed up for. It's what I wanted. Right?*

"Yeah, right," he whispers. He sighs heavily.

Just doing what you gotta do, he thinks.

"Clearly, I didn't think this through well enough."

He makes this drive every day, five days a week, on a rotating basis with three other officers, and he will travel this route several times during his shift, watching for speeders and other careless drivers, people who think that it's okay for them to thumb their noses at the law while jeopardizing the lives of others.

It's a particularly challenging drive this morning as the quickly-accumulating snow is making it difficult to maintain a steady speed, his Michelins unable to find good traction on the already-slick pavement.

"You're the one who put in for the job on highway patrol," Lisa, his wife of twenty-eight years, tells him every time he complains about having to get up early in the winter to clean off the car. Her sarcasm is not lost on him.

"If you didn't want the crappy hours, you should have stayed on regular duty, where you were perfectly content," she quickly adds whenever he brings up the subject.

And she's not wrong, he thinks, his thoughts wandering to a warmer time of year. He dreams of sunshine and hot, sticky weather. He has never been a winter person and the humidity that comes with summer doesn't really bother him. He seldom, if ever, complains about being too hot.

"You just have to take it in stride," he tells anyone when they complain about the heat. "Pace yourself and avoid over exertion. Stay in the shade if you can, and drink lots of fluids, especially rum and beer."

He smiles at the thought, wishing he were somewhere else right now, some place hot with lots of alcohol, free preferable.

I think maybe a trip to Cuba for February or March is just what the doctor ordered, he decides, wondering how he'll convince Lisa to leave their daughters alone for a week—maybe two—so they can go south and bask in glorious sunshine.

No children allowed, he thinks, knowing full well that when he suggests the trip Lisa will insist they bring the girls with them. He doesn't want that. He wants time alone with his wife. He needs time away from the stress, and that includes the children.

It's not that he doesn't love his daughters—Bree and Lauren are his whole world—but he longs for a vacation when he can lie on a beach or sprawl beside a pool, bask in the glorious sunshine and suck back the drinks without worrying about the kids. Even though he knows the girls are old enough and no longer need babysitting, he also knows that he and Lisa would spend every waking hour with them.

Not the kind of vacation I need, he thinks as the snow continues to build up on the highway, the tire tracks made just a few minutes earlier by the vehicles before him quickly disappearing. *And there is no reason why their grandmother can't come and stay with them for a few weeks. She would love that; I know she would, especially since she didn't get to see them at Christmas. She loves to spoil the girls, so why not let her?*

He needs a break, so he hopes he can convince Lisa to leave the girls at home. "But I doubt it," he whispers, aware that he's alone in the SUV. "It would be nice, though. Just the thing to get a fella away from this white shit for a while. And it would allow me to hit the reset button."

Remembering their last trip to Cuba five years ago, he thinks, *you gotta love all-inclusive*, just as the 2018 red Kia Stinger comes into view again.

"What the hell is it with that Kia this morning?" he mutters.

He is certain the car wasn't there yesterday, when he made his final circuit on the route, so it must have been left here sometime between 2 pm yesterday and 5 this morning, when he made his first run.

This is the fourth time this morning that I've driven past this car in the last hour and a half, and it hasn't moved an inch, he thinks, slowing to a crawl as he eases his SUV past the vehicle that's pulled onto the shoulder of the road near exit 18.

Not quite in the ditch, but pretty god-damned close to it, he thinks, doing a quick visual examination of the car that will soon be nearly invisible in the steadily falling snow.

"And where's the driver?" His gut tells him he needs to take a closer look at this one.

There's not a soul in sight and, while he's not sure what's going on here, he knows something's off. He thought that earlier this morning when he first spotted the car, but now its presence is getting the best of him.

Time to check this out.

He switches on the red and blue police lights mounted on the roof of the SUV, which automatically activates the four-way emergency flashers. Seeing the coast is clear, he makes a couple of quick U-turns in the highway so he can approach the car from the rear again. He pulls over just a few metres behind the Kia and comes to a complete stop. In this position, he can see if anyone is moving around inside the car or if anything is happening around the outside of it.

Without knowing why, Warren shudders. *Something doesn't feel right.*

Picking up the mic to the radio transmitter, he calls in: "21C1 will be out with an abandoned vehicle. It's a red 2018 red Kia Stinger, with a Texas plate."

I think. The plate is pretty much obscured from a build-up of snow and dirt.

He continues: "Just west of the Brooklyn Intersection, Highway 103."

"10-4," the pleasantly-sounding dispatcher immediately replies.

Nice woman, Warren thinks, grabbing his force-issued fake-fur hat and gloves from the passenger seat. He pulls them on as he watches the snowflakes land on the windshield and melt instantly before the wipers swipe them away. The defroster has been blasting or the past two hours so their demise was certain.

Those fuckers were goners as soon as they landed on the hot glass. He smiles as he relishes the sight of the melting snowflakes.

"Take that, you little bastards," he says with a chuckle. He knows his deep, ingrained hatred for snow is not normal, or at least that's what Lisa tells him.

But what the hell does she know about it? She just doesn't understand. Some people hate sushi, mowing grass, grocery shopping, gravy on their mashed potatoes or buying new shoes. I hate snow, so sue me.

Opening the car door and pulling his six-foot, three-inch body from the cruiser, Warren quickly scans the surroundings and is relieved to see nothing out of the ordinary. He wonders where the driver has gone and *why did they leave their vehicle here on the highway with a major snowstorm forecast to hit? It's an accident waiting to happen.* His thoughts are grim. *People these days are fucking fools.*

"It will definitely have to be moved before the plows start rolling." Talking to himself is a habit he formed many years ago and, like most idiosyncrasies, it's a hard one to break.

A large transport truck crests a small hill and barrels past him without slowing down, throwing the wet, slushy snow at him.

Instinctively, he grabs his hat to keep it on his balding head. "You prick. If I wasn't busy right now, I'd pull your ass over and you would get one helluva of an earful and a huge fucking ticket."

Moron!

Approaching the rear of the car, he pushes down on the trunk cover with his gloved right hand, something rookies are taught in basic training because, as the instructors say, you never know if someone could be hiding in there, waiting to jump out and do God knows what.

"Nothing," he says, relieved. Moving to the front door of the Kia, he carefully grabs the door handle, gives it a tug and finds it's either locked or frozen solid.

"Oh, for fuck's sake."

I ain't got time for any bullshit this morning. He's relieved, but also puzzled, when the door flies open on this second try. *Who in their right mind would abandon a nice car like this with the doors unlocked?*

He knows there's no cure for stupidity. *And whoever owns this car must be pretty stupid to just leave it here, unattended.*

"Stupid or in a rush ... or up to something."

Glancing around at the isolated, wooded area, he thinks, *but in a rush to do what?*

"There's nothing out here except woods and snow. Where would they go? Unless someone else picked them up?" He shrugs at the suggestion. "Maybe."

With the door open, Warren cautiously sticks his head inside the car and quickly scans the interior, casting his eyes over the front and back seats, their black fake leather still looking like the day they came off the assembly line.

"Nothing," he mutters. "Not a god-damned thing." Pulling his head back out and straightening up, he adds, "This is fucking weird."

He moves to the back of the car and brushes the snow and dirt from the license plate. With the number memorized, he returns to the warmth of his police SUV, instinctively locks the door behind him as he was trained to do and retrieves the mic.

"Dispatch, 21C1. Can you run Texas plate number TLK 4308?"

"10-4 21C1. Stand by."

"10-4," he replies, resting the mic on his right thigh and glancing at his watch.

Fuck, he thinks, realizing that it's only 8:44, which means he still has at least another five hours to put in before his shift ends.

Since it's December 31 and he has the next four days off to make up for working Christmas Day, and Canada Day earlier this year, he's looking forward to kicking back and relaxing for a bit. *Think I've earned a break.*

He's also looking forward to attending Cliff and Julie Graham's annual New Year's Eve party tonight. He and Lisa have been going for the past five or six years. *It's always a blast. Cliff is such a great guy. Glad we met him after we moved here.*

"21C1, dispatch." The voice of the friendly dispatcher brings him to attention.

"21C1 here. Go ahead dispatch."

"That plate has been flagged by US authorities," she reports. "There is an alert on that number."

"What is the alert?"

"That vehicle was reported stolen in Houston, Texas."

"10-4. When was it stolen, dispatch?"

"Five and a half years ago."

He wasn't expecting that information. "Please repeat, dispatch."

"10-4 21C1. That vehicle was reported stolen five and a half years ago in Houston, Texas."

Warren sucks in a deep breath of air and almost chokes as his lungs feel tight. "Dispatch, please send back up and a tow truck."

"10-4. En route."

"10-4," he says, placing the mic back on the dash.

Stepping back out into the biting morning air, he grumbles, "Now, what in the hell do you suppose this is all about?"

He wonders how the car got all the way from Texas to the South Shore of Nova Scotia. "What are you doing here? What have you been doing for the past five and a half years? And where's the driver," he asks.

A loud, cackling noise suddenly breaks the stillness of the frigid winter air. The sound leaves him weak in the knees.

"Shit." His breathing immediately becomes laboured, his lungs suddenly feeling as though someone has reached through his chest and is mercilessly squeezing the organs in their bare hands, choking the life out of him.

"Crows," he whispers. "This can't be good."

2: Party planning

"Take heed, New Year's Eve revellers, Environment Canada has issued a severe storm warning for the entire province as a major nor'easter bears down on Nova Scotia," the radio announcer's nasally voice drones on in the background as Julie reviews her plans for tonight's party.

His voice grates on her nerves. To her, it sounds like the guy is talking with a clothespin clamped on his nose.

"It looks like this is going to be a doozy, folks, so check those generators and snowblowers, and make sure you have lots of gas on hand," the announcer continues. And don't forget to stock up on those storm chips."

She takes a deep breath. *Now this isn't going to be good.*

"According to radar imaging, the storm will pass directly over Nova Scotia and it is expected to arrive sometime in the next twenty-four to thirty-six hours, the announcer continues. "The worst part is that the monster storm may linger over the province for at least a day, and it could bring anywhere between one and one hundred fifty, maybe even two hundred, centimetres of snow in some areas."

Julie shudders at the thought. *Holy Jesus.*

"You better take this seriously, folks. Emergency crews are on high alert and Nova Scotia Power crews are already on standby with emergency centres being set up across the province," the announcer explains.

Julie takes a sip of her black coffee. She likes it strong and prefers instant over perked coffee, especially on a day like this. Perked coffee leaves an aftertaste in her mouth, as if it was burnt.

Maybe we should cancel the party for tonight, she thinks. *That would be the smart thing to do, but if I know Cliff, he won't have any of it. He looks forward to this party every year, and it will take more than the threat of a major blizzard to deter him.*

Turning her attention back to her to-do list, she takes another deep breath and exhales forcefully. "We'll see," she murmurs.

"This one is going to pack a punch," the announcer drones on. "But don't panic."

"Yeah, right," she says, as if the guy can hear her. "You're talking about Armageddon and telling us not to panic. What is wrong with that scenario?"

I hate this guy, Julie thinks, but she listens to his broadcast every morning just the same, mostly to get caught up on the day's news. *It's certainly not for the music they play, if you can call it that.* She shakes her head and turns up her nose, as if someone else can see her. *I can't stand that crap.*

"Homeowners are encouraged to check their emergency supplies and Nova Scotia Power says you should always be prepared for power outages of no less than three days in any major storm, no matter the time of year.

She knows they are prepared for the storm, as Cliff thinks of everything, but power loss is one of her greatest worries whenever.

"Hey, Jules," Cliff Graham, the retired RCMP corporal, says entering the kitchen. "How's it going? I'm getting really excited for the festivities tonight and seeing everyone. It will be great to catch up."

"I know you are, Cliff," she answers. Her voice cracks with concern.

"What's wrong?" he asks, detecting her angst. They've been married for almost forty years, if you don't consider the four years they were divorced, so he knows when something is bothering her. "Aren't you excited about the party?"

"I was." She forces a smile. "Right up until I heard this morning's forecast about the storm."

"Oh that." He shrugs. "I heard that too, but it doesn't sound like it's anything we have to worry about today."

"I don't know. It sounds pretty serious."

He takes a seat across the table from her. "I know you worry when you hear about these storms, but that's part of the plan. They just want to throw us into a panic, so we run out and buy stuff like loads of storm chips." He grins. "I think the weather announcers must be getting kickbacks from the chip companies."

She chuckles nervously. "You think?"

"It will be alright, Jules. That thing isn't supposed to get here for another day or two, so it won't affect the party. And if it does, I've got two good generators ready to go and lots of gas to run them, so we'll be alright." He smirks. "What better place to be in a big storm than hunkered down with a friend who has a huge generator? Besides, a good party is just what everyone will need to take their minds off the mess that's coming."

"I don't know." She grimaces. "It's already been snowing out there for a while. Do you really think anyone is going to feel like partying tonight? I'm not sure I'm in the mood after hearing the forecast."

"You aren't suggesting we should cancel the party, are you?"

Julie looks at him. He raises his right eyebrow, as he always does when he's about to go on a rant. "Come on, Jules, that little bit of snow coming down right now won't slow people down. Have any of our friends called to cancel because they are afraid of a little bit of snow?"

She shakes her head. "I haven't heard from anyone."

"There you go." He smiles as if he has proven a point. "Do you think we can really trust those weather forecasters?"

She squints at him.

He rants on. "Those fucking forecasters and their freaking satellites. They don't always get it right, you know."

She frowns, already feeling defeated by the storm, even though the major blowout is still at least a day away.

"Hey Goggle." Cliff addresses the Goggle Home Nest their daughter Carly gave them for a Christmas present. He grins in Julie's direction. "I hate this technology crap, but I am looking forward to the day when it will fetch me a beer." Addressing Google he adds, "Turn off the radio."

The radio goes silent.

"That will be enough of that shit."

"Turning off the radio won't stop the storm from coming." She shoots him a playful smile.

"Sure, it will." His deep laughter fills the room that Julie completely re-painted a pale green just before the holidays. She had chosen a shade called honeydew, a tone that barely hints at green. "What's that old saying: out of sight, out of mind. Well, in this case it's out of sound, out of mind."

"If only it were that easy."

"You can't let that god-damned forecast ruin our plans. We've been gearing up for this party for a couple of weeks and people are looking forward to it. Shit, *I'm* looking forward to it." He takes a deep breath. "You've got a fridge full of food over there. What are we going to do with all of that if you cancel because of a little snow?"

"A little snow? Have you really listened to that forecast, Cliff?" She stares at him, amazed how her husband can blindly block things out as if wishing them to go away. But he's done that ever since she's known him.

"It will be what it will be." He shrugs. "Let it come. I can handle it."

Leaning back, the kitchen chair straining to hold up his imposing frame, he adds, "Now, what can I do to help get things ready for tonight? I've got to make a run to the liquor store. I'm running low on beer, and if we're going to get snowed in, I don't want to run out," he says with a playful smirk. "Need anything while I'm there? Don't forget, the stores are closing early because it's New Year's Eve."

"Okay, Cliff. You win." She submits to his will. If her husband is intent on having this New Year's Eve celebration, then she decides she may as well embrace it because he will never let it ago. "If you're going to the li-quor store, please pick up four bottles of Champagne. We'll need that to toast in the new year. Better make it six. I don't want to run out." She grins. "And I may need it to help me forget about the snow."

"None of that shit for me." He curls up his nose, a little thing he does when he thinks he won't like something even if he hasn't tried it yet. "I hate that stuff."

"How do you know you won't like the kind of wine I'm getting if you haven't even tried it?"

"I just know." He winks at her. "So, what kind do you want? I know dick-all about buying wine. Why don't you fire me a text so that I get the right stuff for you."

"Get me six bottles of Lightfoot & Wolfville Bubbly White," she tells him, grabbing her phone and shooting him the brand name. "Men," she whispers. "Worse than little kids."

"What the hell kind of wine is that?"

"Oh, Cliff, my dear, we've got to get you some culture." She winks at the burly man across from her. "It's very good wine and it's made right here in Nova Scotia. Just tell one of the clerks what you're looking for and they'll help you find it."

"Will do. Anything else, your Majesty, or will you be satisfied with the wine?"

"All the food and snacks are ready to go. All we'll need is for the people to show up." She pauses. "And you better hope they show up, Cliff Gra-ham, or you'll be eating it all."

"They will." He nods with that self-assured smirk that she's come to adore. "Anything else I can do around here to help before I go?"

"It's all handled, but thanks for the offer. Carly is here, so she can help me do some last-minute straightening up. We'll be good to go once you get back with the wine."

"And beer."

"Yes." She laughs. "And the beer. How could I forget that?"

"Well, that's awesome, honey. I'm always in awe of how organized you are. So glad I married you…twice." He grins. "Speaking of Carly, has she heard anything from that idiot husband of hers? Is the prick planning on gracing us with his presence tonight, or is he too embarrassed to show his face around here? If he's smart, he'll stay away."

"I'm not sure Carly knows for certain what he's doing, but, Cliff, do me one favour, please? If Leo does show up, please don't start anything with him."

"Me? I can't believe you'd turn this around on me. I'm not the one who is the fucking asshole. But if he shows up and starts anything with Carly, I'll end it. I'll end him, for that matter. That's a promise."

"Come on, Cliff. You can't be doing anything of the sort, for Carly's sake."

"It's for Carly's sake that I would put the run to that son-of-a-bitch once and for all. I'll do it for her, if she wants me to, and happily."

Julie knows he means it. "It's not that easy. And you know it. There's a lot to consider."

"Well, I'm pissed at the mere thought of that man having the balls to show up here, after everything that he's done to her."

Julie glares at him.

"You can't expect me to stand back and let him push our daughter around. If he starts anything, I'll throw him out on his god-damned ass." Bringing his left hand to his forehead, he adds, "I've had it up to here with that jerk."

"Just try to remain civil for our daughter's sake," Julie says. She knows that her husband has a short fuse when it comes to anyone threatening his children and grandchildren. She feels the same way, but she also thinks it's better to take a gentler approach rather than having a confrontation, as violence will only make matters worse. "Let's just try to get through one night without an argument, and then we can deal with him in the new year."

"He doesn't deserve civil," Cliff says. "For Carly's sake, I should just lock the fucking door on him and tell him to get lost."

"I don't want him here, either, but we have to at least give him a chance," Julie says, keeping her voice mellow to sooth his rising temper. "That's what Carly wants."

"Why? He's such an idiot…a useless piece of shit. Honestly, I've never really understood what she saw in him in the first place," Cliff says. The first time he met Leo Watkins was seven years ago, when Carly was still in university. "I have no room for him anymore. He's used up all the real estate and I don't care if I ever see him again."

"I feel the same way, but for some reason she still loves him, and she wants to give him a second chance. I've been talking to her about filing for a divorce and staying here with us after the holidays, but I don't think it's working. I just can't seem to get through to her."

"Is he holding her prisoner? Forcing her to stay against her will?"

"I don't know. But you know how it is. Many women in abusive relationships will protect their abuser."

"Whatever the case, it's time that she got away from him. He's already had too many second chances," Cliff says. His eyes narrow in anger as he speaks. "I thought we raised our daughter to be smarter than that."

"We did. The day will come when she sees him for what he really is. But for now, we'll have to go along with whatever she wants."

"I don't have to do anything," Cliff huffs.

She knows he's getting angrier by the second as the tone of his voice is rising and his complexion is turning red. "Now, Cliff. Please don't be like that. Carly and the girls are upstairs, and I don't want them to hear anything."

"Fine." He rises from the chair that looks too small to hold his weight. "I think I'll just go to the liquor store before I say something that will get me into trouble."

"That's probably a good idea." Smiling at him, she adds, "I know you don't like Leo and you have good reason not to like him. I don't like him either. But let's try and tolerate him for Carly's sake."

"You tolerate him, Jules. I'll let him come into the house if that's what Carly wants, but don't expect me to be all warm and fuzzy with the bastard, not after the way he's treated our little girl. As far as I'm concerned, I don't want to ever talk to him or see him again."

Looking straight at his wife, he adds, "When I was in the Force, I saw some things that would make your skin crawl. It would make you want to throw up, that's how bad it was. It's sad what one man will do to his wife and family. Carly doesn't deserve to be treated like that fucking asshole treats her. We have to find some way to convince her to stay with us."

"I've tried, Cliff, believe me. But she's got her mind made up. We just have to give her space and be ready when she needs us."

"Mark my words, Julie. This isn't going to end well."

3: Knock three times

"Good morning, Mom," Carly says as she ambles into the brightly-coloured kitchen, her two small daughters in tow. With their auburn hair and dimpled cheeks, the girls are the spitting image of their mother.

"Where's Daddy? Please don't tell me he's left for town already. I wanted him to pick up something at the liquor store for me."

"Sorry, honey." Julie observes that her daughter looks tired. She can clearly see that the young woman is stressed and the dark circles under her eyes confirm that she has not been sleeping well. "You just missed him, but you could always give him a call. What did you want?"

"I wanted him to pick up a bottle of Grant's Scotch for Leo," Carly replies. Addressing the little girls nipping at her heels, she adds, "You two go sit up at the table next to your grandmother and Mommy will get your breakfast."

"You come and sit right here, my darlings." Julie watches the girls scamper up to the kitchen table. "Nana will get your breakfast." Nodding to her daughter she adds, "I've got this. You go and call your father. I take it that means you've heard from Leo and he's coming tonight?"

"He just called and, yes, he is coming later today. I hope Daddy will be okay with that."

"You know your father, Carly."

"I also know he doesn't like Leo very much," Carly says. Checking to make sure her daughters are secure in the booster seats that sit on top of the kitchen chairs, she adds, "I hope he doesn't start anything tonight."

"I don't think it's your father you have to worry about, Carly."

"Come on, Mom. Not in front of Cara and Cassie."

"I just want you to try to understand why your father feels the way he does." She pauses, studies her daughter's expression and then adds, "Your father may have a rough exterior, Carly, but you and these babies mean the world to him. He will fiercely protect those he loves, and if anyone threatens them, well, then, there's going to be hell to pay."

"I've heard it all before, Mom, and I'm really not in the mood this morning."

Carly pulls her phone from her pocket. "Let me call Daddy and then you and I can go over what you need me to do to help you get this place ready for tonight's soiree."

"I'm not sure how much of a soiree it's going to be if we get stormed out."

"It's not going to be that bad, is it? Leo's driving down from Halifax this afternoon after he finishes work. I hope he gets here before the storm becomes too bad. I'll worry about him driving in the snow."

"Well, then." Julie turns her attention to getting the girls their breakfast. "Maybe he shouldn't come? According to the guy on the radio, it's supposed to be quite a storm. No one would blame him if he couldn't get here."

"You too, Mom?"

"All I'm saying is that with a major storm in the forecast, maybe it would be a good idea to stay off the roads. It would be a lot safer for Leo and you wouldn't have to worry about him."

Carly rolls her eyes. "I know what you're saying."

"You should call your father."

Julie pours Cheerios into two green plastic bowls. Addressing the girls, she asks, "What would you little angels like to drink?"

"Orange juice please," they answer in unison, their lilting voices making Julie smile.

"Okay then. It's orange juice for my two little lovelies."

~

"All right," Carly says, returning to the kitchen a few minutes later. "That's all taken care of."

"Good." Julie is sitting at the table and watching her granddaughters eat their cereal, occasionally reaching across and picking up the loose oat circles that have escaped from the bowls and are resting on the table in small puddles of milk. Smiling at her granddaughters, she adds, "I take it that you caught him then?"

"I did." Carly pours herself a cup of the freshly-perked coffee that Julie had made just for her and joins her mother and daughters at the table. "But I don't think he was very happy to hear Leo is coming to the party."

"I don't suppose he is, but let's not talk about that anymore." She smiles at the little girls. "It's not the right time for that kind of discussion."

"Right. Not the right time." Carly takes a sip of coffee, and asks, "Who's coming to the party?"

"You'll know everyone, or almost everyone. It's the usual crew."

"I assume Kate and Samantha are coming, then? I haven't seen them in a long while and it will be nice to catch up with them."

"They are. We couldn't have a party and not invite them. They're like family to us."

Kate Webster and Samantha Henderson have been part of their lives ever since the Grahams moved to Liverpool many years ago. "You also know Kate's brother, Charlie. He and his wife, Rebecca, are also coming. But I'm not sure if they are bringing Liam or if they are getting a sitter for him."

"Liam must be growing up. How old is he now?"

"Eleven."

"Wow. Where does the time go? I remember when I used to babysit the little tyke. He was such a cute little boy, but hyper-energetic. He could be a handful at times."

"It goes." Julie smiles at her granddaughters. "In the blink of an eye. Just look at how fast these two angels are growing. They aren't babies anymore."

"They sure aren't." Carly reaches out and strokes the auburn hair of her youngest daughter, Cassie. "You know, Mom, Leo and I've been talking about having another baby. He'd like to try for a boy."

"Seriously?" Julie tries hard to bite her tongue as she knows her daughter will be very angry if she says what's truly on her mind. "Now? After everything that has gone on between you two?"

"Yes, I'm thinking another baby might be exactly what we need."

"Funny, I was thinking just the opposite."

"I didn't say we were going to do it." Carly rolls her eyes at her mother again. "I just said we were talking about it."

Julie takes a deep breath. "Please do me a favour, Carly. Don't mention this to your father." She takes a sip of her coffee. "Your father loves these two precious angels more than anything on this planet and you know he would love another grandchild just as much, but he won't like the idea of you having another baby—"

"—with Leo, right?"

"You know how he feels."

"He's made it very clear," Carly says.

"He has his reasons."

"And what about you, Mom? How do you feel about it?"

"You know I would always love another baby, but this isn't about me or your father. It must be your decision, Carly, but are you sure this would be a good time?" Julie smiles at her daughter. "The last six months have been pretty intense, haven't they?"

"Like I said, we're just talking about it." She takes another sip of coffee as the kitchen fills with awkward silence. "Nothing's been decided." She takes a deep breath. "Who else is coming tonight?"

"I'm pretty sure that Kate and Samantha's sons, Hunter and Alex, are coming, along with their girlfriends, Ally and Bree. They are both very nice girls, lovely, in fact. Bree's parents, Warren—your father's brother in arms—and Lisa Hamilton, will be here and, as far as I know, their other daughter, Lauren. She's a cute kid and I'm glad she's doing better."

"She's been through a lot over the past few years."

"She sure has, but I think she's doing better. I'm sure she will enjoy playing with Cara and Cassie. She's a great kid and they'll like her."

"Sounds like you're going to have a full house. Anyone else?"

"Oliver Lewis. You know him, but I don't believe you know his new girlfriend, Dr. Anna Robbie."

"No. I don't believe I've met her before."

"You wouldn't have. She's a psychiatrist who works out of the hospital. She started helping Oliver this summer after that incident at the bridge, when he went missing for three days," Julie explains. "It was the strangest thing."

"Did they ever figure out what happened around all of that?"

"I don't think they know any more than what the news media has already reported, but your father—the cop that he is—believes there was some big conspiracy or something supernatural around the whole thing. I'm not sure I buy any of that stuff. You know him, though. He's into all of that stuff, especially anything that concerns crows."

"Well, whatever happened there, I'm happy to hear that Oliver found someone. He's a really nice man. I've always liked him."

"Me, too, and they seem to have hit it off right away. Oliver's had more than a few rough patches over the years so it's good to see him happy, for once." Julie reviews the party notes scrawled on the pad in front of her. "So, I think that's everyone, not counting you and Leo, and your father and me."

"Sounds like a manageable crowd. And what about the food? Can I help you with anything?"

"No, I think we're all good there. I've been working on the menu for a few weeks. I have already made five dips. I've got hot spinach, crab, baked BLT—your father's favourite—red pepper jelly, which just happens to be my favourite, as well as a pizza dip. I know you like that, so I made that one just for you. I'll just have to heat some of them up when the time comes. And of course, I'll have lots of salsa and nachos. I know everyone likes that."

"They sound delicious, Mom. You have been busy."

"I still have one more dip to make. That's my *famous* Million Dollar Dip. But I want to wait until this afternoon so that it'll be fresh for this evening."

"I love your Million Dollar Dip, but do you think we'll have enough to eat?" She smirks.

"Oh, that's not all," Julie says with a smile. "I've also made bruschetta topped with chopped tomatoes and sweet basil leaves, and sausage rolls, stuffed mushrooms, and hot chicken wings. I've got lots of cheeses, crackers, and all kinds of chips. I also picked up two cold cut trays yesterday and some baguettes. I don't think anyone will go hungry."

"No." Carly laughs. "Sounds like you're expecting to feed an army."

"Oh, well." Julie chuckles. "If we get snowed in, we'll have enough food to last us for a few days."

Turning to her daughters, who have stopped eating, Carly adds, "How are you doing, girls? Done with your cereal?"

They nod.

"Okay then, my lovelies." Julie rises from her chair and reaches out a hand to each of her granddaughters. "Come with me into the den and help me straighten up in there, and we'll let Mommy sit here and enjoy her coffee. How does that sound?"

"You don't have to entertain them, Mom."

"It's no problem. I love spending time with these little rug-rats."

"Okay, then, thank you." Carly smiles. "And Cara and Cassie, you listen to Nana," she adds, watching as the trio leave the kitchen, each girl holding one of their grandmother's hands. "Don't play your grandmother out so she can't enjoy the party tonight."

~

Leaning forward, her elbows resting on the kitchen table, Carly sighs heavily. Smelling the dark roast coffee in her cup, she closes her eyes and thinks about her current situation.

How the hell did I get to this point? Does Leo really deserve another chance? More to the point, can I ever trust him again?...Do I really want another baby right now?

"Jesus," she whispers. "How did life suddenly get so complicated—so confusing?"

She's lost in her own thoughts when three load knocks at the kitchen door suddenly snap her to attention.

"What the hell?" she says, and then yells to her mother, "Someone's at the back door. I'll get it."

Quickly sprinting to the door, Carly pulls back the curtains and peers outside. The yard and driveway are already covered by the quickly-accumulating snow, but there is nobody in view.

"Odd." She shudders.

She cautiously pulls the door open and is stunned as the cold air immediately hits her in the face like a fist. She looks around the yard but again sees no one there.

"That's just freaking weird." She notes there are no footprints in the snow. She shivers, although she isn't sure if it's from the cold.

"Who is it, Carly?" Julie asks, returning to the kitchen.

"It's nobody, Mom." Carly closes the door as cold chills race up her spine. "But I am absolutely positive that I heard someone knocking."

"How many knocks were there?"

"Three. I'm sure there were three very distinct and loud knocks. What does that mean?"

"It's not a good sign," Julie tells her. Taking a deep breath, she adds, "I don't like this."

4: Somebody's watching me

God-damn it, Cliff thinks as he searches the Scotch and Whiskey section of the local liquor store for a bottle of Grant's Scotch. He was having a pretty good day until Carly called a few minutes ago.

I'd like to give him a bottle of Grant's Scotch all right...shove it right down his fucking throat, Cliff thinks.

Feeling a shooting pain radiating from his mouth up to his right ear, he realizes he has been clenching his jaw hard. He only found out in the last few months that his daughter was a victim of domestic abuse, and he's pissed that any man would do such a thing to a woman he professes to love, the woman who is the mother of his children.

That truth has turned him against Leo Watkins forever. He frowns. *The best thing for Carly is to get rid of that piece of shit excuse for a husband once and for all before she becomes another statistic.*

He hates the idea that the man his daughter married is going to be in his house tonight, the same house in which he raised his little girl and watched her become the intelligent, beautiful woman and exceptional mother that she is today. The daughter who gave him two precious granddaughters who melt his heart every time they smile at him.

Taking a deep breath, he tries to control his anger. He knows he will never be able to forgive Leo for cheating on his daughter and, worse still, for hitting her.

"You lay another god-damned finger on my baby girl, and I'll rip your fucking head off your shoulders and pull your fucking heart out through your throat," Cliff told his son-in-law when he learned about the cheating and abuse.

He knows he scared the shit out of Leo, and that was precisely his intention. *Someone had to put the fear of God into that prick.*

As a veteran RCMP officer with thirty years' experience, Cliff has witnessed the pain, heartache and even the death that are the result whenever a man raises his hands against his family. He knows how fast these events can escalate. He also knows there is no such thing as "just a little push," as Leo had tried to explain.

"That better be the last time I hear of you getting physical with my daughter." He had paused for effect and lowered his voice to a growl. "And, if it's not, I promise you that it will be last thing you ever do in this world," Cliff told Leo when he drove to Halifax five months ago to have it out with his son-in-law.

Cliff's eyes roam over the bottles of various Scotches and whiskeys from around the world, lined up on the shelves. *There is no such thing as low-level domestic violence and Julie knows that. I would never have forgiven her if she hadn't told me what Carly had confided in her, and then something more serious had happened.*

He spies the Grant's Scotch on the shelf that's just above his head. *If he steps out of line by even one fucking inch tonight, he's gone because I'll pick him up and throw his fucking ass out in the snow.*

He takes a deep breath. *I should've put the run to that creep the first time Carly brought him home to meet us back when she was still in university. I had bad vibes from him back then and I should've listened to my gut but no, Jules told me to be nice.*

It irks him that Julie would put him in this position. He's sure she knows that letting Leo off the hook goes against everything he stands for, even though she tells him he must do it for Carly's sake. But it's for his daughter's sake that it's best to end the marriage now before something more serious happens.

As he reaches for the expensive bottle of Scotch—*which is way too much to spend on that piece of shit*—Cliff's attention is suddenly diverted to a woman at the furthest end of the liquor isle. He doesn't recognize her in the bulky winter coat with the hood pulled over her head, but he gets the distinct feeling that she is watching him.

Checking me out, Cliff thinks, not sure if he should be flattered by the attention from a young woman or—considering how intensely she appears to be watching him—intimated.

Unsure if he knows the woman, he nods in her direction. In turn, she quickly ducks out of sight behind a shelf.

Now that's odd. Did she just try to hide from me? Cliff wonders. He feels he has seen this woman before, and he wonders why she was watching him.

He quickly moves to the end of the aisle and looks up and down the other rows in the store. He shakes his head, trying to place the woman. *She seemed awfully familiar to me.*

After searching the entire store and not spotting her again, Cliff feels even more puzzled. *Where could she have gone that quickly? Or was it just my imagination? You are getting old, Cliff, so maybe it was nothing.*

He shrugs and returns to get the bottle of Grant's. The incident leaves him feeling uneasy but he decides not to dwell on it. *Got too many other things to do today.*

Pulling the bottle from the shelf and putting it in his cart along with the wine that Julie asked him to pick up for her, he makes his way to the cash registers to pay for his party supplies, the sticker shock from the price of the Leo's preferred brand of Scotch leaves him fuming. *He couldn't just drink something simple, like a normal person. Only the best for him.*

"For Carly," he whispers with a heavy sigh. "Only for her."

~

Cliff slides into the cab of his black Chevrolet Silverado 1500, exhales and pulls the seatbelt across his large body, made even bulkier because of his winter coat.

"Jesus," he says, thinking about the four hundred and twenty-seven dollars he just spent for booze. Even though he's alone in the truck, he says, "Ain't nothing cheap these days. That freaking tax gets you in the end every time—bend over and take it, as they say. What's a fella to do?"

He turns on the truck's ignition. The heater immediately blasts out hot air as Cliff switches on the windshield wipers. *That better do the trick*, he thinks. *There's no freaking way I'm getting out and brushing off that snow. I'll just sit here and wait until it melts.*

Unlike his good friend, Warren Hamilton, Cliff doesn't hate snow. *I'm just too freaking lazy to clean off the windshield. I ain't in the mood for that right now.*

He fumbles with the radio buttons to find something that he likes. *Don't want to listen to any of that shit that Julie listens to.* He remembers that she was with him in the truck the last time the radio was on. He doesn't usually listen to the radio when he's alone, but today, he feels, is a good day for music.

But give me The Doobie Brothers any day over that modern country crap, he thinks, searching for the station that plays classics. *That's when they made good music.*

He settles on his preferred station, surprised when he discovers that one of his favourite songs is playing. *How lucky is that?*

Leaning his head back against the headrest, Cliff is just about to burst into a chorus of *Takin' It to the Streets*, when he notices a tow truck pass by. He sees that it's pulling a red Kia.

Stinger, I think. Maybe a 2018 or 2019. Wonder what's up with that, he thinks as he notices the RCMP SUV following closely behind the tow truck.

That looks like Warren.

He fishes into his coat pocket, finds his cellphone, and makes a call.

"Hey," Warren answers on the second ring. "What's up, buddy?"

"What's happening, Brother?"

"Not much. I'm in countdown mode, just putting in the rest of my shift. I'm really looking forward to your party tonight."

"Me, too. I thought you might decide not to come because of the snow." Cliff clears his throat. "I know how much you hate that shit."

"No way. I've been looking forward to drinking your beer all day and a little bit of snow's not keeping me home."

"I just stocked up. I don't think we'll run out."

"Good thing. I'm ready for a blow-out. I've got four days off after this shift and I plan to make the most of them," Warren says. "Besides, it's New Year's Eve, right? You gotta celebrate in style."

"Exactly. So, what are the roads like out there on the highway?"

"Shitty. I don't think I'd want to be driving too far today. Why? You going somewhere?"

"Not me. My stupid-ass son-in-law is driving down from Halifax this afternoon and Carly will lose her mind until he gets here. Me, I couldn't care less if he gets here or not."

"Come on, Cliff. I know the guy's a dick, but you wouldn't want anything to happen to him, would you?"

"No, I guess not. For Carly's sake," Cliff says. "But seriously, I wouldn't shed a tear over him."

"I get it."

"I'm really not sure how I'll restrain myself if he starts any of his crap tonight."

"I'll hold you back."

"You and what army?" Cliff asks. "Jules has already given me my warning, but you know I'll go full scale ballistic on his ass if he starts in on Carly."

"I'll be there to watch your back," Warren assures his friend. "So, not that I don't like ripping into your son-in-law, but is that why you really called me?"

"I just saw the tow truck go by pulling that red Kia. And then I saw you drive by right behind it. What's up with that? I'm just curious."

"It's the weirdest thing," Warren tells him. "I found the car abandoned this morning on the highway out by the Brooklyn exit. As far as I can tell, it had been there all night."

"I mean, I get it that sometimes your car will break down, but you shouldn't just walk away and leave it alone for a long period of time especially in the middle of a storm. That's pretty dangerous, but you see it all the time."

"Yeah, well, something's up with this Kia. When I had them run the plates, I found out that this car was reported stolen in Texas over five years ago."

"What? Are you fucking kidding me?"

"I'm dead serious."

"So, what the hell's it doing here?"

"I have no idea, but you know how you have those feelings when you know something major is about to happen?"

"I do."

"Well, that's exactly how I felt when I spotted that car. I am positive it means something, and I have a feeling in my gut that it's not good."

"So, what are you going to do?"

"We're taking it to impound, and we've already contacted the Texas authorities to let them know we've found their missing car. We'll wait to see what they want us to do with it. As far as I'm concerned, though, I'd like to figure out who was driving it and where they got to."

"Important pieces of the puzzle. It's going to be hard, though. You don't even know if the driver was alone, or if someone met them out on the highway and took them somewhere. Maybe the driver hitched a ride. They could be long gone by now."

"I know, but I've got to see if I can find them. It's quite the thing to think that a car stolen in Texas over five years ago could end up here. That's not a coincidence. No, there's a lot more to this story, so I'm going to do some digging."

"Well, good luck," Cliff says. He quickly adds, "Just a second Warren. I've got to check something."

"Anything wrong?"

"Not really." Cliff presses the button in the door rest and waits a few seconds as the driver's side window opens, allowing the snow to spill in on him. "I just suddenly had this feeling that someone was outside my truck. But"—he sticks his head out the window and glances around—"I don't see anyone. It's weird though. I could have sworn that someone was out there."

"Little jumpy today, my friend?"

"I wasn't, but all of a sudden I can't shake the feeling that I'm being watched." Pressing the button and watching as the window goes back up into place, he adds, "And I don't like it. If someone wants to talk to me, why don't they just come and see me? I hate these fucking games."

"Trust your instincts, Cliff. And be careful. You know there's crazies out there and you've made a lot of enemies over the years."

"Jesus, Warren. Way to freak me out." Cliff chuckles, although deep down inside he knows that his friend is right. After everything that he's witnessed over his thirty years in police work, he understands that he can't be too cautious. "I'll be careful, but it's probably just my imagination. I've been a little on edge ever since Carly told me that asshole was coming tonight."

"Okay, well, I've got to go. Duty calls. See you later." The phone goes dead.

Cliff leans forward so that he's closer to the large windshield and the heat from the defroster can blast him in the face. He glances around the parking lot, watching as customers race in and out of the liquor store and the grocery store that's right next door. He can't shake the feeling that he's being watched.

5: The nine

When the crows shiver, their bodies adjust to colder temperatures, and they produce five times more heat than normal. In this state, known as torpor, they can maintain a normal body temperature for six to eight hours, even in extremely cold temperatures.

In torpor, the nine are ready for the approaching storm, or at least they are ready for the natural storm that is about to blow in with a vengeance, painting the landscape a bright, stark white.

Most birds in torpor cannot fly, but these are no ordinary crows. They anticipate nature's fury, but it's the other storm that has them on high alert today.

They soar high above the black Chevrolet Silverado 1500 as it leaves the parking lot. There is a sense of urgency within the murder. The members of the flock have seen this type of unusual behaviour in the past. They know when trouble is brewing, simmering, just waiting to boil over like an over-full pot of potatoes.

This pall hangs heavy in the air, and the black birds will return to this human in due course, but for now they must conserve their energy. There are others who may require their help in the coming hours as the monstrous storm front moves in.

As they have done for centuries, the crows will watch over this town and everyone in it. And, whatever is about to happen, they sense that this man will be at the centre of it.

6: Parole violations

"Okay. Thanks, Julie," Samantha Henderson says. "I appreciate the update, and please let me know if there is anything we can do to help."

She pauses, listens, and then adds, "Yes, we will see you later. We're looking forward to it as well."

"Everything okay?" Kate Webster asks as her wife hangs up the phone. "How's Julie?"

"She seems a little stressed right now, which is understandable considering that they are forecasting a major blizzard is about to dump God knows how much snow over us, but I think she's fine."

Samantha sits beside her wife on the beige living room couch. Kate has been there for the past few hours, reviewing notes for a major case that she has been working on for months. It is scheduled for trial on January 3.

"Based on the part of the conversation I heard, I guess the party is still a go for tonight despite the forecast?" Kate quickly smiles before turning back to her papers on her lap.

Samantha nods, gently patting her wife's knee. "It looks that way. Julie said she wanted to cancel because of the storm, but Cliff won't have anything to do with that suggestion. Says he's having a party tonight no matter how much snow we get, and he still wants everyone to come."

"Yup. Of course he does." Kate chuckles, her eyes focused on the file in front of her, as she usually is when she's in the middle of trial prep.

It's a trait that irritates Samantha, but she knows that when her wife is in the zone, she remains laser-focused on the case material. To her credit though, she can still carry on a conversation.

Kate continues, "If Julie suggests cancelling or even postponing the party until the storm blows over, can you imagine how Cliff would react? If he wants to have a party, nothing's going to stand in his way. Not even a major blizzard."

Samantha nods. "Julie says he wasn't even willing to consider putting it on hold for a day or two."

"Well. I can see where he's coming from. This is New Year's Eve, after all, and he's planning a New Year's Eve party. But it won't be much of a party if people can't get there because of the snow."

"Julie says that's what she told him, but you know how pigheaded he is."

"What? Cliff Graham? Stubborn?" Kate laughs. "I never would have guessed."

Samantha grins. "So, considering the forecast, do you think we should just stay home tonight? I did promise Julie we would be there, but if you think it's going to be too bad for us to be on the roads, I can call her right back and tell her we've changed our minds."

"We probably should stay put. That would be the smart thing, but I'd hate to do that to our friends after we promised that we'd be there for them. They are counting on us."

"It would really disappoint them if people started cancelling. If I know Julie, I'm sure she's pulled out all the stops. It would be a shame to let all that food go to waste."

Kate grabs her MacBook Air and clicks on the weather app.

"According to the forecasts, the snow we're having right now is just the outer bands. Looks like the major part of the storm isn't supposed to hit here for another twenty-four to thirty-six hours or thereabouts," Kate says. "If we go to the party, we can always leave early if it looks like the storm is getting any worse."

Samantha nods.

"In the meantime," Kate says, "what are we doing for the rest of the day until it's time to get ready to leave? I don't really feel like going anywhere right now." Glancing at her wife, she adds, "I want to finish reviewing these files, but I'm almost done if you want to do something."

Samantha shakes her head. "I was thinking that maybe, when you're done with your work, we could clean up this place and put the Christmas decorations away. That would give us a jump start on the New Year."

"Really? But we always do that on New Year's Day. That would kind of be breaking with tradition, wouldn't it? I know how you feel about traditions."

"Does it really matter?" Samantha smiles. "It's only one day. Let's just get it done and then we won't have to worry about it tomorrow. We'll be able to shovel snow and maybe even relax and get ready for the new year ahead. God only knows what that will bring."

"Okay." Kate places her files on the coffee table in front of the couch and then gives her wife a quick kiss on the cheek. Pulling her closer for a hug, she says, "Good thinking, but first I want to talk to you about some-thing."

"Now what?" Samantha asks, pulling away. "Whenever you say you want to talk to me about something these days, it's always bad news." She takes a deep breath and then asks, "*Is* it more bad news?"

"Well." Kate hesitates. "It's certainly not good news."

"Oh, Jesus. What now?"

Kate takes a deep breath. "It's about Gwen."

"Lily's daughter? That Gwen?"

Samantha hates discussing this topic. The memories of her best friend Lily's brutal murder that left Alex an orphan will haunt her forever. They'd adopted Alex, as was Lily's wish, and that, to Samantha, was Lily's greatest gift. "What is she doing now?"

"That's just the thing," Kate says. "I don't know. In fact, no one knows."

"What are you talking about, Kate? Isn't she in Ontario? I thought the last notice we received from Parole Services said she was living in a halfway house in Oakville and reporting to her probation officer twice a week."

"She was...until she wasn't."

"I don't understand." Samantha wipes her eyes with the back of her right hand. She always gets emotional when they discuss Gwen.

"I got a call late yesterday afternoon from Parole Services. Gwen failed to report for her last scheduled appointment," Kate explains. "When they sent officers to the house to check on her, they couldn't find her. We are on their notification list so they wanted to give us a 'heads up' just so, you know, we could be on our toes."

This information is hard for Samantha to hear, and she is trying hard not be angry with her wife for withholding the news until this morning. Samantha knows she tends to fret over things and understands that Kate probably didn't want her to worry unnecessarily, but that still doesn't ex-cuse the secrecy.

"What do you mean *they couldn't find her*? Wasn't it part of the condi-tions of her release that she reports to them twice a week?"

Kate nods. "Along with a long list of other conditions that she had to follow, and it seemed like she was doing everything she was supposed to do, until now."

"Jesus Christ, Kate." Samantha pulls back from her wife, her anger boiling over. "And you thought it would be a good idea to wait until now to tell me this?"

"I know I should have told you yesterday, but the woman from Parole Services seemed to think they would locate Gwen by last night and she said she would call me once they had her in custody. But seeing as I haven't heard from anyone yet this morning, I felt you ought to know."

"You felt I ought to know?" Samantha fires back at her wife. "Do you think?"

"I was wrong," Kate replies, her voice mellow and even-keeled, forever the voice of reason. "I should have told you right away when Parole Services called."

"Yes, Kate." Samantha rubs her eyes again. "You should have, but you always think you need to protect me, but I deserve to know about these things, especially when it could affect Alex."

"I'm sorry. I just didn't want you to worry."

"Worry? Why would I worry? Should I worry that Alex's deranged half-sister, the same one who wiped out his entire family, is running around lose somewhere doing God knows what?" Samantha takes a deep breath. "Oh my God, Kate, what about Alex? Is he in danger? Will she come back here after him?"

"I don't think we should jump to any conclusions. It's not likely she'll come back here after all these years. Besides, how would she even get here? It's not like she has any money for travel."

"You don't know that."

"Well, there's a good chance she doesn't have any money as she just got out of prison," Kate counters.

"Come on, you know how devious she is." Samantha tries to calm her nerves but it's not working. She feels like the walls are suddenly closing in on her. "If she wants to come back here bad enough, she will find a way to make it happen."

"What would she want to come back here for?" Kate asks. "Her mother is gone, and her brothers have moved away. The last I heard was that they have cut all ties with her, which makes sense, considering what she did. The only person left is Alex, and she doesn't even know him. He was just a young kid when she went to prison."

"I can think of one good reason for her to come back—money. Alex did inherit a substantial fortune when his parents died. You know that Gwen has always felt she deserved a part of that money. I could see her coming back to get what she thinks is hers."

Kate sighs and then nods. "You are right about that."

"I never understood how she got out on parole in the first place. Why didn't she have to serve the entire twenty-year sentence, which I always thought was too lenient, considering her crimes."

"Because the judge mandated that she had to serve two-thirds of the sentence, which meant she could get out after thirteen years if she followed the rules and did what she was supposed to do, so they let her out with certain conditions," Kate explains. "That's pretty standard practice in this country."

"Well, it's not fair. We see how well Gwen follows the rules."

"We sure do. I'm really sorry about keeping this from you. I was wrong to do that."

Samantha bites her bottom lip, something she does when she's angry, then says, "Yes, you were."

"Are we okay?"

"We'll talk about that later. So, what do we do now? Do we just sit here and wait for Gwen to knock on our front door and ask for money?"

"I'm not sure there's anything we can do except wait to hear from Parole Services."

"Let's not tell Alex about any of this," Samantha says. "I don't want to throw this at him right now, not after everything he's been through this year."

"I don't know, honey. Maybe we should tell him." Kate pauses. "You want to do to Alex what I was trying to do to you—protect you. Is that a good idea?"

"It's not the same thing and you know it. It's different."

"I'm not so sure about that," Kate answers. "Haven't we gotten ourselves into a mess before when we've kept things from Alex *for his own good*?"

"Good point." Samantha thinks about the situation. "I wonder what Cliff would say, if he knew what was going on? Think we should talk to him? We've always trusted him."

"Might not be a bad idea. He always has good advice and somehow manages to see things from a different perspective."

"I'll call him right now."

7: Dreams

Watching the murder of crows circling just above the trees in the snow-covered backyard, Alex Goodwin sighs heavily.

What are you guys up to, he wonders, observing the large black birds swoop and glide on the cold air currents. He knows the mysterious sentinels are always nearby and are forever on alert, fully in tune with the world around them.

Waiting. Watching. Ever ready to react...to protect him.

"Do you see something?" he whispers, leaning closer to the window as if to join them, his hot breath immediately fogging up the cold glass.

Quickly counting the cluster of black birds, he says, "Nine."

For a kiss, he thinks. He frowns, unsure how to interpret that.

"Hey, fellas. You seem restless or agitated. Is something going on?"

He understands that he and the crows are connected on a different plane than this reality. They seem to know what he is thinking and always seem to understand what he is saying. "Tell me, should I be worried?"

"Should you be worried?" The female voice breaks his connection with the crows.

"Yes." He spins around to address his girlfriend.

Ever since the tragic events of this past July, when their best friend, Ozzie Merrick and Ozzie's father tried to kill him, Alex and Bree Hamilton have become very close. She witnessed the attack that night on the bridge. She knows exactly what he's gone through.

"Should I be worried?"

"About what?" She reaches for his hand. "What should you be worried about, Alex?"

He joins her as she sits on the edge of his bed. "I have no idea if there's reason to worry, but whenever I see a large murder of crows hanging around like that group out there, I automatically assume there's something serious brewing."

"I know, Alex." She squeezes his hand gently. "And I know that whatever it is, you will get through it...we will get through it together."

"You're so confident." His mouth twists in a half smile. "But I am not so sure."

"Look at what you've already gone through and you're doing okay now." Bree's voice, gentle and soothing, always has a calming effect on him. "You've been through a lot—more than any seventeen-year-old should ever have to endure—yet here you are. Safe and sound."

"Yes, here I am, lucky to be alive."

He releases her hand, rises from the bed, and moves back to the window to peer out into the pristine whiteness, where the black birds provide a stark contrast to the falling snow. The presence of the crows makes him restless, uncomfortable as if every nerve ending in his body is firing on all cylinders, sending tiny shockwaves throughout his lean body. It feels like he's on fire.

"But something feels off today. When the crows are circling like they are right now, it usually means they are trying to send me a warning."

"About what?"

"I have no idea, but I get the sense there's something brewing. It started when I woke up this morning. It felt like the ceiling and walls were closing in on me, and the feeling in my gut has grown stronger as the morning has gone by," he explains. "It's nagging at me, and I can't shake it. And then the crows showed up, so I know it's all connected. I'm sure they have a warning."

"Or maybe you're just being paranoid," Bree suggests. "Not that you wouldn't have good reason to be paranoid after your past experiences with the crows, but there is another way to look at this, you know."

"How so?" He cocks his right eyebrow in her direction.

"Well, why don't you come back over here again and let's talk about it?" She lightly pats the bed beside her.

He smiles at her. She's been good for him over these past six months, helping to get his life back on track following the devastation of his friend's betrayal. He knows she cares very deeply for him, and he returns the affection. She keeps him grounded. He has never felt like this for anyone before and he believes they could have a long-term relationship.

Moving back to the bed, he chuckles, "All right. If you insist."

She takes his hand again and squeezes. "You know, Alex, I like you very much."

"I like you too, very much."

"And I know that being involved with you also means that I will be involved with the crows."

"I guess."

"No guessing. I've been around you long enough to know that the crows are a big part of you and will always play a large role in your life. I accept that it's part of the package."

"And?"

"And nothing." She smiles at him. Speaking softly, she says, "I understand that if we're going to be romantically involved, then the crows will also be in our lives, and I want you to know that I'm okay with that." She smiles again, her green eyes sparkling. "I know who you are, what you've been through and what those black birds mean to you."

"I can't change that, Bree."

"I'm not asking you to change anything, and that brings me to my point." She takes a deep breath. "Whenever you see the crows clustering around, you automatically think it means something dark and evil is about to happen."

"It usually does."

She shakes her head again. "Maybe you should start to look at the bright side of things."

"Is there a bright side with the crows? Just look at everything that's happened to me in the past."

"It is true that trouble usually follows the crows." She glances out the window as if looking for inspiration from the crows that are gathered in the backyard. "But isn't it also true that by the crows sending you messages, you are always better prepared for whatever is coming at you?"

He nods. "Yes. I suppose I am."

"So, isn't that a positive thing?"

He pauses and considers his girlfriend's observation. Finally, he says, "Yes, that is one way to look at it."

"And that's how I choose to look at it. Whenever I see the crows behaving like this, I know you will be okay because they are there to protect you." She squeezes his hand again. "Look at the challenges you've already survived with their help. It's a miracle you are even here today, and it is because the crows have intervened over the years. They are your guardian angels—your dark and sometimes twisted guardian angels—but they have always pulled you through the darkest times in your life."

"That's a valid point," he concedes. "But it's also true that the crows wouldn't have to protect me if there wasn't so much bad shit happening around me all the time. It's a bloody curse."

"I think it's this simple, Alex," she says. "You have a choice. You can either dwell on the dark forces, the evil and all the bad things that can, and probably will, happen, or you can look at the bright side of things and accept that this is your life. Most importantly though, you must believe that you can get through whatever comes your way."

"With the crows' help?"

"Yes, with the crows' help." She leans in and gently kisses him on the cheek. "And with my help. Just like those crows, Alex, I will always be here for you."

"How can you be so positive that things will turn out okay?"

"Because—and you are going to think I'm crazy..."

"No, I won't. You're the sanest, most grounded, intelligent person I know."

"Don't be so sure." She chuckles nervously.

He knows that's something she always does when she has to discuss an uncomfortable topic with him.

She continues, "You haven't heard what I'm about to tell you. You may want to reserve that judgment until I'm done."

"Okay. So, tell me."

Looking him directly in the eyes, she blurts out, "Because I have seen into the future."

"What?" He pulls back, shocked. "The future? Come on Bree. What are you talking about?"

"See?" She winces. He can see her face is twisted in pain with the thought that he doesn't believe her. "I told you that you'd think I'm crazy."

"I honestly don't. I have seen enough strange things to know that I should never jump to conclusions or make any hasty judgments about anything. You just caught me off guard."

She forces a smile, but he believes she's on the verge of tears.

Taking a deep breath, he says, "What do you mean, you've 'seen into the future'?"

"In my dreams." Her voice conveys the passion she has for the young man sitting on the edge of the bed with her. "I have dreamed of a future with you, and honestly, I like what I see."

"How?"

"I don't know how or why it has been happening, but I think it must have something to do with the crows. I think their influence is rubbing off on me. Is that even possible? Would they really have that kind of power to allow me to see the future?"

"I don't know. But I suppose it's possible. I've—we've—seen how powerful they are. They must know how important you are to me. Maybe they have found a way to reach out to you. Maybe they are trying to reach me through you."

"Well, I like to think so because, if they have found a way to do that, then that means you and I are even closer than I thought we were." She smiles. "That gives me a whole lot of faith that we are destined to be together."

"So then," Alex asks, "if the crows have found a way to reveal the future to you, what have they shown you?"

She gently touches his sharply-chiselled face and brushes the white strands of loose hair away from his eyes. "They've shown me that you and I are going to be together for a very long time."

"And how do you feel about that?"

"I love the idea of us sharing our lives together." She speaks softly. "You and I…and our babies."

"Babies? What are you talking about? I know you can't be pregnant because you and I haven't, you know, even done it yet"

She chuckles softly. "I'm not pregnant right now, Alex. In the future. In my dreams I see that we have four babies together. I see three tiny girls, triplets, as a matter of fact, and they are the sweetest, most perfect babies I have ever seen. I know they are our babies."

"And you think that is our real future?"

"I do." She smiles. "I really do."

"How can you be so sure? Maybe it's just that you have a vivid imagination."

"No, it's definitely more than that," Bree says. "It's real…they are real. I even know their names."

"Their names?"

She nods. "Their names are Piper and Bailey, and the smallest one is named Sydney. There's also a fourth baby, a boy. Seth is his name."

"How could you possibly know all of that?"

"I just do."

"Wow, Bree." He takes a deep breath and then exhales. "There's a lot to unpack here."

"Oh, I'm not done yet."

"There's more?"

She nods again. "I've been receiving messages from Sydney."

"Messages? Like what?" He can sense her sudden hesitation. "What is she saying?"

"It's not words," she says. "It's more like a feeling that I get when I dream of her. For some reason, she and I seem to have a special bond that I don't have with the other girls."

"You have got to give me more, Bree. Just tell me whatever it is."

"Okay." She takes a deep breath. "I feel that Sydney is giving me a warning of imminent danger."

"Imminent danger from what?"

"Unfortunately, that's the part that I just don't know. All I get is a feeling that, despite everything you've gone through—everything we've gone through—there's still some kind of threat that is very real."

"A threat to who?"

She hesitates then whispers, "I believe there's a threat to you. But I don't know if that threat is present now or if it's in the future."

Alex rises from the bed and moves to the window again. He stares outside into the cold whiteness and ponders her comment. "So, if your dreams mean anything, then the fact that the crows are hanging around out there this morning *does* mean something. They are trying to warn me, aren't they?"

"Maybe. You know anything is possible with them."

"So let me ask you this." He turns to face her. "How long have you been having these dreams about our future and the little girls?"

"I don't know. Maybe a week or a little longer."

"How many dreams have you had?"

"Three or four, I think. But you know what dreams are like."

He can see that she is now wondering if she has done the right thing by telling him about the dreams.

She says, "Sometimes, the next day, you can't even remember what you dreamt, and sometimes you can only remember bits and pieces. Most of these dreams are kind of like that, but some of them are also very vivid. Those are the ones that I can remember in detail."

"Why didn't you tell me about this before today?"

"I was afraid to tell you because I thought you would not believe me," she says. "I didn't want you to jump to any conclusions."

"I wouldn't do that," he says. "So, what do you think this all means? If the crows are involved, what are they trying to tell me? They've sent me lots of warnings over the years, but they've always been directly to me, not through another person. This is all very weird to me."

"It's all very weird to me, too."

She rises from the bed and joins him in front of the window. They watch the crows as they glide over the snow-covered backyard. "This is all new to me, Alex. What do we do now?"

He puts his arm around her slender waist and pulls her closer to him.

"I don't know."

As they watch the crows swoop and glide through the rapidly-falling snowflakes, he adds, "If I'm reading the signs correctly, this storm means trouble and I'm not talking about the natural kind of trouble."

"Should we tell someone?" Bree asks. "Maybe your mother or Oliver? He's always helped you in the past. Maybe he'll know what all of this means."

Alex shakes his head. "I don't think we should tell anyone just yet."

"Are you sure that's the right thing to do? What if we wait too long and something terrible happens to someone—to you? I would never be able to survive that."

"What if we tell them and then it turns out to be nothing? We'd get them all worked up over nothing. I think Mom and Oliver have been through enough for a while," he answers. "My sense is that we should keep this information to ourselves for now, but at the same time remain on high alert and be ready for anything."

"Anything?"

"Yes." Alex hugs her tightly. "Anything. You know how this works."

8: Strawberries and cream scones

"What is that wonderful aroma? It smells delicious," the strikingly-beautiful blonde says as she enters the cottage-style kitchen that Oliver had recently remodelled.

He looks up and winks at her. "And good morning to you, beautiful lady. How are you doing on this lovely snowy morning, Dr. Anna Robbie? Did you sleep well?"

Anna laughs. "I sure did. I was exhausted."

She has been seeing Oliver for the past few months since ending her professional relationship with him, and today she finds him sitting at the counter in front of his laptop, reviewing a backlog of email messages he had received and neglected over the holidays.

"I slept like a log, thank you, my wonderful Oliver Lewis." She smiles and kisses him on the nose. "And no wonder. After that workout you put me through last night. You played me out. But don't get me wrong." She grins, her blue eyes sparkling. "I'm not complaining. In fact, it's just the opposite. All I can say is, *wow*."

"Happy you approve."

"Oh, I approve, all right. You are nothing short of amazing, you lovely man. And speaking of amazing, do I smell fresh-baked scones?"

She sidles up to him and puts her hands on his shoulders. "I do, don't I? And if I'm not mistaken, it smells like strawberries and cream scones. Oh my God, Oliver. I love scones, and strawberries and cream are my absolute favourite. You are incredible."

"You're the incredible one." He smiles, his eyes drinking in the beauty in front of him. She exudes poise, self-confidence, and class. He shakes his head. After everything he's gone through this past year, he can't believe he was so fortunate to fall in love with such an intelligent and beautiful woman. He had been alone for so long after his last great love left him that he hadn't thought he would ever fall in love again.

"How could you possibly know what flavour they are?"

"Oh, baby. I can tell," she almost coos. "I've got the nose of a blood-hound when it comes to scones, especially strawberries and cream scones. Don't tell me you were up early enough that you had time to make some. I didn't hear a thing. Guess I really was exhausted."

"You never so much as flexed your toes when I got out of bed two hours ago." He wiggles his eyebrows.

She giggles.

"And yes, I sure as heck did make them. I wanted to surprise you."

"Well, you surprised me all right." Her smile melts his heart.

"I'd do anything for you. I thought about making gingerbread in honour of the holidays and all that, but then I thought that's just too corny, so I went with the ones I hoped you'd like. Besides, I'm kind of over Christmas."

"We've only been together a few months, Oliver, but you already seem to know me so well. I don't recall that I ever told you that I even liked scones. Did I?"

"Come on, Doc. You, of all people, should know me better than that. You are a psychiatrist, after all. Can't you see inside my head? Don't you know by now that I pay attention to the people I care for?"

She leans forward and lightly kisses him on the lips. "I am glad that you do. Though it's hard to believe you had the energy to bake anything after our lustful adventures last night."

"I've also done the dishes, shovelled the walkways, put in a load of laundry and answered a lot of these work emails," Oliver says. "Looks like I'm going to be busy in the new year...if I stick around town long enough to do all the work, that is."

"So, about that," Anna says, making her way to the stove where the scones are cooling. "When are you going to tell your friends about your plans?"

"I'm not sure yet." He goes to the counter to pour her a cup of the dark roast coffee he made in the French press. "Try this. The coffee goes well with the scones."

"Oh my God, Oliver," she moans after taking a bite of the pastry. "These are amazing. I think I love you."

"Glad you like them."

"Scones were a big part of my childhood in England. I've such fond memories of morning tea with my grandmother."

She sighs and Oliver notices she suddenly looks sad. "Grammie raised me after my parents were killed in a car crash, leaving me an orphan. We always had scones with morning tea every Sunday. My grandmother insisted on it." Adapting a thick English accent, she continues, "'*It's the English way,*' she always told me."

Closing her eyes she adds, "These are to die for. Where did you learn to make these?"

"I'm a mystery man of many talents....An enigma." He laughs.

"Oh no you don't, mister," she says in between bites of her scone. "Time for you to 'fess up."

"Okay. Okay."

He pours the freshly made coffee into two blue ceramic cups. "You know how I told you that I had a brain tumour about fifteen years ago and I almost died?"

"Yes. And I absolutely marvel at your miraculous recovery, and also how you act like it's no big deal."

"It was a long time ago and I'm fine now." He shrugs. "Thankfully, the cancer never came back. Anyway, after I was cured, I left town and spent the next few years travelling around the globe. I spent some time in Europe, just wandering around and working when I had to, and learning how to cook and bake. It's no big deal, really. But it was a wonderful time in my life. I learned a great deal about the world...and myself."

"Ooooh, baby. It is a big deal." She takes another bite. "It's a very big deal."

"Here's a coffee to wash them down." Oliver hands her a cup.

Taking a sip of the hot, richly bold liquid she closes her eyes. "Where have you been hiding all my life? I think this is the best coffee I've ever tasted. How come you've never made this for me before today?"

"I don't know, maybe because I was holding back for a special occasion. Now, why don't you take your coffee and your scones into the living room and relax by the fireplace? I have a nice fire going, and it's pretty cozy on a snowy day. I just want to finish up these emails and then I'll join you."

"Oh no, mister," she says. "You aren't getting away that easy."

"What do you mean?"

"I'm wondering why you haven't told your friends you're moving to Halifax in the new year, or have you changed your mind about coming with me?"

"Oh no, nothing like that. I still want to come with you, very much, but I was just waiting until after the holidays to tell everyone. They've all gone through so much this past year that I didn't want them to focus on me. I wanted them to relax and enjoy their downtime, but I will tell them when the time is right."

"Aren't your friends all going to be at that party tonight? Maybe that would be a good time to tell them."

"Do you think? I wouldn't want to spoil everyone's fun. It's supposed be a celebration, after all."

"What makes you think you're going to spoil everyone's fun?" She places her cup on the counter and wraps her arms around his neck. "You know, Oliver, I bet everyone is going to be very happy for you that you're moving on with your life."

"You're probably right."

"So why do I sense the hesitation?"

He glances around the small but comfortable kitchen, as if trying to avoid eye contact. "I know this is the right move for me. I know we started our relationship when I was as your patient, but I've fallen madly and passionately in love with you. I've never felt this way before about anyone."

"But?"

"But you have to understand that this town has a special hold on me and my type."

"Your type?" Her eyebrows knot together. "You mean the crow stuff, right?"

"Yes, the crow stuff. I've told you all about it, and if you love me, then you will understand that I have a certain role to play in this town. It is a big part of who I am and it's very important to me. I take my responsibility very seriously."

"Right." She sighs. "You're a 'Protector.'"

He nods. "I know you don't believe in these legends about the crows and what they can do and the power they have."

"I'm still not sure I understand what it all means."

"It means that there are certain people in this town who know they can count on me to be here whenever they need me."

"Like Alex Goodwin?"

"Precisely." He watches her reaction. The last thing he wants to do this morning is to send the wrong signal to the woman he loves. He started seeing her romantically after she declared him to be sane earlier this year following some deeply intimate sessions in which he explored his 'manifestations', as she called them.

He continues, "I really want to go to Halifax and be with you as much as I can, but I am torn about leaving this place. I never know what's going to happen or when. The crows don't work on a fixed schedule."

"Halifax isn't all that far away, Oliver. You can be back here in less than two hours if Alex really needs you. And you aren't planning on selling your house right away, so you'll always have a place to come back to, should you have to stay awhile."

He nods. "You're right."

"Listen to me, Oliver." She wraps her arms around his waist and pulls him closer to her. "I'm not trying to mess up your life, but you and I have talked about this. You know I'm crazy about you, and I can see us having a good life together, but I can't pass up on this extraordinary opportunity I'm being offered. The chance to work in one of the most elite psychiatric clinics east of Montreal is something I can't just walk away from. I am hoping you will come on this journey with me. I really want you in my life, and you deserve to be happy."

"I really want that too." He pulls her close and kisses her gently on the forehead. Looking into her sparkling blue eyes, he adds, "I have to wrap my head around all of this, but I will find a way to make it work."

"No pressure." She strokes the back of his head. "I want you to do whatever makes you happy. If you decide to stay here, we can try to make it work, but I'm always afraid about long-distance relationships. I tried that once and it ended in disaster. I can't do that again."

Oliver shakes his head. "I don't want that, either. If I'm going to be with someone, then I'm going to be all in." He nuzzles into her neck, giving her a gentle kiss. "I want to be with you every night. I want to hold you and kiss you goodnight and wake up beside you the next morning. If that means moving to Halifax, then I promise you that I will be there. I'm in this relationship one hundred percent. The past few months have been among the happiest times of my life, and I am not going to do anything to jeopardize that."

"Then, my sweet," she says with a smile, "please tell your friends what's going on. You owe them that much, and I'll be right there with you. I know they will be happy for you."

"So, in other words, you got my back?"

"I sure do. For now, and for always."

"No matter what?"

"Absolutely." She kisses him again. Pulling away she adds, "No matter what, especially if you keep making scones like this for me."

"It will cost you."

"What's the cost?"

"Oh," he says with a laugh. "You'll see."

"Let's go back to the bedroom right now so I can give you a down payment." She takes him by the hand.

He doesn't resist.

9: Terminal

Dr. Charlie Webster tiptoes into the darkened room. He cautiously approaches the bed where Rebecca, his wife of seventeen years, is resting and, although he has never considered himself to be a religious man, he says a silent prayer for her—for them.

He knows she didn't sleep well. He had felt her tossing and turning beside him, so he doesn't want to disturb her this morning. He will let her sleep for as long as she wants to.

She needs to rest, he thinks, looking at the outline of her slender body under the rose-coloured duvet. *If it wasn't snowing so hard right now, I'd pack up Liam and take him to Kate's place for a few hours so that we don't disturb her, but it's too messy out there right now to be on the roads.*

As his eyes adjust, he studies her face, looking for any signs that she may be in pain. *Besides, what if Rebecca needs me? I need to be here for her.*

Ever since she received the devastating diagnosis three days ago, she has only slept a few hours, and he knows that exhaustion will not be good for her in her weakened state. She will need every ounce of strength she can muster if she is going to fight this thing—this dreadful disease that's slowly eating away at her body.

She's a doctor, so of course she knows what this prognosis means, he thinks, reminding himself to keep his emotions in check when he's talking to her. *Getting myself worked up in front of her is not going to fix this and it's not going to help a god-damned thing, so come on, Charlie, keep it together for her sake. The last thing she needs right now is for you to lose your shit. That will only make things worse—if that's even possible.*

He's about to feel her forehead to see if she's running a fever when her eyes suddenly snap open and she stares up at him. She's still beautiful, even in the subdued light and without a bit of make-up, but he's always thought she is naturally beautiful.

He swallows as he feels like someone just punched him the guts. The tears are close, but he digs deep, fighting the urge to cry right then and there.

"What are you doing?" Her voice is weak.

"I just wanted to check on you." He tries to remain calm, hoping that he can somehow soothe her worries.

"You don't have to be quiet, Charlie. I've been awake most of the night." She sounds hoarse, her dry, raspy throat making her words nothing more than a whisper. "Too much on my mind to sleep, I guess."

"Sorry, Becca."

He sits on the edge of the bed and takes her right hand into his hands, gently massaging the palm as if the motion will help her relax. "I wish there was something I could do to help with that. Why don't you let me give you some citalopram to help you relax? Maybe you can finally get some sleep. Your body needs the rest. You need all your strength to fight this thing."

"No. I don't want anything." She shakes her head, her long black hair matting on the pillow. "We are both doctors. We know there's nothing that either of us can do about this. All I want right now is a glass of water, if you wouldn't mind getting it for me, please."

"Not at all." He gently places her hand back on the bed and goes into the ensuite bathroom.

"I was thinking about the party tonight," he says as he watches the water from the cold-water tap swirl down the drain. He wishes he could make her sickness disappear just like that water. "I'm going to call Julie and Cliff and make our apologies. I don't think we should go anywhere today. It's calling for a lot of snow, and I didn't think you would be up for a crowd."

"No, you won't." Rebecca gingerly pulls her body into a sitting position, taking it slow. "You will do nothing of the sort, Charlie Webster."

He returns to the bed and passes her the glass of cool water. Watching her every move, he says, "You can't honestly tell me that you are thinking about going to the party, all things considered."

"Yeah. I can."

He watches as she takes small sips, and he sees her struggle to swallow. He wonders if her throat is sore. He knows she will do everything in her power to hide her pain from him. He also knows that Rebecca has always shielded him from anything that might cause him discomfort.

"And, yes," she adds after a few slow sips. "We are definitely going to the party."

"Don't you think you need some time to come to grips with what you just heard? Besides, it's not like you've had much sleep over the past few days. You must be exhausted," he says. "I know I am completely wiped out, and I think what you really need right now is a good, long sleep. Things will look a little different once you've rested."

"Listen to me, Charlie Webster. You and I know what the future holds for me, and no amount of sleep is going to change the inevitable. But I refuse to give up. I am going to fight this thing for as long as I possibly can, and I need you to support me in this. What I don't need right now is for you to handle me with kid gloves. I don't want this disease to change the way you look at me...the way you treat me...the way you touch me. I want to live whatever life I have left to the fullest."

"But—"

"No buts." She raises her eyebrows as she always does when she wants to emphasize her point. "I may be sick, but I am still the same person I was before I started getting those pains in my back three weeks ago. The only thing that has changed is that I'm dying. I don't want to be treated like a baby or an invalid all of a sudden. I'm still perfectly able to function like an adult, so, for now, you have to give me that."

Charlie sighs and looks at his wife, her pallid complexion and sunken, dark eyes telling him just how sick she really is. He recognizes the signs.

"Of course," he whispers. "Whatever you want. You know I will always support you no matter what happens. I am here for you one hundred percent of the way, but I just didn't think you would be ready to see people just yet, let alone talk to anyone about this."

"I'm not sure I am," she admits. "But we can't hide it. It's nothing to be ashamed of. It happens to a lot of people, sadly."

"I'm not ashamed of anything. Certainly not of you or what you're going through. But I think our family and friends will know right away that something is wrong when they see you. There will be a lot of questions. Are you ready to deal with all of that?"

"Will they?" She shakes her head and takes another sip of water. "I don't think we should make any decisions on what we do based on what other people may or not think. Besides, I've been looking forward to getting out of this bed and out of this house for a while now."

She pauses and looks at him over the rim of the water glass. "I need to do this, Charlie. I have no intention of being trapped in this bed for whatever time I have left. I refuse to give in to this thing. It may slow me down and it may eventually kill me, but it's not going the change the person I am."

He thinks about her request. "Okay, if that's what you really want, we will go to the party, but what will we tell people when they start asking questions? You know what my sister is like. Even if you can hide your illness with makeup and a smile, she will know that something is up. I have never been able to hide anything from her."

"It is not only what I want; it's what I need." Her eyes tell him that this is important to her. "And if anyone asks questions, we'll just tell them that I've had the flu but that I'm feeling much better now. I mean, it's not like I'm contagious or anything."

She takes a deep breath. "Besides, this party may be the last social function I get to attend."

"Please don't say things like that." He rubs his eyes with the backs of his hands, his emotions finally getting the best of him. "I can't even think about that."

"Please don't cry." She reaches up and pulls his hands away from his eyes. "Come on, Charlie. Please listen to me." Her voice remains calm and to the point. "I have terminal cancer We must accept that diagnosis for what it is, which means by this time next new year, I won't be here."

"You don't know that." He sniffs back his tears. "You can fight this. You are a strong woman. They are coming out with new drugs every day. With the right management and treatment, you could last many, many years."

"I could," she agrees. "But it's not likely."

"You can't give in to this thing, Rebecca."

"I'm not giving in to anything," she says. "I am facing the truth. We know the life expectancy for people with pancreatic cancer is around five years after diagnosis, with the right treatment and if it is caught early enough. That's not the case for me. The life expectancy for stage four pancreatic cancer is very low, three to five months at the most. You know I have very few options."

He becomes stubborn. "I am not an oncologist, but there must be a way to treat this."

"If only the tumour had showed up when I had my physical three months ago there might have been a better chance of slowing it down, but now, as Dr. Hagerty said, it's too late for surgery. It is already infecting other organs and, soon, my body will begin to shut down." Rebecca's voice is void of any emotion. "Dr. Hagerty said I can do chemotherapy and be sick as a dog for maybe six months, if I'm lucky, or I can manage the pain and all the other symptoms and live six months...or whatever time I have left. Either way, the end result is going to be the same."

"You have to try something, Rebecca." Charlie is amazed, almost shocked, by how relaxed she seems about all of this.

"Do I?" She smiles at him. "You have had patients who have been in my shoes and you've seen what they've gone through. I don't want to be sick for whatever time I have left. I want to try to live my last months or days as best I can, not with my face stuck in a toilet bowl or so heavily drugged that I don't even know my own name." She shakes her head. "That's not for me."

He rises from the bed. "I won't accept that, and I refuse to lose you. You must fight this, and you have to fight like hell. I know you can beat this, if you don't give up."

"Is that what you would tell me if I was your patient? Or are you saying that because I'm your wife?"

He looks at her but doesn't answer. The tears trickle down his cheeks.

"I know this is hard, sweetheart, but they are the facts, and we have to face the truth," she says. "What I need from you right now is for you to stand beside me and to be strong and to respect my decisions. I need you to be there for Liam. He's only eleven and will not understand what's going with me. You must keep it together for his sake—and for my sake."

"Yeah, well, that's easier said than done." He tries to keep his emotions in check. "I wish it was me who was sick instead of you."

She shakes her head. "You wouldn't want that, and I don't want that. I just need to know that you are going to be there with me."

"Of course, I'll be with you." He kneels beside the bed, leans forward, and places his head on her lap, his emotions causing his body to shake. "Where else would I be? You are my soulmate, Rebecca, my best friend, and my crutch—the person I always lean on."

Sniffing back the tears that are streaming down his face, he whispers, "You are my one true love, and I don't know how I will get through the rest of my life if I l lose you."

"Listen to me, Charlie Webster." She pushes her long, slender fingers through his thick, brown hair. "I know you'll get through this. You are the bravest, smartest, most vibrant person I have ever met. The only way that I can be at peace when I die is to know that you and Liam are going to be okay. You will struggle, no doubt, but you must do this. For me."

"I don't know that I can." Finally giving into the emotion that is chewing him up, he sobs. "How can I face a future without you in it? You've been the best part of my life for more than twenty years and I need you. Liam needs you. How will I ever handle him?"

"You will be his father and you will help him to work through his emotions." She places her hand on his back, letting it rest below his neck.

"Liam is a smart kid, so count on him to help you. He'll show you the way."

"He'll show me the way?"

"Yes. And you know other people will be there for you. Oliver is your best friend. He will help you however he can, so use him, lean on him for support. Tell him what you need to tell him. Don't keep anything bottled up. And Kate and Samantha will step in to help you any way they can. If I know your sister, she will be like a mother hen. I know Kate will be there for anything you need."

"How can you be so calm?"

"Acceptance." Her voice remains mellow. "Am I sad that I won't be with you anymore or that I won't be around to see Liam grow into the wonderful human being that I know he is destined to become? Absolutely. My heart breaks when I think of you and Liam without me in your lives. But I have counselled many terminal patients, and I've seen them react with the full spectrum of emotions. In the end, no matter how we feel or what we want, the only thing we can do is accept the truth, and that's what I've done. My early death is imminent."

Pausing and gently lifting his head from her lap, she looks into his brown eyes. "Now, my darling, you have to do the same."

"I can't promise that I will be as calm about this as you seem to be, but I will try," he tells her, blinking quickly as the tears flood his eyes.

"I know you will, and part of that acceptance is telling our friends and family what's going on," Rebecca says, adding, "You'll have to tell Kate very soon. She is very astute, and she cares very much about you—about us. You owe it to her."

He grimaces at the thought of telling his sister that his wife is dying. "Yes. I know you are right, but I will do it after the party. I don't want to ruin anyone's evening."

10: What do we do next?

"I don't know if I can do it, Hunter." The young, blonde-haired woman struggles to keep from crying, her bottom lip quivering as she speaks. "I don't think I can handle being around other people right now." She shakes her head. "I'm just not ready."

"Come on, Ally." The young man with the wispy, reddish-auburn hair is shocked. They've been together for two and a half years and he's never seen her in such an emotional state. "We have no choice. I told my mom that we would go to the party with them tonight, and if I tell her that we've changed our minds, she will ask all kinds of questions." He grim-aces. "You know what she's like."

"She does seem to have the ability to read your mind. But maybe she will understand."

"I cannot keep any secrets from her. It's like she can see right through me."

"Can't you just tell her that I don't feel well?" Ally suggests.

Leaning against the bathroom vanity, he can see she is trying hard to keep her emotions in check.

She continues, "Just tell your mom that something I ate made me sick, or that I must have picked up the flu somewhere and that it just hit. Or tell her I want to stay home because of the snow." She sighs. "I don't really care what you tell her, Hunter, but I'm not ready to face anyone right now."

He stands close to her and pulls her into a warm, comforting embrace. "If I thought for one minute that I could lie to her and get away with it, I would have been doing that a long time ago." He smiles. "It's her super-power. She's like a freaking human lie-detector."

"All I know is that there is no way I can go to any party tonight." She hugs him tightly. "Not when I feel like my world is imploding around me. I can't pretend that none of this is happening. If you think your mother will see through your lies, then just wait until she sees me. There is no way I will be able to hide this from her."

"I know it's a lot to ask, but I will be right there with you. I'll keep her away from you."

"Come on, Hunter. You can't be with me all evening." She sighs. "Besides, if you can't lie to your mother about not going to the party, how do you think, we're going to keep this news from her?"

"Shit. You are right." He kisses her on the cheek and releases her from his embrace. "I'm so dead. She's going to kill me."

"No, you're not. You make it sound worse than it has to be. It's just that we have to come up a plan on how to talk to your mother—to our parents."

Putting the toilet cover down and taking a seat, he looks up at the woman whom he loves very deeply, despite their young ages. "Jesus, Ally, what am I going to tell her? She's going to lose her shit when she finds out."

"You think your mother is going to lose it?" She rolls her eyes. "What about my mother? She thinks I'm a good Christian girl who's still a virgin. She will definitely lose her mind when she finds out that I'm pregnant." She takes a deep breath. "She will completely disown me."

"No. She won't do that."

Tears flow from her eyes and trickle down her cheeks. "Yes, she will. I've heard what she's said about other young girls who have gotten pregnant before they were married. She will absolutely cut off all ties with me. What are we going to do?"

"Let's not do anything drastic," he urges. He squints at her. "You would never do anything like—"

"Like what? Have an abortion?"

A look of desperation crosses his face. "I wasn't saying that you should do that."

"Good. Because I could never have an abortion. Maybe it's my Catholic upbringing but I think the guilt would kill me." She rubs her eyes. "But that still leaves us with the problem."

"Whatever we do, we are in this together. Totally. We will do this as a team. Just you and me and, no matter what anyone else says, we will find a way to make this work."

"How? We're both in university." She attempts to stifle her emotions. "We can hardly take care of ourselves. There is no way we can afford to take care of a baby on top of rent and tuition and all the other stuff that comes with an apartment and a family. I just don't see how we can swing it."

He takes her hand. "Listen to me. We love each other and that's all that matters. We will figure this out." He smiles. "And I promise you that you are going to finish university. You have always wanted to be a teacher and I will see to it that you will get your degree, no matter what."

"How?" Her tears start again. "How am I going to finish university if I have to take care of a baby?"

"I haven't worked out the details yet." He squeezes her hand gently. "But if it comes down to it, I will quit university and stay home and take care of the baby."

"I don't want you to do that. You have worked so hard to get where you are."

"Yes, I can. The fact is, I don't really like it, anyway. I've only been going to classes because I know that's what my parents want, but I've never wanted it. I'll quit for a few years, get a part-time job and take care of the baby. I will take a night shift, if I have to, to make things work. Even though it will be tight, I'm sure we will manage. You will continue to work towards your degree." He smiles. "And I'll be a stay-at-home dad....I like how that sounds."

"You would do that for me?"

"I absolutely would to that for you—for us. I would do that and more to make you happy, no matter what it takes."

She sucks in a deep breath and then exhales. "Oh Hunter. I love you so much, but your mother is not going to be very happy about any of this. She's always been worried about me getting pregnant. You know that. She's had that discussion with us many times and now we've fulfilled her worst fear."

"Oh well, good for her." He shrugs. "These things happen, don't they?"

"Well." She half smiles. "They don't *just happen*."

"No." He chuckles. "But you know what I mean. So, then, what do we do next?"

"I think the next step is for me to make an appointment with my doctor in the new year and, after that, even though it's my worst nightmare, we have to tell our parents."

Hunter studies her face, thinking about what happens next. "No," he finally says. "I don't think we should wait to tell our parents."

"What are you talking about?"

"Let's tell them right away. Why put it off? We know it must be done, so let's get it over with. Let's just rip the Band-Aid off and deal with it straight on."

"You don't want to wait until we hear from the doctor? What if the home tests are wrong? Maybe I'm not doing it right or maybe something else is going on with my body."

"You've done three of them. I'm sure you are doing it right. We know you are pregnant, so let's tell them right now, as in tonight. What a great way to start the new year."

"I can't believe how well you're taking this news, Hunter," she says. "I thought you would lose your mind when I told you."

"Trust me, Ally, my mind is blown."

"I'm glad you're excited, but I'm not sure I am ready to tell anyone."

"I know this is scary." Hunter pulls her close again for another hug. "But I was taught that if you have a problem or something unpleasant to do, the worst thing you can do is put it off. The best way is to do it promptly, honestly and with integrity." He looks into her eyes. "And that's what I intend to do. Face our parents and deal with the consequences. Delaying the inevitable will only make it worse."

"Okay." She sighs, resting her head on his chest. "If that's how you want to handle things, then that's what we'll do, but I don't think tonight is the appropriate time. This is supposed to be a party, so let everyone enjoy it."

"I understand that, but like I said, my mothers, especially Samantha, will know that I'm hiding something. She'll keep poking and prodding and pushing me to tell her what's up," he says.

"My God, Hunter, your mother is not at all like that. I've never seen her push you that hard. Of course, as a good parent, she's always watching out for you and paying attention to what's happening in your life, but it's because she cares. She's not some kind of Nosy Nelly."

"No." He shrugs. "I guess she isn't quite that bad."

"I think you are too hard on her." She rubs her hand over his muscular chest. "Be thankful that she cares so deeply about you."

"That's how you see it?"

Ally nods. "It has always been clear to me that she will do whatever she has to do to protect you and to help you reach your best potential. She's not at all like my mother, the saintly Martha Bradford, the Bible-thumping, holier-than-thou, died-in-the-wool Catholic whose idea of a good time is sitting in a sewing circle and doing needle point while she passes judgment on everyone, especially on the members of her own family."

"My God, Ally." Hunter chuckles. "You make your mother sound like a character out of some black and white movie about cranky old Catholic nuns."

"Don't laugh at me, Hunter Henderson-Webster." She pulls back from him. "You don't know the half of it."

"So, tell me." It is clear to him that he has hit a nerve.

"You have no idea what it was like growing up with her as my mother. You don't know what she's really like, because you only get to see the nice person that she wants people to see, not the religious zealot that she really is. I've told you how she's belligerent and bossy and manipulative. Beside all of that, she's extremely judgmental of people—especially girls —who don't follow the rules. Girls like me who break the rules have our place, you know? And that place is in Hell."

"I know you've always told me how she drives you nuts, but aren't all parents like that?".

"Not like my mother. How is that you can't see her for what she really is? I would never say she was physically abusive, but she's certainly mentally and emotionally abusive. Just ask my sisters, if you don't believe me. My childhood was pure hell."

"I believe you. I know you always seem very uncomfortable whenever we're around her. Like maybe you are ashamed of her or something."

Ally shivers. "I can just hear her now when she finds out I'm pregnant. 'Allison Marie Bradford'—she always uses my full name when she's mad at me—'you little whore. I thought I raised you to be a good girl,' she'll say. 'I thought you were still a virgin, but you've been seduced by the pleasures of the flesh and now you'll have to pay for your sins.' She will never forgive me for getting pregnant before I'm married. I will always be a tramp or a slut in her eyes. She may never speak to me again; probably disown me. She'll have nothing to do with our baby."

"Is it really going to be that bad?" Hunter pulls her to him.

"Oh yes. That bad and then some."

He takes her chin in his hand and gently tilts her face towards his. He gives her a sweet, gentle kiss. "What matters is that I love you with all my heart and I will be there for you and the baby, no matter what."

"You promise?" Tears stream down her cheeks that are flushed a bright red, as they always are when she's angry or upset.

"I do." He looks into her eyes. "I don't care what anyone says—our mothers included. If this is happening, then it's meant to be, and if it's meant to be, then it also means that you and I are supposed to be together. I believe it is fate."

"Okay, Hunter." She sighs, trying to fight back her tears. "If that's what you think, then let's tell our parents."

11: Superstitions

Carly Graham-Watkins does not consider herself to be an overly superstitious person, but she's felt on edge after hearing three loud and very distinct knocks at the kitchen door this morning. Only when she checked, there was no one there. Her mother, on the other hand, believes the three knocks were an omen of bad luck or even a sign of death.

"When I was a little girl, my mother and grandmother would lose their minds whenever they heard something like that," Julie told her. "They believed it was a sign that someone close to them, maybe even a family member, was soon going to die."

Carly had heard these old wives' tales many times before. While growing up, Julie freely shared her knowledge of such things. She told Carly that such traditions were an important part of her culture.

"According to superstition—and the older generations believed this stuff—three knocks at the door or a window was considered to be death coming to call," she explained following that morning's incident. She pointed out that such omens are called forerunners in Maritime folklore.

"There are times when you might even hear three knocks coming from somewhere within your house, but you can't locate the source. That's also a forerunner, and these signs are not be taken lightly. I saw my mother become very distraught on one occasion when she heard a forerunner, and you know what, two days later, one of her brothers died. That's not easy to dismiss: I don't believe in coincidences."

While Carly isn't sure what she believes, she will admit that the strange occurrence this morning has left her with a sense of unease unlike anything she has ever felt before. Watching her two young daughters play with their Miniland dolls Santa brought them for Christmas, she feels an overwhelming sense of sadness has suddenly embraced her. She's tried, but she can't shake the heaviness that now rests in her chest. It feels like someone is kneeling on her, making it difficult to breath.

Remembering her father's dire warnings that something bad was going to happen if she remained with her husband, it feels that her life has crashed around her. She wonders if there is any correlation between the three knocks and what has been happening in her life. *The past six months, ever since I discovered Leo is cheating on me, have been pure hell*, she thinks.

"It was only one time," he insisted after she overheard a phone call he was having with another woman while he was in the bathroom with, he had thought, the door locked. "I promise it meant nothing and it only happened because I was out of town, drinking, and I was missing you," was his excuse. "One thing led to another, and we got carried away. It meant nothing. Please, you must believe me. Please forgive me."

"Forgive you?" She was stunned by his audacity. "If it meant nothing, then why are you continuing to have conversations with this woman?"

He tried to worm his way out of it, but he couldn't explain why he was still in contact with the woman whom, according to him, he met while he was at a conference in Toronto. Apparently, this woman, whoever she is, is from the St. John's office and it sounded to Carly like they were making plans to meet up again.

"If it meant nothing, why were you planning another rendezvous?" Carly asked, continuing to press him for details. "If it meant nothing, why were you laughing and giggling into the phone when I walked into the room? If it meant nothing, why did you do it in the first place?"

Oh, he apologized all right. Profusely, in fact. He begged for her forgiveness but, try as she might, she can't forget the excitement she heard in his voice when she overheard the phone conversation back in July.

Since then, their relationship has deteriorated to the point that now she is considering leaving him. His solution to their problems is to have another baby, but she can't see herself bringing another child into the mess that is their marriage.

She has been trying to make things work for the sake of the girls, but it's hard to forget what he's done. Every time she thinks of him being with another woman, she feels like she could vomit. She's even gotten to the point where she has blamed herself for his infidelity, but, as her mother told her, Leo is the one who cheated, not her.

She knows she should tell him to hit the road. He's shattered her trust and broken her heart, and even though he gives her this song and dance about how he only ended up with the other woman in a moment of weakness, she doesn't believe him.

"How can we continue to live like nothing ever happened if I can't trust you?" she asked him and, in the heat of passion and anger, she pushed him. She knows she should not have provoked him, but, much to her surprise and disappointment, he shoved her back, causing her to lose her balance and fall, hurting her wrist and bruising her cheek just below her right eye, when she hit it on the corner of the coffee table.

She's not sure he meant to push her, but the physical contact was crossing the line for her. Sure, she pushed him first and she knows she should not have done it, but she had good reason and he hardly felt it. She was angry over what he had done, and he never flinched.

She's a lightweight compared to Leo. He's much larger than her, but she never, in a million years, believed Leo would ever lay a finger on her. Considering their physical differences, if Leo were to ever really haul off and hit her, he would likely hurt her. She cringes at the thought.

He should never have done that, no matter if he felt I provoked him, she thinks. *Which I hardly did. Besides, he deserves more than a little shove.*

"No man should ever raise a hand to a woman," she remembers her father, telling her, his words reverberating in her head. "Any man who does that is a coward and can never be trusted to not do it again."

"Mommy, Mommy," her daughters call to her from across the den. "Come and play with us."

"In a minute, girls." She smiles at the two auburn-haired girls who are her whole life. "Just give Mommy a few minutes to finish her coffee, then we'll play. Does that sound okay?"

"Yes Mommy," Cara, the older daughter, replies.

Carly watches her little girls giggle amongst themselves. They are oblivious to the turmoil that is swirling in their lives, and that's the way Carly wants it. That's the way it must be. It breaks her heart to think of how upset they will be if they lose their father. No matter whatever else Leo has done, she knows he loves his daughters, and they adore him.

She tells herself that her daughters are the only reason she continues to stay with Leo. Her father, though, continues to tell her that for the sake of the girls, she should get away from that—to use his words—cheating and abusive son of a bitch as quickly as she can.

Staring at the cold black coffee at the bottom of the ceramic cup that she's been holding for the past half hour, she tells herself that Leo would never hit her again, and he would never lay a finger on his daughters. But she knows her father isn't wrong. She has heard the stories and read the news reports. She knows that abusive husbands will always promise to never do it again, but they almost always do it again.

Now she has some decisions to make, and while she thought she had decided she would stay with Leo for the sake of their daughters, now she isn't sure that's the right decision. She feels like the walls are closing in on her.

"You and the girls are always welcome to come stay with us until you get back on your feet," her mother has told her many times. "Stay as long as you have to. You and the girls will always have a home with us."

She knows her parents mean well, and she appreciates their concern, but the mounting pressure she feels from them to do what they want her to do is making it more difficult for her to think clearly and make her own decisions.

What do I do?

"Jesus." She jumps as her cellphone suddenly rings, snapping her out of her stupor. Glancing at the small screen, she recognizes her husband's number. She takes a deep breath and answers.

"Hey, you." Her throat is so hoarse and dry that she can hardly speak. Quickly taking a sip of the cold, black coffee she stifles the urge to gag. "How is the weather in there?"

"Hey, babe," he answers. She hates it when he calls her that because it makes her feel like his possession, his "plaything." But he won't stop using that word even though she has asked him many times to do so. "It's still snowing in here," he says. "What's it like down there on the South Shore?"

She glances over her shoulder and out the window. "It snowed pretty hard all morning, but it looks like it is finally starting to slack off a bit. Based on the forecast, though, I have no idea how long that will last. Have you changed your mind about coming down tonight?"

"No. I'm just wrapping up a few things, then I'll be heading out."

"Text me when you leave the city so that I'll know you're on the road."

"How are things down there?"

"What do you mean?" Even though she knows exactly what he's implying, she wants him to say it.

"Come on, babe. You know what I mean."

"Not really. I already told you the snow is slacking off right now, but the roads still look pretty dicey."

"That's not what I mean, and you know it." He sighs. "I mean with your parents. How is your father today?"

She takes a deep breath. "Good, I guess. They are getting everything ready for this evening's festivities. Mom's busily cleaning around the house and Dad is outside cleaning off the driveway or something. Actually, I'm not really sure what he's up to, but I guess he's fine."

"Are you sure?" Leo asks. "How did he take it when you told him I was coming tonight? Do you know if he got my Scotch?"

"I don't know. I haven't been talking to him since he got back from the liquor store, but I did ask him to get it. If they had it in stock, I'm sure he got a bottle."

"Man, I hope so. Gotta have the good stuff to ring in the New Year with."

She can imagine him smirking.

"Your father still pissed at me? He hardly said two words to me when I was there for Christmas with you and the girls. I hoped he would have forgiven me by now."

"You have to give him time, Leo. You hurt him—all of us—pretty bad," Carly tells him. "I may be able to swallow my pride and give you a second chance, but Dad's not made that way. He has seen too many bad things because of his line of work, and he knows how quickly these things can devolve and, the next thing you know, someone can be hurt or maybe even killed."

"I told you I will never do anything like that again."

She can detect the urgency in Leo's voice but she's not sure if it's guilt she hears or just him trying to cover his own ass.

He continues, "I told you I was sorry. What more can I do to make your father see that?"

"I don't think there is anything you can do to make him like you after what you've done. Tonight, the best thing you can do is stay away from him," she says. "Try not to push any of his buttons. I've seen Daddy angry and, believe me, you don't want to see that."

"Why do I have to be the nice one?"

She can hear the agitation building in his voice. She knows that when he thinks he's right and everyone else is wrong, he can become difficult to deal with. "I've tried to make amends with your father. Don't you think that he should also give a little and try to meet me halfway?"

"Remember, you are the one who pushed him off the deep end, so you are going to have to go around him when you're here. And for God's sake, don't say anything to him that will piss him off tonight. You are already on thin ice with my dad."

"Maybe I should just stay put right here in Halifax and celebrate the New Year all by myself."

She recognizes that this hurt-puppy routine is the normal ploy that he engages when he's trying to get her to sympathize with him, especially when he's trying to force her to side with him over her father. The tactic may have worked with her over the years, but not today.

"That's your decision. I can always tell everyone that you decided to stay in the city because of the crappy roads and weather forecast, if that's what you want. I'm sure everyone will understand."

"Don't you want me to come to the party, Carly? You don't want to be with me on New Year's Eve?"

"I'm not saying that." She's growing tired of this verbal sparring. "I am just saying that if you don't think you can come here tonight and be civil to my dad, then maybe it's best that you not come at all."

"So you are on his side, then."

"I'm not on anyone's side." She feels the anger building in the pit of her stomach. "Please don't do this today. I am not in the mood."

"It sounds to me like you've already picked your father over me."

"I really don't feel like arguing right now. Can we just stop?" She doesn't want to cry in front of her children, but she feels the tears welling up in her eyes.

"I'm not saying anything, babe."

"All I'm saying is that you should really think about tonight, and I'll be fine with whatever you decide to do," she says. "Of course, the girls would be happy to see you, but if you can't make it tonight, they will be okay."

"And what about you, babe? Will you be happy to see me?"

"Don't push me, Leo. Just decide what you're going to do and let me know. I'll see you tonight if you get here. If not, I'll see you when I get home."

"When will that be?"

"I'm not sure. In a few days. I told Mom that I would stick around for an extra day or two to help her clean up the house and put away the holiday decorations. Then I'll think about coming home."

"You *are* coming home, aren't you, babe?"

"Are you really asking me that question, Leo?" She can't believe how annoying he can be when he's trying to force her to decide on something he wants. "I've got to go. Cara and Cassie want me to come and play with them and I promised them I would be right there."

"You are just going to cut me off?"

"Just let me know what you decide to do about tonight," she says. "Now, I've really got to go."

"Right. Sure, babe." She hears him sigh. "Go play with the girls and I'll figure things out."

He disconnects the call.

"Damn it." Carly sighs. "That didn't go well."

As she turns off her phone, she hears her mother calling her name.

"Hey, girls," she says to her daughters. "You play with your dolls for a few minutes. I hear Nana calling me from the living room. Do not touch anything and do not leave this room. I will be right back."

The little girls don't answer, almost oblivious to their mother's words.

"Yeah, right," Carly whispers, pulling herself off the couch. *When it comes to a competition between those dolls and me, the dolls will win every time.*

She joins her mother in the living room, where she's doing some last-minute dusting before their guests arrive in a few hours. "Yes, Mom. What do you want?"

"What?" Julie stops what she's doing. "What are you talking about?"

"You called for me to come here, didn't you? I just assumed that meant you needed some help with something."

She sees her mother shake her head. "Sorry, honey, but I didn't call you."

"I just finished talking to Leo and I heard someone—I thought it was you—calling my name." She pauses. "Are you saying you didn't?"

"It wasn't me," Julie says, and Carly can see her mother immediately become flustered. "If you heard someone calling your name, then this isn't good."

"What do you mean?"

"It could be another sign," Julie explains, flopping into a thickly-padded easy chair next to the fireplace. "They say that when you hear someone calling your name, and you can't locate the source, it's a sign that someone you know is going to die. When you combine that with the three knocks that you heard this morning, that isn't good."

"Come on, Mom. You've got to stop talking nonsense like that. The girls might hear you. You might scare them."

"Well, Carly, I don't know what to tell you, but that is the old superstition." Julie keeps her voice decidedly low. "I'm just telling you what I heard when I was growing up."

"Jesus," Carly whispers. Returning to the den to be with her daughters, she thinks, *That's just what I need to worry about, on top of everything else. God-damn it.*

12: Overtime

This sucks, Warren Hamilton thinks. He fishes into the pocket of his bulky winter coat to find his cell phone so he can call his wife. The last thing he wanted to do today was to work overtime. *Today of all days.*

He shakes his head and accepts that overtime is part of the job. He knows it comes with the territory, but he doesn't have to like it. *It is what it is.*

It's already twenty minutes after two and he would like nothing better than to walk out of the detachment and leave all this stress behind for a few days.

He has been an RCMP officer long enough to know that anything can happen, and it usually happens when you least expect it. *But why does it always seem to happen whenever I'm getting ready for holidays?*

He's ready for his four-day break, but he knows he can't just walk away from the detachment while he's waiting to hear back from Texas authorities about that stolen 2018 red Kia Stinger that was mysteriously abandoned outside of town.

There's definitely something way off about this whole thing, he thinks as he waits for Lisa to answer her phone. *Come on.* His patience is wearing thin. *Just answer the phone.*

"Yes, Warren," Lisa says after the third ring. "What's wrong?"

"What makes you think there's something's wrong?" He's a little annoyed that his wife believes she knows him so well that he's so predictable; but the truth is, he's more miffed that she's actually right about this call.

"Because you never call me on your personal phone unless something comes up, so what's happening?"

"Well. It looks like I'm going to be stuck here for a bit longer."

"Oh Warren. Today of all days. What's going on?"

"Just waiting on some calls, but they are important so I can't leave right now."

"Do you think you'll get away in time for the party?"

"Jesus, I hope so." He'd be disappointed if he were stuck here more than an hour. "Cliff said we could come by any time after seven and it's just after two right now, so if I'm out of here by five, that still gives me lots of time to get home, get cleaned up and make it to the party with lots of breathing room. I'd like to get there a little early to give Cliff and Julie a hand with any last-minute preparations if they need help."

"I was hoping you'd be home this afternoon to help me put away these Christmas decorations. I want to have the house cleaned up before we go to the party, so that we don't have to deal with the mess tomorrow."

"It's not like I planned it this way." Warren smiles sheepishly, thinking that maybe he's lucky after all to have to stay at work a bit longer, as he hates putting away the Christmas decorations. "Why don't you get the girls to help you?"

"Because Bree isn't here. She's at Alex's, of course. I took her over be-fore lunch. It seems like she lives there lately. I don't know that I like that so much. Alex seems like a good kid, but we've all heard the stories about him, and it seems like trouble follows him everywhere. Do we really want our daughter getting that close to him?"

"Come on, Lisa. Just cut him some slack." Warren pauses and con-siders his next comment as he doesn't want to upset her. "My advice is to not make a big deal out of this and ruin things for Bree. She seems really happy to be with him, and if you mess with that, she will hold it against you. If you go looking for trouble, you usually find it."

"I'm not looking for trouble. What kind of a bitch do you think I am?"

He can sense that he crossed a line with that last comment. Always en-gaging his mouth before engaging his brain.

"All I'm saying is that she has to watch herself with him."

"She's a smart kid. Let's give her some credit that she'll make wise de-cisions."

"You always side with her."

"No, I don't. And if you aren't looking to pick a fight with her, then why do I have to choose a side? Just let her be and trust her. She will do the right thing."

"How can you be so sure?"

"I think we've raised her right. Besides, I have talked to Cliff about Alex," Warren says. "He has known Alex for a long time. If there is one person in this town who can give us an honest, objective opinion about that kid, it's Cliff."

"So, what does he think?"

"He says we shouldn't worry. The kid has seen more than his fair share of trouble over the years, but through it all he has remained grounded and kept his nose clean," Warren says. "And you know Kate and Samantha. They are very protective of Alex. I think Bree is pretty safe with him, so give her some room, okay?"

"I wasn't saying Bree wasn't safe with him."

He can hear the frustration, maybe even a little anger, in Lisa's voice.

"I'm concerned about the amount of time she's spending with him. That's all."

He thinks it's time to shift the conversation. "So, if Bree isn't home and I'm stuck here, it's just you and Lauren on clean-up duty for this afternoon. Put her to work. She's a good little helper."

"I would, but she's not feeling all that well. I think she's coming down with a cold or something."

"I don't like to hear that," Warren says. He can't bear the thought of his little girl getting sick again. Her immune system hasn't fully recovered yet and she seems to catch everything going around. "We'll just stay home if she can't go to the party. It's probably too late to get a sitter for tonight."

"If she doesn't feel up to going, I'll stay home with her and you can go tonight. I wouldn't have fun at a party if she's not feeling well," Lisa says.

"That wouldn't be very much fun for you, so, if she's not up to going, we'll all stay home."

"Let's wait a few more hours and then we'll see how she's doing. She was up pretty late last night so she could just be overly tired. We'll see how she is feeling when you get home. Any idea how much longer you're going to be at the detachment?"

"I am hoping it won't be too long. I'm just waiting to hear back from an outside source, and you know you can't rush those things. It could be three minutes or three hours."

"I know you can't tell me anything about what you're working on, Warren, but can you at least tell me if it's serious. Should I be worried?"

"About me?"

"Yes, about you." He can imagine her rolling her eyes. "Who else would I be worried about every day when he goes off to work? The mailman?"

"I've told you a million times, Lisa, that you don't need to worry about me. Everything is okay right now."

He's about to tell her he will be home as quickly as possible when the private detachment phone line rings. It's the number they give to other police forces and officials when they are waiting to receive information for an investigation. "The other phone is ringing so I have got to go and answer it as there is no one else here right now. I will see you when I see you."

He disconnects the call before she has chance to respond, but he knows she's used to that. He also knows he'll catch hell from her later for cutting her off.

I wish she wouldn't let that little stuff bother her so much after all these years.

Quickly grabbing the private office phone, he says, "Constable Warren Hamilton here. How can I help you?"

"Constable Hamilton," a gruff voice with a very heavy southern drawl responds. Warren can tell right away from the gravel in his voice that this guy is a heavy smoker. "Sergeant Earl Boone with the Houston PD here. We hear that you have recovered a 2018 Kia Stinger that was reported stolen down here."

"That's right, Sergeant," Warren says. "There were no papers or any other means of identification in the vehicle, but the plates confirm that it is your missing car. What can you tell me about it?"

"Not a helluva' lot." The Texan cop pauses to cough. "The report says that it was stolen from the airport parking lot over five years ago. It was a brand-new vehicle at that time, not long off the assembly line. Hardly had any miles on her."

"Do you have any leads on what happened?"

"Nothing." Warren can hear him wheezing. "You have to understand, Constable, that Houston is a big city, and we receive lots of reports of stolen cars every day. Once they're gone, we hardly ever find them again because they are either taken out of the city and sold, or they're taken to chop shops and broken down for parts. I was surprised that you guys found this one. We had written if off because, like I said, it has been more than five years since it disappeared. Where did you say you are again?"

"Just a small town on the south shore of Nova Scotia," Warren tells him. "If you do a quick Google search and find Halifax, then we're about an hour and a half drive from there towards the southernmost tip of the province."

"I did do that before I called and no offence, Constable, but what in the hell is our stolen car doing all the way up there in the middle of nowhere?"

"I have no idea." *Offence taken*, Warren thinks. "That's why I wanted to speak with you. I wanted to see if you had any ideas about that."

"No. Not a clue," the Texan says. His accent is so thick that Warren can hardly understand some of the words. "It wasn't my case so anything I know about it is coming right out of the file."

"Can you tell me if the car's owner has any connection with Nova Scotia? That may tell us something."

"Just a second." He puts Warren on hold.

Sounds like this is a waste of time, Warren thinks while he waits. He wonders what his next step will be if this call doesn't pan out.

A few minutes later Sergeant Boone returns to the call. "Sorry for making you wait. Says here that the car was owned by a seventy-nine-year-old woman who passed away a few years back. She was a born and raised Texan. I'd say it's not likely that she had any connection to your neck of the woods."

"So that's it?"

"Yes-sir-ree-Bob." Sergeant Boone chases his comment with another loud coughing fit.

Warren waits for the officer to catch his breath.

"Sorry about that. Where was I? Oh yes. I was saying now that the car has been located, we'll mark the file closed."

"It may be closed for you," Warren says. *Clearly, this guy doesn't care anything about this car or wonder what it's doing in Nova Scotia.* "But it's still very active for us. We'd like to know how the vehicle ended up here and who was driving it. There must be some kind of connection to our province, something that's not obvious."

"Sorry, Constable, can't help you with any of that."

And clearly, you don't want to, Warren thinks. *Wouldn't want to take you away from your smokes.*

"Anything else, Constable?"

"I guess not. I should just let you go as you must have better things to do. After we are done with the forensics and paperwork, will you guys want it back?"

"Not likely, but that's not my call," Sergeant Boone answers. "My guess is we'll ask you to dispose of the vehicle, crush it or whatever you guys do with discarded vehicles up there. It's not worth shipping it back to us."

"Sometimes we junk them. Other times we may put them up for auction, depending on what shape they're in."

"The suits higher up the food chain can work that out." The sergeant chuckles. "That's way above my pay grade."

Poor excuse for a joke, Warren thinks. "Okay, Sergeant, thanks for your help."

"Thanks for letting us know you found the car and Happy New Year," the sergeant says as he hangs up.

Well, that was fucking useless. Thanks for all your valuable help—not!

13: A face in the window

Now that the snow has slacked off to just a few flurries, Cliff decides it's a good time to clear the driveway to make way for guests to park when they come to the party in a few hours.

I'll get to you in a minute, he thinks, eyeing his yellow Cub Cadet two-stage gas snowblower that he left standing in the corner of his garage after its tune-up a few weeks ago. It's ready to tackle the job that everyone knew would soon be coming but no one really wanted.

But, he thinks, remembering how badly his buddy Warren Hamilton hates the snow, *it's not so bad if you're ready for it.* There was a time that he also hated the winter, but he learned to accept it. He chuckles. *You just gotta embrace it and buy yourself one of these babies.*

The machine may be a few years old, but Cliff is proud that it still looks and performs as it did on the day he bought it. He gives it his personal attention, just like he does all his machines. This year, he gave the snowblower a complete overhaul and installed new spark plugs and starter, even though the old one still worked just fine.

He loves tinkering with small engines. It's a skill he picked up from his Old Man when he was growing up in Newfoundland.

"It still purrs like a kitten," he tells anyone who will listen as he brags about the snowblower. *So, I'm proud of my machines. Ain't nothing wrong with that.*

Addressing the Cub Cadet, he says, "I'm coming for you, baby. Just give me a few minutes."

I have something more important to do right now.

He removes two bottles of Scotch from the liquor store bag that he just brought home and left in the garage while he took the other booze inside the house. One bottle contains the expensive brand that his son-in-law asked for, the other being the cheapest bottle of whiskey he could find in the store. He places the bottles on the workbench.

Locating an empty water jug, Cliff opens the expensive bottle of Scotch and carefully pours the honey-amber-coloured liquid into it.

Man, that smells nice, he thinks, as the delicate aroma of the expensive Scotch fills the garage. He chuckles. *I hope no one walks in here right now or they'll think I'm getting a head start on the celebrations.*

He savours the smell. *I'm not much of a Scotch drinker, but I might actually like this. May have to try it later.* Even though he is alone in the garage, he adds, "Someone's gonna have to drink it."

Next, he opens the cheap bottle of whiskey and pours the liquid, with its slightly darker tones, into the bottle that had contained the more expensive Scotch.

"Shit." He curls up his nose. "That doesn't smell quite as nice." *Smells like perfume. I wouldn't drink this crap.*

Replacing the cap on the expensive Scotch bottle and twisting it tight, he looks at it, studies it. He's pleased with his handiwork. *Leo will never know the difference.*

He then drains the expensive Scotch from the water jug into the bottle that had contained the less costly whiskey and secures the cap.

Holding both bottles up to the light he whispers, "Take that, you son of a bitch."

Placing the expensive bottle containing the cheap whiskey back in the liquor store bag, Cliff thinks, *I'm done catering to that asshole. Ain't going to happen again.*

Thinking of Carly, he knows that Julie and his daughter would be pissed at him if they knew what he had just done, but as the official barkeeper this evening, he's pretty confident they will never find out. And if someone asks him why the new bottle is already opened, he'll just lie and tell them he opened it to enjoy the smell.

Cliff stashes the bottle containing the more expensive Scotch on a shelf under his workbench behind several other bottles and boxes, and then stands back to look at the inconspicuous hiding place.

"There," he whispers. "No one will ever find it under there."

That stuff's too good for that bastard. He grins. *Now to get that snow moved out of the way before everyone shows up looking for a place to park.*

He's just about to push the start button on the Cub Cadet when his cellphone rings. Slipping the silver-coloured Samsung Galaxy from the pocket of his navy Canada Goose winter coat that Julie gave him for Christmas, Cliff scans the small screen to see who's calling.

"Kate Webster," he mumbles as he's not used to getting calls from the lawyer. Usually, it's Samantha he hears from. "I hope she's not calling to tell me she and her family aren't coming tonight. That would be a real disappointment."

He pushes the talk button. "Hey Kate, my friend," he says, trying to remain chipper. "What's up?"

"Hey, yourself, Cliff," Kate answers. "Are you busy right now?"

"I'm always busy. But I can certainly make time to talk to you, if that's what you're asking. What's on your mind?"

"Samantha's here with me. I have my phone on speaker so we can both hear you. Are you alone?"

He immediately wonders what's up as it wouldn't take two people to cancel out on the party. "I'm out in the garage and there's no one else here. What's going on, ladies?"

"Well, Samantha and I want to talk to you about Gwen, Lily's daughter."

"I know who she is." Images of the bloody carnage that the young woman helped to unleash in this town more than thirteen years ago flash through his mind. He quickly shakes them off and asks, "What's she done now?"

"That's just the thing," Samantha says. "No one knows for sure."

"What are you talking about? Her probation officer should know everything about her—what she does, where she goes, who she's with, everything."

"You'd think that," Kate says. "But no one knows what she's up to because no one knows where she is."

"What the fuck?" Cliff blurts out. "Sorry, ladies. But what the fuck? How can her probation officer not know where she is?"

"It appears," Kate explains, "that when Gwen failed to make her scheduled check-in a few days ago, officers went to her boarding house to check on her, but by the time they got there, Gwen had already left. She had cleared out."

"And no one has any idea where she went?"

"Apparently not," Kate answers. "They can't locate her."

Cliff sighs. He hates to hear that the system has failed, but he knows that's an all-too-common occurrence.

"The thing is," Samantha says, "we're quite worried because we don't know if she would come back here."

"Do you think she would?" Cliff asks.

"I do, yes."

"Why? Her family is all gone and there's nothing left here for her."

"But there is," Kate tells him. "Alex is here, and he is her half-brother.

Besides that, Alex inherited most of Lily and Josh's money after they were killed. He can't touch the bulk of it until he turns twenty-one, but it is a considerable fortune, so Gwen may figure some of that money belongs to her, and we're afraid she might come after it. Or him."

"Jesus." Cliff answers. "I hadn't thought of that but, in light of her past actions, I suppose it's possible."

"That's just the thing. We know what she's done in the past, so we know what she is capable of," Kate continues. "Even though Probation Services saw fit to parole her, I'm not convinced that was the right thing to do."

"You don't think she is fully reformed?" Cliff asks.

"No." Cliff can sense the certainty in Kate's voice. "No, I don't. But I do think that she's capable of manipulating people and making them think she has been reformed."

"The bottom line," Samantha adds, "is that we don't trust her, and we are afraid of what she might do if she comes after Alex."

"Yeah, I hear you. So how can I help?"

"We were hoping that you could use some of your resources to help us find her," Kate says. "We are really worried about what this could mean for Alex."

"You do remember that I am retired, don't you?" Cliff senses his friends' anguish. "But I do have a few contacts in the business who may be able to help."

"That would be great," Samantha says. Cliff can hear the desperation in her voice. She adds, "We would appreciate whatever you can do and we're willing to pay you for your services, obviously."

"Absolutely not," Cliff answers. He has known these two women for a long time, and he has always had a soft spot for them. "That won't be necessary. I'm not really sure how much help I can be, but I will put out some feelers. It will be like throwing spit balls at a wall and seeing which ones will stick, but you never know."

"We know this could be a long shot," Kate says. "But we didn't know who else to call and we just couldn't do nothing. We're just worried about Alex."

"I'm sure he's not in any danger," Cliff says. "But you can't be too careful. I'll make a few calls. Just remember, though, I can't promise that I can get you any answers."

"We understand." Samantha says. "We're just relieved that you are there for us. Without you to talk to about this, we would be lost."

"Understood." Cliff is slightly embarrassed by the comment. "I'll do my best," he promises. Taking a deep breath, almost afraid to hear the answer, he asks, "So, in light of what you just told me, are you guys still planning on coming to the party tonight?"

"We are still planning on being there," Samantha says. "We can't let this thing with Gwen control our lives."

"We've already told Julie that we would be there," Kate adds. "And unless something major happens, that is still our plan."

"That's good. Looking forw—What the fuck?"

"What is it, Cliff?" the women ask in unison. "Something wrong?"

"When I looked out my garage window just now, there was a face right there, staring back at me," he says. Making a quick beeline to the garage door, he adds, "I've got to check this out. Bye."

He ends the call with his friends, throws open the garage door and sprints outside, the brisk air immediately slapping the exposed skin on his face.

Moving to the side of the garage where the window is, he glances around the yard. The grey mid-afternoon sky creates an ominous atmosphere. As the snow-laden storm clouds move in, it all feels oppressive and heavy to him.

He sees no one.

"What the fuck?" He scans the surrounding neighbourhood. He shivers again as icy chills race up his spine. He's sure he saw someone out here.

"God-damn it," he whispers. On the ground below the window, he spies a set of footprints in the snow that confirm someone was, in fact, just here.

Bending to study the footprints, Cliff is angry that anyone would have the guts to spy on him.

He suddenly recalls the woman he had noticed checking him out in the liquor store. He can't shake the feeling that she was surveilling him. He's been in police work long enough to know what that looks like.

The problem is, with the snow and the fact that whoever was just here a few minutes ago was obviously wearing boots, I may never know even know if it was a man or a woman, where they came from or where they went.

How the fuck did you move so quickly? he wonders. *Where in hell did you go?*

Doing another quick scan of the yard, he exhales, a cloud of breath forming in front of his mouth.

"I don't know who the fuck you are," he says, hoping the cold air will carry his words to whoever was just spying on him. "But if I catch you creeping around my property and spying on me or my family, I'll blow your fucking brains out."

Turning to head back inside his garage, Cliff stops suddenly when a series of low-pitched, guttural caws and cackling calls pierce the frigid air. He's heard these noises many times over the years, and he knows exactly what's making them.

"Crows." *Sounds like a lot of them.*

He scans his surroundings. The sounds are like ice water running through his veins.

That's just what I need right now on top of everything else that's happening.

He moves quickly to the garage door and ducks inside. After all the dealings he's had with the crows, he knows this visit means one of two things—"Either something good is about to happen or this town is about to get the shit kicked out of it again."

It's usually the second one.

14: When nine crows take flight

The nine crows in this murder have spent most of the day travelling from one location to other, vigilantly observing those they are destined to safeguard.

The dangers are real, and dispersed widely throughout the town. There are many threats targeting those under the flock's protection, but, for now, those dangers remain obscure, hidden behind a cloud of deceit and subterfuge.

Those who pose the dangers lurk in obscure places. They hide in the shadows and crouch around the corners, waiting for their opportunity to pounce. When that opportunity presents itself, they will strike, usually with deadly intentions and often with fatal results.

Watching from a distance, the crows have seen the retired police officer struggle over the years as he comes to grips with his own fate and their existence. He doesn't know how to react to them—are they friend or foe? He doesn't understand that while he often feels threatened by their presence, they have always been his greatest allies.

The crows have tried to communicate with him, to connect with him on many occasions, but he has not always received the messages as intended.

For whatever reason, he rebuffs their overtures. He has not been as receptive as others in this town. Instead, he resists, throwing up roadblocks.

This human—this man—is powerful. He is strong-willed, determined, set in his ways, and not easily swayed from his beliefs. He is a practical man who deals only with facts and absolutes. The crows know that, to reach him, they must find another way, for it is important that he receive their message. Futures are at risk....Lives hang in the balance.

The crows know what they must do. They will be persistent. They must find a way to get to him.

The nine remain forever on alert, vigilant and ready to react. Forces which threaten or pose danger to those they are destined to protect ought to take heed, for these black birds—these sentinels that have watched over this town for the past three centuries, defending the weak and the vulnerable—will not stop until their work is done.

That is their way. That is their sworn duty. That is their responsibility and their purpose.

When nine crows take flight, they are always on a mission. That mission today is to watch and strike, when necessary, but, above everything else, to protect.

15: Forerunners

Carly finds her mother in the kitchen, where Julie is watching Cliff through the back door window as he pushes the yellow snowblower down the long snow-covered driveway. It's the same driveway where Carly learned to ride her bike many years ago.

For a second, her mind flashes to those bright summer days filled with sunshine and laughter, when her father would chase after her. She would giggle as her tiny legs pedalled as quickly as they could to escape the "monster" that was going to "get" her.

It was so much fun. She sighs, almost wishing she was that little girl again.

"Hey, Mom. Do you have a few minutes to talk?"

"Of course, my darling girl," Julie answers. "Always."

Her mother turns from the door and smiles at her. "I was just about to make myself a cup of tea. I need a little pick-me-up before the last-minute rush to get ready for this evening." She nods toward the table. "Why don't you sit down, and I'll make one for you, too."

"That would be nice. Thanks. How's Daddy doing out there? Looks like we had more snow this morning than anyone was counting on, but nothing like what they are still calling for over the next few days."

"Oh, you know your father." Julie chuckles. "He's in his glory out there. He's happy as long as he can push that snowblower. As soon as there's a flurry in the sky, he gets all fired up."

Removing two large ceramic cups, one blue and one green, from the cupboard, she adds, "I swear to God that man is infatuated with that freaking snowblower. I've never seen a man love a machine as much as he loves that one. It's not normal."

Carly laughs as she takes a chair at the table. "Maybe you have competition, Mom."

"I think you may be right." Julie drops Red Rose tea bags—her preferred brand since she started drinking tea when she was thirteen—into the cups, followed by boiling water. "I'm surprised he doesn't bring it to bed with him."

"Oh, Mom." Carly laughs. "It isn't that bad."

Julie retrieves the milk cartoon from the refrigerator while the tea steeps. "I don't know. Sometimes I wonder about him. He is getting older, you know. I'm afraid he may be losing it. Maybe senility is sitting in."

"I can just see it now." Carly says. "Do you think he will be out there much longer?"

Julie glances out the window and watches as her husband methodically manoeuvres the snowblower down one side of the driveway then back up the other side. She then turns her attention back to the cups, removes the teabags and then adds a splash of milk to each cup. She adds a level teaspoon of sugar to Carly's cup.

"I'd say probably another hour or so. That's a big driveway and there's a lot of snow to move."

"Right." Carly exhales.

A cup in each hand, Julie joins her daughter at the table. "Why? Something going on that you don't want your father to hear?"

"Not really. Well, maybe. Yes, I guess so."

"What is it, sweetheart? Are you alright? Are the girls okay?" Julie asks. She slides one of the hot cups to her daughter. "Those two precious angels are so much fun to have around. Your father and I just love them to pieces. If something is wrong, I hope you know that you can talk to us about anything."

"Everything is just fine with the girls." Carly forces a smile that is actually more like a grimace. "They are both down for naps. They were exhausted and I hope they sleep for a few hours, so they aren't cranky tonight."

"What's going on, then?"

"You will be angry."

Julie shakes her head and takes her daughter's hand. She squeezes gently. "I promise you that I won't be angry."

Carly exhales. "I am so confused right now." She quickly brushes away the tears that trickle down her cheeks. "I just don't know what to do."

"What's going on, honey? Let me help you."

"So, I talked to Leo earlier. It was just before lunch."

"And? What did Leo have to say?"

"More of the usual."

"I see. How did that make you feel?"

"I don't know, Mom. That's why I'm so confused."

"How so?"

"He talks a good game."

"He sure does. Always has. In fact, your father always said that Leo's mouth is his greatest asset."

Carly forces a smile. "Daddy calls 'em likes he sees 'em.... And he isn't wrong about that."

"My God. Don't tell your father that he was right about anything. It will go straight to his head, and I'll never hear the end of it." Julie laughs and Carly knows her mother is trying to relieve the tension.

"He was all apologetic and said all the same old things," Carly says. "Leo knows what he did was wrong, so now he apologizes and expects me to forgive him, but I can't forget it that easily."

"Of course, you can't. Leo hurt you very badly. You need time to heal."

Carly shakes her head and glances at the back door as if she's expecting someone to walk in. "That's just the thing, Mom. I don't think I can forgive him. Truthfully, I don't *want* to forgive him. I've tried really hard to get in a good space about this, but every time I try to forgive him, I just picture him with another woman, and I want to vomit."

Julie sighs. "You didn't deserve this."

Carly snuffs back the tears that are close to bursting through the emotional dam she's built around herself. "He betrayed me." Her words are soft, almost a whisper. "How can I ever forgive him and move on as if nothing happened? I'm not sure I can ever trust him again."

"I can't tell you how you could do that, and I won't tell you that you have to forgive him. Only you can decide that. But I think your father and I have made it very clear how we feel."

"Yes. And I know you are both right."

"Sometimes, when the people we love break our hearts, the pain runs so deep that we can't stand to be around them," Julie says. "You may never find it in your heart to forgive Leo."

Carly brushes tears from eyes.

"I know it's hard, Carly," Julie continues. "But you must listen to what your gut is telling you and then follow your heart. Look what your father and I went through all those years ago. Love can be hard, and both people in a relationship must nurture it. Leo squandered your trust and destroyed that sacred covenant between a husband and wife."

"Maybe it's time that I accept it's over between Leo and me."

"I thought you told me that you and Leo were thinking about having another baby. What happened to that plan?"

"It wasn't a plan." Carly closes her eyes. "That was all Leo's idea, but I know this is not the right time to have another baby. I am nowhere ready for that."

"So, then, what are you going to do Carly? What's your plan? What do *you* want? Is Leo still coming to the party tonight?"

"He is, or he was, as of an hour ago."

"What are you going to tell him when he gets here?"

"I'm thinking that I will tell him that I have decided to stay here with you and Daddy for a while, if the invitation is still open."

Julie smiles. "You and the girls will always have a place here with us. You can stay as long as you like. You know that."

"Thanks, Mom." She sighs and looks at her mother. "I know that, but I never want to assume anything. If this situation with Leo has taught me one thing, it's that I should never take anything for granted."

"Oh, my God, Carly. You know we are always here for you," Julie says. "All you have to do is say the word."

She nods. "Please don't tell Daddy about this. I know you guys don't keep any secrets from each other, but I should be the one to tell him."

"Of course, you should be. But don't worry about what your father will think. He is behind you one hundred percent. He wants what's best for you and the girls." She pauses and then asks, "So how do you think Leo will react?"

"He will be pissed." Carly's bottom lip quivers just as it did when she was a little girl trying to hide her feelings from her parents. "He wants me to come back to Halifax with him and pretend like nothing ever happened. Once I tell him I'm staying here, I expect he'll storm off and go back to the city. He will think I betrayed him and find a way to put the blame all on me."

"Let him go. The best thing he can do right now is give you space to think clearly. You don't need him pressuring you and telling you what you should do."

"Right." Carly says. She takes a deep breath and then exhales. "So then, I guess that's settled."

"My darling girl. I hate to see you suffering like this. You don't deserve to be treated this way."

"I know, Mom. But it's done now, and I have to figure out what's next for me and the girls."

"Exactly. You know you can stay here as long as you need to. Those babies upstairs need stability." She pauses. "And safety."

"Thank you so much. That's my thinking, too." Carly takes another sip of her tea and smiles at her mother. "I know you have things to do to get ready for tonight, but there is one more thing, if you have time."

"Of course, honey. Everything is pretty much handled. What's up?"

"I wanted to talk to you about some strange things that have been happening around here today."

"Strange? As in someone knocking three times at the back door even though, when you checked, there was no one there? Strange, as in someone saying your name in your ear even though no one did?"

Carly slowly nods. "That kind of strange. But there was also the howling dog."

"The howling dog?" I don't know anything about a howling dog."

"That's because I didn't tell you." Carly looks into her mother's eyes. "I knew you would say it's another sign or something like that, and I didn't want to freak you out."

"I am already freaked out," Julie says. "But go ahead."

"It was last night—this morning, actually—around three o'clock. Like most nights lately, I wasn't sleeping very well, and I swear to God that I heard a dog howling outside my bedroom window. Since you don't have a dog, I thought it was pretty weird. I also thought maybe it was a neighbour's dog and something was wrong with the poor thing, because it was a very mournful sound, like maybe the animal was in distress and needed help. So, I got out of bed, went to the window, and looked out, but I couldn't see any dog anywhere. The moon was pretty bright and there was hardly a cloud in the sky, so I'm sure if there had been a dog, I would have seen it."

"You know, they say these types of things come in threes," Julie says dryly. She takes her daughter's hand again. "Three is an important number in Nova Scotian superstitions. Bad luck always comes in threes. Deaths in a family or neighbourhood always comes in threes. Signs of death always come in threes. My grandmother always said that it had something to do with the Holy Trinity."

"Come on, Mom. Now you are really freaking me out."

"This isn't good, honey," Julie whispers. Carly can tell her mother is struggling to keep her emotions under control. "Hearing a howling dog, when there's no dog present, is another sign."

"Another sign of what?"

"Death." Exhaling forcefully, she adds, "You've experienced three signs of death in the last twenty-four hours. This is very powerful."

"Sorry, but I didn't think it meant anything and I know how you worry about these things, so I just chalked it up to my overactive imagination." Carly offers an apologetic smile "What do you think all of this means?"

"I was raised in a family environment where all the superstitions seemed second nature to me," Julie says. "Maybe your current state of mind is making you more receptive to these 'happenings,' as the older folks called them, but I think it's only natural. Those three things that have happened to you are all signs that a death is going to occur and, if I'm being honest, that has me very worried."

"I know I've always told you that I don't believe in this stuff, but right now, I'm not so sure what I believe any more. Would you say these things are like premonitions?"

Julie nods. "In a way. Premonitions are usually visions you have in your head, but these signs—forerunners—are more tangible. They are something you see, like the image of a person, or sounds, like knocking or someone whispering your name or a dog howling. You haven't seen anything, have you? Because if you have seen a forerunner, that would be another powerful sign."

"Honestly, Mom, I haven't seen anything. If these things are all signs of death, is there any way to figure out who is going to die?"

Julie squints, as if she's thinking. "I have no idea, but according to legend, these signs indicate that a death is going to occur within three days, and it always means it will be someone close to you, maybe even a family member."

Carly sighs. "I don't need this right now. Why am I receiving these messages all of a sudden?"

"I've always heard that anyone can receive such messages," Julie says. "However, ever since you were a child, I have felt there was something special about you. I think you are more receptive to these forces than most people."

"Really? Why?"

"I have never told you this, but when I was pregnant with you, your great-grandmother Mae—that would be your grandmother's mother—became very ill. She died on the day that you were born, actually about an hour before you came into this world. According to the legends, if a birth and death in a family happen on the same day, then there is a chance that your souls may connect somewhere out there in the universe. It's like you are two souls that reunite in another realm."

Carly looks at her mother with disbelief. "Come on, Mom. You don't really believe that, do you?"

"I don't know." Julie says, shrugging. "That's what the legend says. But remember how I always told you that I believed you were an old soul trapped in a young body?"

"I do." Carly smiles but it's more like a cringe.

"Well. Maybe there was some truth to that."

"So I'm an old woman?"

"Not at all," Julie says. "You are an old soul. And there's nothing wrong with that. It just means you are more grounded, wiser, and more in tune with your surroundings than a lot of other people. It's actually a good thing."

"I don't feel so wise these days."

"Don't sell yourself short, Carly. You are a very intelligent, vibrant young woman. Sure, you are going through a rough patch, but you will get through this."

After a moment, Julie adds, "You would have loved Grandmother Mae, and she would have loved you. She was kind and generous. She always knew when something was bothering me and exactly what to say to make me feel better. She used to call me Jellybean. I thought that was such a fun nickname. She was a sweet woman and I see a lot of her in you."

"I wish I had met her."

"I believe she is with you," Julie says. She takes her daughter's hand again. "I know it seems hopeless right now, but we will get through this together."

"I hope so, Mom, because I can't take much more."

Julie smiles at her daughter. "Someone is watching over you—maybe even your great-grandmother Mae. Trust me. You'll be fine."

"How do you know?"

"I just know."

"I love your optimism, Mom. It gives me hope."

16: Brothers

There, Cliff thinks. He turns off his Cub Cadet, stands back and admires his handiwork. *That's a beautiful thing. Glad to have that all done, at least until the next round.*

Surveying the neat banks of snow that run along both sides of his long, paved driveway, he almost bursts with pride. "Good job, buddy," he says to the snowblower. "Let's get you back inside for a little rest before the big storm hits tomorrow. If it's going to be as bad as they say, I'll need you to be in tip-top shape."

"Cliff Graham. Are you really talking to that stupid machine?"

He hadn't seen Julie come out onto the back steps.

"What am I going to do with you?"

"What?" Cliff feels sheepish. He knows he fusses over his machines to the point of obsession, but tinkering with them is how he passes his time. Furthermore, he tells anyone who will listen, it's a good stress-reliever. He remains coy. "I don't know what you mean."

"Oh Cliff, you are just too funny." Julie laughs. "Maybe you two would like to get a room."

"Keep it up and I may just sleep in the garage tonight with this baby." He smiles at the woman standing in front of him, wearing nothing but a thin navy turtleneck on one of the coldest days so far this winter. "You need something, or did you just come here to freeze to death?"

"I was just checking to see how much longer you were going to be out here."

"A few more minutes. Why?"

He sees her wrap her arms around her tiny body to stave off the bitter winds. "I just wanted to let you know that I was going to take a shower so I can make myself pretty for our guests." She laughs in that playful manner that he loves.

"You don't have to make yourself look pretty, my lovely wife." He's sure that, after all these years, she knows he means what he says. If there is one thing people like about Cliff, it's that he holds no punches. "You're always pretty in my eyes."

"You're only saying that because I'm your wife and you think you have to."

"I wouldn't lie about that. You will be the most beautiful woman at the party tonight."

"Okay, mister. Flattery will get you everywhere."

"You need me for something?"

"The girls are having a nap and Carly's in the kitchen, having a cup of tea with me. I thought maybe you would like to come in and spend a bit of time with her before the party."

"Does she need company?"

"I don't know. I just thought she might like to have someone to talk to, that's all."

"I see." Cliff studies his wife's facial expression to see if she is trying to tell him something without actually saying a word. He's getting a strange vibe from her right now. "And you are sure that everything is okay?"

"All I'm saying is that you should try to find some time to talk to her."

She glances away as an RCMP vehicle pulls up the driveway. "Is that Warren?"

"I believe it is. I'll go see what he wants. Can you please tell Carly that I will be right in?"

"Of course." She turns toward the door. "Tell Warren I'll see him later."

Cliff heads toward the Ford Explorer, watching as the driver's side window goes down. "What's up, Brother?"

"Not so much," Warren answers, poking his head out the window. "Just finished my shift."

Cliff glances at his watch and sees that it's just after three-thirty. "A little late, aren't you? Someone forget to tell you it's New Year's Eve?"

"Had to finish up some paperwork, but now I'm ready to kick back and relax for four days. I need a break."

Cliff nods. "So, why are you way out here this afternoon? You live in the other direction."

"Picking up Bree at Alex's house because, as you know, Lisa isn't comfortable with driving in the snow. After that, I'm heading home to get ready for the party. Since I was driving past, I thought I'd see if you need help with anything. I figured I'd find you out here playing in the snow."

"That'd be me." Cliff chuckles. "Just one man and a mighty machine out here against the natural elements. I know you hate snow, Brother. I used to hate it, too, but you can't stop it from coming so you have to find some way to adapt to it. It's either that or you'll be miserable for four months."

"Guess I'll be miserable for four months," Warren says.

Cliff smirks. He knows his friend is a lost cause when it comes to him ever embracing winter. "So, listen," he says. "I am glad you stopped. There is something I want to talk to you about, if you have a second."

Warren nods. "What do you need?"

"It's not me, actually," Cliff says. "It's for Samantha and Kate."

"What's going on with them that they need help from the police?"

"It really involves their youngest son, Alex. He was adopted, you know."

"I knew that. He's dating my daughter, remember? I know everything there is to know about that kid."

"Of course, you do." Cliff is sure Warren would have done a deep dive on Alex Goodwin the minute the kid showed any interest in dating Bree. "I'd do the same thing if any boy was interested in my daughter," he says. "Wish I had dug deeper a few years ago."

"Leo?" Warren asks.

"Yes, the little prick." Cliff sighs. "Anyway, enough about that asshole. The events that left Alex an orphan took place more than thirteen years ago, so you don't know any of the other people involved."

"Not personally, but I've read the files," Warren says. "And, of course, I've heard all the stories. It is a small town, after all."

"It is that." Cliff chuckles. "There are no secrets here."

"I know you were the lead investigating officer," Warren continues. "It would have been a tough case."

"It was horrible. One of the worst cases I ever had to work on." Cliff takes a deep breath as images from that horrific June day flood into his memory. "Since you've read the file, you know that Alex's half-sister, Gwen Pittmann, was involved with the murders, and she was sentenced to serve twenty years for the role she played."

Warren nods.

"Well, she was recently paroled after serving thirteen years," Cliff says. "A condition of her release is that she is supposed to check in with her probation officer on a regular basis—"

"And they lost her."

"Exactly."

Warren shakes his head. "This fucking system only works half of the time."

"But the thing is, now Gwen has disappeared, and no one knows where she has gone. Kate and Samantha are freaking out because they think she may show up here."

"Here? Why?"

"It's simple," Cliff says. "Alex came into a great deal of money when his parents died and Gwen, who is Lily's daughter by her first husband, figures some of that money belongs to her. Kate and Samantha asked me if I can help them find the girl and I'm wondering if you guys have heard anything or received any bulletins about her."

Warren shakes his head. "You know how it works. We're only notified if a dangerous offender, like a pedophile, is released on parole and there's a chance he may be a threat to re-offend. We're not usually told about people like her when they're released. It's a good thing that family members and victims keep track of those dealings, because they can't always count on the system to get it right."

"Yeah, I knew it was a long shot, but I thought I'd ask."

"I can ask dispatch to issue a bulletin if you'd like. Just to put everyone on alert."

"Would you do that?"

"For sure. Just give me a second." Warren lifts the mic from its mount on the dash of the SUV.

Cliff listens as his friend asks the dispatcher to call up the file for Gwen Pittmann and then to issue an all-points bulletin stating that the girl's whereabouts are currently unknown but that there's a chance she may be heading to Nova Scotia.

"There." Warren returns the mic to the stand. "That should do it."

"Thanks, Brother," Cliff says. "Samantha and Kate will be relieved. I owe you one."

"You can pay me back with a beer later." Warren chuckles while glancing at the digital display clock in the dash. "I guess I should be on my way, because Lisa is expecting me. Lauren is not feeling well, but I'm hoping that won't affect anything for tonight."

"Damn. Anything serious?"

"I hope not. Lisa thinks it's probably just the start of a cold, or maybe she's just overly tired cause she was up late last night, but you know we can't be too careful with Lauren," Warren says. "It's been a few years since her last treatment, but we're always afraid that she'll relapse." He takes a deep breath. "I couldn't handle that."

"Is there any chance that she could relapse?"

"Doctors say that, with the type of childhood leukemia Lauren had, there's a very good chance it will never come back. When she had her annual check-up a few months ago, they said she was all clear, so we're thankful for that. But we'll always worry about it."

"I'm sure you will." Cliff studies his friend's face, looking for any signs of emotions but Warren Hamilton is a pro at hiding his feeling. *Just like most cops*, Cliff thinks. He says, "Okay, Brother, but please let me know if there is anything I can do to help, and by I, I mean me and Jules. You know we are always here for you guys."

Warren smiles. "You do the same."

"Well, then," Cliff says. "Now that you brought it up, I'm not really looking for any help but there is something I want to tell you about."

"What's going on, Cliff?"

"Since we are sharing secrets, I want to tell you about something weird that's been happening today."

"There seems to be a lot of *weird* going around."

"How do you mean?"

"You know that stolen red Kia Stinger that I found abandoned out on the highway?"

Cliff nods.

"Turns out the official owner is deceased and, according to her file, she has no known connection to Nova Scotia. Isn't that something?"

"It is something," Cliff agrees. "But it's not clear what."

"So, Brother, what's really going on with you?"

"It started this morning when I was in the liquor store," Cliff explains. "I swear to Christ that I spotted a woman checking me out."

"Doing surveillance on you?"

"Yes. Weird, right?"

"Very weird."

"Then I was in the garage a little while ago, and when I looked out the window, I swear to God there was someone there looking back in at me. It damned near scared the shit out of me."

"Holy fuck. For real?"

Cliff nods. "By the time I ran outside, they were long gone and I couldn't see many footprints."

"And I thought I was having a strange day. No one wants to have a stalker. What can I do to help?"

"Nothing right now. But just keep this between us. I haven't told Jules about it, because the last thing I need right now is for her to freak out. It's probably nothing, anyway."

Warren squints at his friend as if he's thinking. "Come on, Brother. You and I have been around this business long enough to know that you can't dismiss anything. You have to be ready for all possibilities and anticipate the worst. That's police work 101."

"Believe me, I know the playbook. I practically wrote the damned thing, and I'm always prepared," Cliff says. "But I don't think it's anything to lose my shit over. Probably just some busybody being nosy. You know what people are like." He takes a deep breath and exhales. "Now you should be on your way before your wife kicks your ass. You are already running late."

"Right. I'm going. See you tonight," Warren says as he puts the SUV window up, starts the vehicle and heads down the driveway with a wave.

Love that guy, Cliff thinks as an icy wind suddenly blows up and leaves him shivering. He shudders despite his thick, duck down insulated winter coat. *It feels like someone just walked over my grave.*

"Well, partner," he says to the snowblower, "let's get you back into the garage."

Glancing upwards, he freezes in place, shocked to see a flock of crows circling overhead.

"Now fellas," he says as he counts the large black birds. *Nine. I'll have to ask Samantha what that means. She always seems to know about that crow stuff.*

"I want you to listen to me." He hopes the cold wind will carry his words to the crows. He's learned over the years that, for some reason, the black birds seem to understand what he says. "I don't want any trouble right now. Please leave me and my family alone."

He watches a few minutes longer while the crows continue to circle above him. Then, as if on cue, they quickly fly off to an unknown destination, leaving him feeling empty.

He feels the blood drain from his head and extremities as the beating of his heart hits a fever pitch, threatening to burst from his chest. "Please, not again."

17: Warnings

Warren Hamilton is a veteran RCMP officer, with almost twenty-five years of experience under his belt. He believes he is a good cop and through his experiences on the job he has honed his skills, but above everything else, he has learned to trust his gut.

His instincts have rarely failed him over the years, and right now his gut's telling him to pay attention to the warnings that have presented themselves today.

It started this morning with the red Kia that he found abandoned on the side of a road. That discovery is not sitting well with him, nor is the fact that it was stolen more than five years ago in Texas.

What the hell is up with that? he wonders.

Pulling into the driveway at Samantha and Kate's house, where Bree has spent most of the day with her boyfriend, Alex Goodwin, he can't shake the feeling that there is something very important about that mysterious vehicle.

Then there's all the stuff that Cliff just told him about Gwen, who has seemingly fallen off the face of the earth.

Will she come back here, as Samantha and Kate fear? Is she dangerous? Would she target her half-brother? Is Bree in any danger by hanging out with Alex?

Warren considers the questions. Should he prohibit Bree from seeing Alex until this matter is resolved and Gwen is located? He knows Bree wouldn't be happy about that, and she can be a feisty one when she's angry.

Just like her mother. He smirks at his weak attempt at levity. *Clearly, there's nothing here to laugh about. And what about that crazy shit that's going on with Cliff?*

Warren blows the horn to let his daughter know he is waiting for her.

A stalker, or someone following him? Someone spying on him? What the hell is that all about?

Warren knows Cliff is still a good cop, even though he's been retired for a while, but he's worried about him. He believes Cliff will be careful. *But it's hard to prepare for the unknown.*

Glancing around the affluent neighbourhood, Warren can't help but to be impressed by the many opulent homes that line the quiet street. He believes the modest bungalow where Kate Webster and Samantha Henderson live looks a little out of place amongst the upscale properties that some of the town's wealthiest and most influential residents call home.

Not that there's anything wrong with living in a modest home, but not really what you'd expect the town's mayor to live in, he concludes. However, he notes that since he's gotten to know Samantha, he has never once felt that she put on airs, so her modest home seems like a good fit for her.

Hell, I live in a modest home, but what else would you expect on a cop's salary?

But he's okay with that. If money fuelled his existence, he would never have gotten into police work in the first place. Instead, he's always felt that police work was a calling, something he felt compelled to do.

At least we're not starving or living in a tent, he tells himself. *But there are days when I wish we had the money to do the things we want to do, like those renovations we've talked about for years but never seem to have the cash to do.*

That's why he's sure Lisa will shoot down his idea for a trip to Cuba this spring, *even though we both could use the break.*

He understands why his wife keeps a close rein on the finances. It has been especially tight since Lisa took a leave of absence from her job as a critical care nurse four years ago, when their youngest daughter, Lauren, became ill.

But he knows that was the right thing to do. *We needed someone to be home with Lauren and with Lisa's medical training and experience, she was the obvious one to put her career on hold for a few years.*

No regrets, he thinks. Lauren's health came first, and it always will. Now, remembering the struggles his youngest daughter went through to overcome leukemia, he just hopes she's going to be okay.

He's been worrying ever since Lisa told him this morning that Lauren wasn't feeling well. *Please, God. Don't let her be sick again. I can't go through that again and I don't want to see her have to deal with that pain again.*

Come on, Bree, he thinks, trying hard not to become impatient. He smiles at the thought, because no one has ever accused him of being a patient man.

But I've got things to do.

He thinks about the missing Gwen Pittmann. He cringes as the images that are part of the official record flash through his head.

Not pretty, he thinks.

He's read the file several times since his daughter started dating Alex, so he is fully versed on the tragedy that left the young boy an orphan. The conversation he had with Cliff just a few minutes ago, however, re-kindled his interest in that case.

He's just about to hit the horn again when he sees his daughter emerge from the bungalow and walk toward the Explorer.

Finally.

"Hey, honey," he says as Bree slides into the passenger seat. "Did you have a nice visit with Alex?"

"Yes." She pulls the seatbelt snugly around her tiny frame. "There. Good to go."

Warren puts the Ford into reverse and eases the vehicle back down the driveway. "Do anything exciting?"

"Not really. Just the usual."

Warren gets the distinct impression from her tone that his daughter does not want to talk to him.

"Everything okay between you and Alex?"

She nods. "Everything is fine. Why?"

"I don't know. You just seem a little distracted or something."

"No. Everything is fine."

"Okay, honey. If you're sure."

She glares at him. "Why do you and Mom always do that?"

"Do what?"

"Why do you always look for trouble?"

"We don't do that." Warren puts the vehicle back in park. "If we ask you questions, it's because we care about what you're doing, and we worry about you. Nothing more."

"Well, it feels like you're prying."

"So why does it seem like you're upset or mad about something?"

"I'm not."

Warren nods. "Yes, you are, and I want you to know that if something is bothering you, you can always talk to me and your mother." He pauses. "Let's try something else. How are Kate and Samantha?"

"They are okay, I guess."

"Are they still planning on attending Cliff's party tonight?"

"I guess so."

"How about Alex? How's he doing?"

She puts her head down. "He's okay, too," she mumbles.

Warren detects a change in his daughter's tone and demeanour. Whatever is going on with her, it involves her boyfriend.

"You and Alex have a problem, Bree?" he asks, gently.

"We're perfectly fine. Stop trying to cross-examine me. You've spent far too much time in Provincial Court."

Warren touches her left arm. "You're right. But I can tell something is bothering you. I am not going to let this drop. Let me help you."

"Fine," she whispers. "If you must know, Alex is worried that the crows are acting up again."

"The crows?" Warren didn't see that coming. "Why would he be worried about crows?"

"Come on Dad." She rolls her eyes. "I've told you that Alex seems to have this special bond with the crows around here."

He nods. "I still don't understand it, but I remember that you've told me about it."

"He thinks that the crows are trying to tell him something, maybe a warning."

"Can they do that?" Warren asks, his eyebrows knotting together.

"Yes. It's like they can tell him when something is wrong, and he just gets it. He's been getting these vibes from the crows that something bad is about to happen."

"Do they give him any idea about what that's going to be?"

She shakes her head. "It's not that specific, but they've got him worried. When the crows are warning him, they are usually pretty accurate."

"Is there anything you can do help him?"

She shakes her head again and Warren can see that she is really upset.

"Is there anything *I* can do?"

"I don't think so."

"He's been through a lot this year, Bree. In fact, he's been through a lot during his entire lifetime. Maybe all of that is just coming to the surface," Warren suggests.

"It's more than that, Dad," she says. "And if he is worried, then I'm worried for him."

"I don't like seeing you upset like this," Warren says. "Maybe you should give him some space."

"Don't."

"Don't what?"

"Don't even suggest that I stop seeing Alex."

"I know Alex is special to you and he seems to like you a lot, but take it from someone who has had more than his fair share of issues to deal with: sometimes we need space to get our heads straightened out. That's all I'm suggesting."

"Now you sound like mom."

"Okay, Bree." Warren puts the SUV into reverse again. "Let's not argue about this right now. I've got to get home. Lauren wasn't feeling well this morning so I'm anxious to see how she's doing."

"Wait a minute, Dad," Bree says sharply.

He hits the brakes. "What? Did you forget something?"

"No." She points toward the east-side corner of the bungalow. "But did you see that?"

"See what? I don't see anything."

"There was someone there, just a second ago. Kind of hanging around the house. It seemed kind of creepy to me."

Warren recalls what Cliff told him about someone lurking around his property, and puts the vehicle into park again. "Are you sure?"

"Yes."

"Tell me what they looked like."

"I didn't really get a good look."

"Was it a man or a woman?"

"I don't know." She shakes her head. "They were wearing a bulky winter coat, and they had the hood up."

"Okay, Bree," Warren says. "I am going to have a look around and you are going to stay in this vehicle. Under no circumstances are you going to open the door. Do you hear me?"

When she doesn't answer right away, he asks again, "Do you understand what I am saying, Bree?"

"Yes, Dad. I promise I'll stay right here."

"Good," he says. "And keep the doors locked. I won't be long."

After he gets out of the vehicle, he locks the doors with the button on his remote and heads up the driveway towards the house.

Noting that several crows are now flying over the house, Warren flinches. "Nine," he says after doing a quick count.

He wishes Cliff were with him right now. *He would know what the hell nine crows means.*

18: Phone calls

"Wait. Wait." Oliver gives the woman next to him a quick kiss on the lips and rolls around in the bed to look at his phone. "Just give me a second. I've got to see who this is."

"Whoever it is can wait," Anna whispers as she wraps her arms tightly around his neck. "We're not done yet."

Trying to catch his breath, he smiles. "It might be important."

"More important than me?"

"Nothing is more important than you." He snatches his cellphone from the bedside table. The screen immediately lights up. "Alex? Wonder what he wants?"

Anna sighs. "I think that's my cue to take a shower."

She slips out from under the cotton sheets, grabs her robe from a nearby chair and wraps it around her slender body.

"Please don't go. I don't have to take this."

"Yes, you do." She stops in the bathroom doorway, turns, and shoots him a playful smile. "See what your young friend wants, and when you're done, feel free to join me in the shower...if you'd like to."

His broad smile betrays his thoughts. "I'd like to, very much. I'll only be a minute."

"Don't keep me waiting too long."

Watching as she disappears into the bathroom and gently closes the door, Oliver takes a deep breath. *You are one lucky man, Oliver Lewis*, he thinks, as the cell rings again.

He considers letting the call go to voice mail but decides he better answer. He knows that if Alex is calling, it could be important.

Oliver and Alex have a special bond that was forged over events that unfolded earlier this year, when he helped to fend off a mortal enemy that had been after the boy's family for centuries. He's told Alex that if he needs anything he should call him, no matter the time of day. As Alex's protector, Oliver believes that is his sworn duty.

"Hi Alex," he answers.

"Can you talk, Oliver?"

"For a minute. What's up?"

"The crows are at it again."

"What?" He sits up straight in the bed. Alex now has his undivided attention. If something is going on with the crows, it could be serious. "How so?"

"They've been hovering around here for the past few days, and I know they are trying to tell me something."

"Why are you just calling me now? That's not the deal."

"I know, but I didn't want to bother you. You've already been through a lot."

"We've been through a lot, Alex, and you are not bothering me. Have you had any visions?"

"Not yet, but I can sense something is going to happen."

"Right. How many are there this time?"

"Nine."

"What does that mean?"

"According to the old legend, it's 'nine crows for a kiss,'" Alex says.

"That's an odd one. Any guesses as to where this could be going?"

"I don't have a clue. But remember, there is always the possibility of a hidden message in the number of crows."

"Right." Sensing the worry in the young man's voice, Oliver asks, "Are you okay?"

"Yes," Alex quickly answers. "Just a little on edge, I guess."

"Understandably so," Oliver says. "Do you want to meet up and talk about it?" He glances longingly toward the bathroom door, as he hears the shower running. "I could come over right now, if Kate and Samantha would be okay with that."

"No, I don't think you need to do that," Alex replies. "I really just wanted to give you a heads up."

"Are you going to be at the party tonight?"

"I'm planning to be there, as of right now, anyway."

"Then why don't we take a few minutes tonight to have a chat?"

"I don't want to ruin your party."

"You won't be ruining it for me. If you need to talk about this, then we'll find the opportunity to talk. We both know that when the crows are trying to tell you something, we better pay attention. Your safety is my top priority."

"Okay then, we'll talk about it." Alex sighs. "The crows see all. They know all."

"It seems that way. Is there anything else going on?" Oliver asks. "You sound stressed over the crows, and I don't like it. They don't mean you any harm."

"Past events suggest that I should be worried whenever the crows become active because it usually means there is a possible threat to me or someone I care for. Maybe we should all be worried."

"We will deal with this," Oliver assures the young man. "No matter what it is, I'll always be here to help you."

"Will you?" Alex asks. "I don't expect that you'll be around forever. You have your own life. You don't need to be preoccupied by some teenager who always seems to have some kind of trouble going on in his life."

"What are you talking about?"

"I'm happy you've found someone that you like being with, someone who makes you happy. You deserve that and you should be with her. You don't have to worry about me. I'll be okay."

Oliver wonders if the kid could have possibility picked up that he has been talking to Anna about moving to Halifax with her. *But how could he possibly know that?*

He adds, "I will always be here for you. It is my sworn duty as your protector. My destiny."

"I want you to be happy, Oliver."

"I am happy. In fact, I'm happier now than I have been in a very long time." Oliver pauses. "What's this really all about? Are you sure you're doing okay?"

"Yes, I'm fine," Alex insists. "Gotta go now. I'll see you tonight."

Oliver hears the call end.

Shit, Alex. What was that all about? He hears the shower stop. *Just as well.* He shrugs, hoping Anna won't be upset with him. *I'm not really in the mood anymore.*

~

Samantha answers her phone on the first ring. "Hi, Cliff. What's up?"

"Hey, Sam. Is Kate there with you?"

"She's in the basement putting away some Christmas decorations, but I can get her if it is urgent."

"It's not urgent. I just wanted to let you and Kate know that I have put out a few feelers about Gwen, like I promised I would."

"And?"

"It has only been two hours so nothing to report yet."

"Right."

"The chances of Gwen showing up here after all these years are pretty slim, don't you think? She's got to know there is nothing here for her."

"I'm not sure," Sam answers. "And we can't take any chances."

"No, I guess you can't be too careful when it comes to the boy, but it won't do any good to worry about this," Cliff says. "If she shows up here, we will handle it."

"How?"

"I guess that will depend on what she does, if she comes here at all."

"I can't just sit here doing nothing. There must be some way of finding her."

"They are looking, Sam. Warren knows what's going on. He's had them issue an all-points bulletin so every police officer across Nova Scotia is on the lookout for Gwen. If she's anywhere in this province, they will find her."

"How can you be so sure?"

"Because I trust the officers," Cliff says. "They are trained to watch for this sort of thing. There is no way she can stay hidden forever, not with all the modern technology they have at their disposal. If she's out there, they'll spot her."

"So, in the meantime, what are we supposed to do?"

"Just stay on your toes," Cliff says. He knows that telling Samantha Henderson to sit tight would be an exercise in futility. "Stay alert and call the police right away if you see anything suspicious. And most importantly, if you see the girl, do not approach her. You don't know if she's dangerous, especially if she's desperate."

"Thank you for helping, Cliff. I appreciate that."

"You're welcome. You know I'm always here if you need anything."

He had initially called because of the person lurking around his property and, even though he can't be sure if that has anything to do with Gwen Pittmann, he was going to give Samantha a heads up just in case. But now, after hearing how worked up she is, he's not so sure that's a good idea.

Why tell her something that's going to upset her even more than she already is? And I may be jumping to conclusions, because why would Gwen Pittmann be stalking me?

Instead, he asks, "Are you guys still coming tonight? Looks like the snow has stopped so everything should be fine."

"For now, at least, that's the plan," Samantha says. "We are all looking forward to it. I think everyone could use a little bit of fun right about now."

"I hear you, friend. I've got the driveway all cleared off, so you guys won't have any problems finding a place to park."

"Anyone cancel because of the weather?"

"Not yet," Cliff says. "I just hope it stays that way, because Jules has whipped up one shitload of food. I have no idea what we'd do with everything if people cancelled." He chuckles. "I'll be eating well for a week."

"Let's hope it doesn't come to that."

"Let's hope not. My waistline couldn't handle it."

"And you really don't think there's anything to worry about with Gwen?"

"Well, who can say for sure what someone in her position will do, but I honestly don't believe that she would show her face around here again," Cliff says.

"I hope you are right Cliff."

"Try not to worry, Sam. If she shows up here, we'll grab her and then she will go away again for a long time."

"You sound certain."

"You have been around long enough, Sam, to know that there are no guarantees with anything like this, but I am certain of one thing."

"And what's that?"

"You and your family have lots of friends in this town," he tells her. "If someone comes after you, then they come after all of us."

"Is it really like that?"

"It sure is. You and Kate have done a lot of good and people are watch- ing out for you.

"Thank you for saying that. Even if it's not true, I do feel better know- ing that we have people like you in our corner."

"We have been through a lot together over the years, you, me, and everyone in this town."

"We sure have."

"Those bloody crows have taken us on one helluva roller coaster ride, haven't they?"

"Indeed." She chuckles nervously, recalling the events of past years. "They sure have."

"And not always for the good, right?"

She says quickly, "What's up, Cliff? Is something going on with you and the crows again? Is that what you really called for?"

"Honestly, Sam." He should have known that she would have detected something. "I'm not sure. But yes, I think so."

"What is it?"

"Ever since this morning I've been seeing a flock of crows hovering around me. More than usual, if you know what I mean."

"A murder."

Cliff pauses. "Yes. I hate that name, but there has been a *murder* of crows hanging around me today."

"How many are there?"

"There are nine crows."

"Nine crows for kiss." Sam exhales. "Let me think on what this might mean, and we'll talk about it later this evening. That okay with you?"

"For sure. See you later then."

"Okay, Cliff," she says, ending the call.

"Nine crows for a kiss," she whispers. "What's up with that?"

19: Ghosts

The idea that she may have some kind of special, otherworldly connection to her long-dead great-grandmother Mae has left Carly feeling cold, confused and alone. She's now questioning everything she's ever believed, including her very existence.

It was all nonsense, wasn't it? She sighs.

Her thoughts are swirling as she considers what her mother told her. Forerunners, supernatural occurrences, the connection to an old woman that Carly never knew.

A woman who died on the same day I was born and is supposedly now reaching out to me from the Great Beyond? How do I make sense of all that? Could be pure coincidence or does that really mean something special? Is it even possible that there is some kind of cosmic connection between the two us?

She shivers at the thought. She isn't comfortable thinking of such possibilities, as she considers herself to be a rational person. The idea of anything paranormal has always seemed like fiction to her. Or, at the very least, old wives' tales and superstition. But now she isn't sure, as something definitely seems off to her.

I always thought people who delved into the supernatural were a little off kilter, she muses, but quickly decides that description does not fit her mother, who she has always felt is one the smartest, wisest and most grounded people she has ever known.

She is organizing the clothes her daughters will wear for this evening's festivities. The girls are excited about the expected visitors and have been awake for about half an hour now. To Carly's relief, her parents took their granddaughters downstairs to play and for a snack, but mostly to give her time to shower and get ready for the party.

Mom is so convincing when she talks about this stuff, and she makes me want to believe that maybe there is something to it. Besides, who can really say for sure what's real or not?

"There have been too many signs to just simply ignore them," Julie told her a few hours ago and ever since then Carly has been reviewing everything—an invisible barking dog, someone saying her name in her ear when there was no one else in the room except the girls, and three knocks at the back door even though there was no one there.

I'll admit that's some pretty weird stuff. She shudders. *And maybe it's nothing more than coincidences.*

"But what if it's not?" she whispers, even though she is alone in the room. "What if it really means something? What if all of those things are signs that someone is going to die?"

She looks at the knee-length red dress she has chosen to wear this evening, not that she has much choice, as it's the only one she brought with her from Halifax.

"Not really crazy about how it looks, but it will just have to do."

She suddenly catches a glimpse of someone walking past the open bedroom door. "What do you think, Mom? Do you like it?"

She waits for her mother to answer then asks again, "Mom? What do you think? Got a second to pop in here and have a look at this dress for me?"

When no one responds, Carly moves quickly to the door, pokes her head into the hallway and asks, "Mom, is that you? Are you out here?"

God-damned it, Carly, she thinks when she doesn't see anyone in the brightly-lit hallway with its rose-coloured paint and two windows, one at each end, both of which are casting thin shards of light onto the hard-wood floor. "Come on, girl. Get a freaking grip," she says. "You're losing it."

"Who's losing what?" It's her father's voice.

"Daddy?" She spins around and watches as he ascends the stairs. "You scared the crap out of me."

"I did? How?" Cliff asks. "I was just coming up so that I can get ready for the party."

"You didn't just walk past my room?"

Cliff shakes his head. "I was downstairs. Are you all right, Carly?"

She sighs heavily. "I guess. But honestly, Daddy, I just don't know."

"We have some time. Want to talk?"

"Not really."

"I can listen to whatever you want to talk about."

"That's the thing, Daddy. You won't just listen." She rolls her eyes.

"What do you mean?"

"You *know* what I mean. You never want to listen to my side. You only want to convince me that your side is right. You always have an opinion, and you're not afraid to tell me what you think."

"I'm sorry," he says.

It's clear to Carly that her father is holding back his temper. She knows he tends to cut lose when they talk about something he doesn't like, and lately that something is Carly's husband.

"Let's talk, and I promise I won't say anything to upset you," he says.

"Can you do that?" She moves back into the bedroom and takes a seat on the edge of the bed. "Can you promise me that we can talk, and you won't lose your temper?"

"I promise." He follows his daughter into the room.

"Okay, then." She pats the bed beside her. "Sit right here and let's just be honest with each other while keeping our cools. Deal?"

"Deal." Cliff drops on to the bed beside his daughter. "What do you want to talk about?"

"Me, Daddy," she replies as tears are already welling in her eyes. "I want to talk about me."

"I'm listening." He keeps his voice low and mellow.

"You know things aren't good between Leo and me."

"That's an understatement."

"Daddy." She stares at him. "You promised."

"Sorry." Pretending to pull a zipper across his mouth, he looks at her and smiles.

"I know Leo has given you lots of reasons not to like him," Carly says. "But he is my husband and the father of my babies. The truth is, despite everything he has done"—she eyeballs him—"Promise me you will never use what I am about to say against me?"

Cliff raises his hand and crosses his heart, his face solemn.

"Some part of me still loves Leo. I don't know exactly why. I've thought about it a lot. I don't know if it's because some part of me is broken, or if I'm still thinking of how I felt when we were first together. But, while some part of me still loves him, a larger part of me despises him and what he did to me. There. Remember: not a word."

Carly knows it is taking every ounce of restraint her father can muster to keep from commenting. Instead, he just nods.

"And I may always love him," she continues, "but I don't think I can live with him any longer."

"May I say something?" Cliff asks as she struggles to keep her composure. "Please."

She nods. Tears stream down her face.

"I can see Leo has hurt you very badly. And if he has done it once, there's a very good chance he will do it again."

"Daddy."

Cliff raises his right hand in a gesture for his daughter not to talk. "Just let me say what I want to say and then you can give me hell. Okay?"

She nods.

"The thing is, sometimes the people we love hurt us and that pain can run so deep that it can never be repaired. I think that's what Leo has done to you. Sometimes when someone hurts us that badly, we have to walk away from them. Honestly, I think that's what you need to do with your husband, because you will never be able to trust him again and you can't live like that. If you stay with him, you'll be miserable, and that won't be good for you or the girls."

He pauses. She can see he is studying her face for any type of reaction and, seeing little, he continues, "I know people make mistakes and some people can change their ways, but I don't believe your husband can do that, because he will never accept that what he did was wrong. I know it's an old cliché, but, as they say, that leopard will never change his spots."

He takes a deep breath, waiting for her to blast him, but she remains quiet, almost stoic.

"And I know what I am talking about, even though you might think I'm a buffoon by times," Cliff says, offering her a smile. "Now you can let me have it."

"Oh, Daddy." She wipes her eyes with the backs of her hands and returns his smile. "You aren't a buffoon. Yes, sometimes you express your opinions a little too loudly, but I respect you and I always want to hear what you have to say."

"Really?"

She nods. "You're the best father ever and the girls are very lucky to have you for their Papa." She gathers her thoughts, then adds, "I know you're right about Leo, and that's why I have decided to stay here for a while after the holidays."

"Here? As in here with us? Your mother and me?"

"Yes. Is that okay with you?"

"You know it is," Cliff says. "You don't even have to ask. I assume you've already talked to you mother about this?"

"I have."

"Just wanted to make sure we are all on the same page"

"Like you, she thinks this is right thing to do."

He nods. "So then, if that's settled, what now?"

"This is going to be the hard part. I have to find a way to tell Leo."

"He's going to be pissed." He gently wipes her tears away.

"Oh, boy," Carly says, her voice cracking. "That's a major understatement."

"I'll be glad to tell him for you," Cliff says, and Carly knows her father is serious. "I'll meet him at the front door and tell him to turn around and go back to Halifax because he's not welcome here. If he doesn't leave, I'll be happy to show him the way." He winks. "Nicely of course."

"No, Daddy. This must come from me."

Cliff nods. "But do me a favour. Don't tell him when you're alone in a room with him."

"He won't hurt me, Daddy."

"He's already hurt you," Cliff says. "You don't know how he's going to react."

"I have a pretty good idea."

"So do I and that's why I don't want you to be alone with him. I'm not saying you need an audience when you tell him, but try not to be too far from other people. He's going to lose his mind when he hears this, so please give me a heads up when you're ready to do it, and I'll keep an eye on him."

"Yes," she agrees. "The thought of telling Leo that we are through feels like someone has stabbed me in the heart. It hurts so bad that I want to crawl back under the covers and hide away from the rest of the world."

"If this is what you have decided, then you have to tell him so you can start putting your life back together."

Cliff puts his large arms around her to pull her in for a hug. "And," he whispers, "it's best that you do it sooner rather than later. Get it over and done with instead of letting it fester until it breaks you."

Carly nods. "Besides, I've got enough other ghosts to deal with today that I don't need Leo hovering around me and making promises that he won't keep. I have reached my limit with him."

"We all have a breaking point. But what do you mean about ghosts?"

"Oh, it's nothing."

"It didn't sound like nothing," he says. "Please tell me if there's something else bothering you."

She hesitates but finally asks, "Do you believe in the supernatural, Daddy?"

He looks at her, caught off guard by her question. "Never really thought about it very much." He shrugs. "Are you having trouble with ghosts? I didn't think you believed in that stuff."

"I didn't think I did, either, but, I'm almost thinking that maybe I do. I mean, who can say for sure what's real or not, right?"

"That's what your mother always said," Cliff replies. "You know how she feels about that stuff. And we know that some types of ghosts are real, so, while I would say you can't really dismiss anything, I am not sure I am ready to believe in the paranormal."

"I'll tell you what Mom tells me: keep an open mind."

20: Party-goers

A heavy pall hangs over the town, the dark, dense clouds riding low in the waning light of this, the last night of the old year. As a new year dawns, their ominous presence in the early evening sky signals that bad weather is quickly moving in.

Those who have been paying attention believe the dark clouds are a sign of impending tragedy. Those who refuse to take heed, however, are tempting the fates.

According to forecasters, the storm isn't supposed to hit for at least another twenty-four hours, but forecasters don't always get it right. The dark menace is brewing, churning, and boiling like a witch's cauldron.

As the sky continues to turn hateful, the winds begin to muster to their promised brutal force and snow clouds gather, threatening to re-lease their pent-up fury at any moment on this quiet, unassuming com-munity of less than five thousand residents.

Some have taken heed of the warnings, hunkering down in their homes or wherever they feel safe. The celebrations, however, will go on at the Graham house. The hosts have promised that everyone will be safe there no matter what the storm throws at them.

But the nine crows that have been watching as the events have unfol-ded throughout the day are not so sure about that. An uneasiness stirs within the murder.

The crows watch quietly from their high perches, hidden within the snow-laden branches of the stately pine trees that surround the Graham property. The large black birds remain on high alert and they watch the party-goers arrive.

Most of these party-goers seem oblivious to the dangers that lurk within the shadows, waiting there to spring forth and deliver violence upon the targeted ones.

The crows know that danger has been stalking around this town all day, zeroing in on its would-be victims, waiting for the opportunity to strike.

The nine have tried to warn them but, as typically happens, most of these humans ignore their overtures, believing instead that the crows as more of a nuisance than the guardians that they are.

The crows know there are some in this crowd who appreciate their true intentions. These select humans understand that the crows are watching and waiting. And when the danger emerges from the darkness, the nine will do everything within their power to protect them.

It is their way. It is their sacred duty.

21: Time to mingle

"Well," Cliff says with a smile. He pulls his wife aside from the crowd of friends who have assembled at their invitation and hugs her tightly. "See. What did I tell you? Everyone came and they all seem to be having a great time."

"Don't gloat, Cliff Graham," Julie whispers. "It is not your best quality."

"I'm not gloating." He grins. "Okay. Maybe I am gloating just a little bit."

He laughs while assessing the guests gathered in the living room and den. From where he and Julie are standing, near the kitchen, he can see clearly into both rooms.

Watching as their friends and family chat, laugh, drink, and enjoy the spread of food Julie has prepared, he adds, "I'm glad we did this. I really think everyone needed a blowout. A lot of bad shit has gone down over the past twelve months."

"It really has been a lot to deal with," Julie agrees. "Everyone just needs to regroup and try to put it all behind them."

Cliff nods. "They deserve it. We deserve it."

"All right, mister." She winks playfully at him. "I'll agree that everyone is having a good time."

"Why wouldn't they? We throw a great party. We're all safe and sound, with friends inside a cozy house. There's lots to drink and the food is fantastic. You've really outdone yourself this year with the munchies. There's just so many choices, and I especially like it that you've included a lot of my favourites." He grins. "I don't think anyone will go away hungry, and if they do, that's their own fault."

"Thanks, sweetheart, but I think you're a little partial." Standing on her tippy toes so she can give him a kiss on the cheek, she adds, "I did it all for you. You look forward to this party every year."

"No, you didn't." Cliff stoops to return her kiss. "You enjoy this party as much as I do, and you know you do. You just won't admit it."

She nods. "Yes, I guess I do. Even when events and circumstances conspire to tear us down and test our resolve, this special event brings us all together. I think it gives us the chance to step away from the stress, gather our thoughts, and regroup so that we can face a new year filled with hope and the belief that there will be a better tomorrow."

"That's deep. I guess I didn't realize how much this party means to people," Cliff says. "But do you really think things will be better tomorrow?"

"Yes. Maybe not on January 1 or even the next day, but someday. But besides all of that, it's just wonderful to see everyone here, being so happy."

"Speaking of happy, I wonder where Carly has gotten to? She seemed upset today. I guess she has good reason to worry."

"It's a lot for her to deal with."

"It sure is." Cliff takes a deep breath. "I wish I could remove all that crap from her life. Most of all, I'd like to remove that pain in the ass that has caused her so much grief."

"Me too, but all we can do is be there for her," Julie says.

"Have you seen her in the last little while?"

"She and the girls are in the kitchen, and Lauren was with them. She's helping to occupy Cara and Cassie. She's such a sweet girl and the grand-babies just love her," Julie answers. "I take it that Carly told you about her decision?"

"She has." Cliff remains stoic. He's not willing to show his emotions and maybe embarrass himself or upset the guests. "What do you think about that?"

"I know it's hard on her, and it will be hard on the girls because they love their father, but I believe she is doing the right thing. She's given Leo a lot of leeway these past few months, but she knows she can no longer trust him. I don't think there's any coming back for them."

Cliff takes a deep breath. "Speaking about that prick, I wonder where he is? It's almost eight-thirty and he's still not here. I imagine the roads are pretty dicey and I wouldn't want anything to happen to him, for Carly's sake...and for his sake. I may not like him, but I don't want to see him get hurt."

Julie scans the rooms. "If he's here, he hasn't shown his face yet. Maybe he's too embarrassed to talk to us."

"Good," Cliff says. "I don't care if I ever see him again. Maybe he de-cided not to come after all."

"It's just like Leo to make Carly worry about him by driving down here in the middle of the snowstorm. Why didn't he leave earlier, when it wasn't snowing so hard, or just stay in Halifax?"

"Don't get me started, Jules." Cliff is trying hard to restrain himself as the mere thought of his son-in-law attending this party or even being in this house, is driving him crazy. "You know Leo. He's got to make a grand entrance, as if he thinks the world revolves him."

"Yeah right," Julie scoffs. "What a jerk."

"Cliff decides it's time to change the subject before he loses his temper. "I am glad to see everyone else has made it. Except for the doctors. Charlie phoned to say they were running a bit late but would be along as soon as they could."

"I'm sure they'll be here shortly," Julie says. "I haven't seen Charlie and Rebecca in a while, so it will be nice to catch up with them."

Cliff nods. "I was worried that maybe Warren and Lisa might not make it. He told me earlier today that their little girl isn't feeling too well, and he's worried that maybe the leukemia had come back."

"Yes. I was talking to Lisa about that," Julie says. "And she's worried, too. She told me that Lauren was really lethargic last night and even this morning, but she rested all day, and she seems to be doing fine now."

"That's good, right?"

"I think so. But I don't know much about how that disease works," Julie says. "Lisa told me they're hoping that she was just overtired from all the holiday activities, but she's making an appointment in the New Year with their doctor, just to have Lauren checked out. They can't be too careful with her. They may have to leave early, depending on how Lauren is feeling. They don't want her to get over-tired again."

"Poor kid." Cliff sighs "Doesn't seem fair that someone her age has to face something like that."

"Life isn't always fair, Cliff. You know that better than anyone."

"Sure do." He recalls past events but quickly shakes them off.

"These life events are forks in the road," Julie points out. "You may want to go one way, but these events pull you in another direction. The thing about life is that no matter what you want to do, there's a master plan that has everything all laid out for you. You may veer from the road every now and then, but eventually you'll reach the destination that was the point of that plan in the first place."

"You do believe that don't you?" He smiles at her.

She nods. "I mean, just look at our friends. They've all been through so much, especially these past few months, yet they all ended up right here this evening because that's where they are supposed to be. I look at it as an opportunity to recharge."

"Yeah, well," Cliff chuckles. "Maybe it is serendipity, but none of them might have ended up here if I had listened to you this morning. Remember? You wanted to cancel everything because of a little snow."

"But who can say if that whole debate this morning wasn't part of the master plan?"

"Jesus, Jules. Don't do that." He laughs and hugs her tightly. "It's too freaking hard on my head when you play those kinds of games. Just let me get a few more beer into me before you get all philosophical on me."

She laughs. "You think a few beers are going to help?'

"Probably not." He grins. "But when you wax poetic like that, you sometimes lose me."

"Oh sweetheart. You big cuddly brute." She wraps her arms tightly around his hefty frame, that makes her look like a child standing next to him. "You are just too funny."

He glances around the room, then says, "Putting Leo and everyone else aside, I did want to ask you if you think Carly is *really* okay. She seemed very upset when I talked to her earlier, which I understand, but I got the feeling that it was more than that. She seemed really worried about something, and I'm not so sure it's all about her marriage."

Julie shakes her head. "You are right about that. The truth is, she is worried about all the strange things that happened to her today and, frankly, so am I."

"I know what you're going to say. She asked me earlier if I believed in ghosts and that sort of thing, but you know how I feel about that stuff."

"I know you think it's nothing but old wives' tales." She rolls her eyes. "But I'm telling you it's more than that."

"I don't think it's a good idea to encourage Carly to believe in that stuff," Cliff says. "I know how deeply you feel about your beliefs, but don't you think she has enough on her plate to worry about right now?"

"You can't just dismiss these things, Cliff, just because you don't understand them. For some reason, whatever forces are in play seem to be working overtime with our daughter. One occurrence is usually powerful enough to send a clear message, but when it comes in a group of three, like she's experienced, then that's some pretty powerful signs right there."

"I didn't think Carly believed in all that mumbo-jumbo stuff."

"It's not mumbo-jumbo stuff."

Cliff raises his right eyebrow. "I'm sorry, honey. I didn't mean that like it sounded."

"You just have to keep an open mind."

"So, do you think Carly believes?"

"I think she always did, but she didn't want to admit it. I've always felt that she had a special connection with the other side, but she was never willing to open herself up to receive it. Somehow, though, it appears that those forces managed to break through today, and now they are sending her some strong messages."

"What do you mean? Messages about what?"

She takes a deep breath, glances around the two rooms and exhales. "Death. She's been receiving signs all day warning her that she is going to be dealing with a death in the very near future, and maybe a death of someone close to her. Quite honestly, Cliff, this has me worried."

"Come on Jules." Cliff sighs. "You can't really believe in all this stuff, do you?"

"Yes, Cliff. These warnings usually come true."

He can feel her anxiety level rise when she talks about Carly's experiences. "That powerful, huh?"

"Very powerful." She nods. "Powerful enough that Carly actually came to me about it, and she's never done that before."

"So, what can we do about it?"

"Nothing," she says. "There's nothing we can do except wait and see how this all plays out. If something is going to happen, it will happen over the next three days."

Cliff nods. "In light of everything else that's happened today, I'll never dismiss anything even when it seems strange or weird."

"What do you mean? What else has been happening today?"

"I don't want to get into it right now because this isn't the time. But let's just say that there have been a number of crows following me around today."

He hears the breath catch in Julie's throat. "Crows? Really? How many?"

"The last time I counted, there were nine."

"My God, Cliff. Why didn't you tell me about this before now?"

"Because I didn't want you to worry. Honestly, it could be nothing more than just a bunch of black birds following me around. There is a lot of snow out there and they're probably scavenging for something to eat. Let's not worry about it tonight."

She looks at him. He sees her eyes are squinting like they always do when the wheels are turning. "What does it mean when you see nine crows?"

"According to Sam, it's nine crows for a kiss." He fears he may have made a mistake in telling her about this.

She shakes her head. "I don't understand."

"When I get the chance, I'm going to talk to Samantha about this. If there is anyone in this town who knows about the crows, it's her."

"This is really freaking me out, Cliff." Julie takes a deep breath and exhales. "What do we do about them?"

"I'm not sure we do anything." He can see that his wife has become very upset. "Don't do that, Jules," he cautions. "Don't lose it. We don't know that there's anything to worry about."

"I've been in this town long enough to know that if the crows are hanging around, that's not a good thing. It always leads to trouble, and I don't think these people can take much more."

"I know, sweetheart. I get a little scared whenever I see those black birds hanging around, but for now, all we can do is stay on our toes and be mindful of anything that seems out of the ordinary."

"Shit, Cliff. Everything that's happened today seems out of the ordinary."

"Good point." He hugs his wife tightly. "We have guests so for now, let's enjoy the party and then we will face whatever comes our way."

"I don't know if I can do that."

"Yes, you can," he says. "I know you. You can get through anything that the crows throw at us."

"Okay." She sighs. "You are right. Put on your party face, my dear. Let's go mingle."

22: Late arrivals

No sooner do Julie and Cliff finish their conversation than the front door swings open and Leo Watkins strolls in, seemingly without a care in the world. Stomping his snow-covered boots on the front entrance floor as if to announce his arrival, he offers no apologies or explanations to anyone for being late.

Cliff resists the urge to rush right over and throw him out the door on his ass. He tells himself to calm down. *Remember, this is a party and you promised Julie and Carly you'd be civil tonight.*

He grits his teeth and watches as Leo makes his way across the room, shaking hands, smiling and chatting up the other guests, pretending to be someone important. It's as if he's running for elected office. Cliff wishes he could save his friends from such unpleasantness.

"Hey parents-in law," Leo says, as he approaches them with a swagger. "How's it going, Dad? Did you miss me?"

"We're fine." Cliff says tersely. He hates it when that prick calls him *Dad.*

Forcing a smile, a gesture that makes him want to vomit, he thinks, *I missed you like I'd miss a fucking hole in the head.*

With the tension thick in the air, Julie moves quickly to defuse the situation. "Hi Leo."

She reluctantly gives her son-in-law a hug to avoid an awkward situation. She quickly pulls away as the cologne he's wearing makes her stomach churn. He continues to use the strong-scented "toilet water", as Cliff calls it, even though Carly has repeatedly asked him not to as the smell bothers her as well.

"How were the roads?" Julie asks politely. "Bad driving, I bet."

"Nah. They weren't too bad, so I could handle it," Leo brags. "They were snow-covered for most of the drive along the 103, but I just plowed on through. I wouldn't let a little bit of snow stop me from being with my girls on New Year's Eve."

Of course, you did. Cliff rolls his eyes.

He holds back what he'd really like to say and replies, "We thought maybe you had changed your mind and decided to stay in Halifax, like most normal people would do in the middle of a major snowstorm. Think maybe you could have called if you were going to be late?" He's unable to bite his tongue any longer. "Carly was worried about you, but I wouldn't expect you to worry about her feelings."

"Cliff." Julie glares at him.

Leo either didn't catch Cliff's snide comment or, if he did, decides to let it slide. *Which wouldn't be like him, as he's always looking for a reason to argue.*

"I had some work that couldn't wait, so that delayed me." Leo glances around the rooms where people are partying. "The snow didn't keep these people away, but I don't see Carly anywhere. Do you know where she is?"

"She's in the kitchen with the girls," Julie answers.

"Good. I'll pop in and let her know I'm here." Addressing Cliff, Leo says, "I could sure use a Scotch after that shitty drive."

"I guess I can handle that." Cliff sighs. He is surprised that his often-brazen son-in-law just didn't go to the bar and help himself without asking, as he usually does. Remembering the little switcheroo he had performed this afternoon, he laughs abruptly. "I guess you want some of the good stuff, right?"

"Sure do. That would be great."

"Yes sir. I'll get that for you right away." Cliff turns and moves toward the bar. *I wouldn't want you to overexert yourself.*

He pulls the expensive bottle containing the cheap whiskey from the bottom shelf. *I've got just the thing for you, Your Majesty.*

He opens the cap and pours some of the honey-coloured liquid into an eight-ounce glass. He grimaces. *Man, this shit smells putrid.* He glances at Leo across the room chatting up his wife and curls up his nose. *I wonder if this is what skunk piss smells like.* He chuckles at what he's done.

Returning to his wife and son-in-law, Cliff thrusts the glass into the younger man's hand. "Here," he says. "I hope you enjoy it because I bought it just for you."

Leo grasps the glass and immediately gulps down a healthy mouthful. He coughs as the liquid passes down his throat. "Jesus," he says between gasps. "What the hell was that?"

"It's the good stuff just like you ordered." Cliff tries hard not to sneer.

"Are you sure?" Leo sniffs the glass. "That was more like gasoline. I don't know if it's possible for Scotch to spoil, but I don't think this stuff tastes right."

"I got you what you asked for," Cliff says, but thinks, *you got what you deserved.*

Leo takes a second, smaller sip. He cringes. "This doesn't taste like I remember it. This is anything but smooth."

Cliff nods toward the bottle he left on the bar counter. "I just bought it this morning and it wasn't cheap; I'll tell you that much."

"Okay, boys." Julie interrupts. "Cliff, why don't you be a good host and go talk to some of our friends and, Leo, why don't you go and find Carly? I'm sure the girls will be happy to see you. They stayed up late just for you."

"All right." Cliff bends to give his wife a quick kiss on the forehead. He whispers, "I know what you just did."

She smirks. "What?"

He steps back and winks. "I'm going. Over and out."

"Behave yourself but have fun," she says, as Cliff heads into the den, where Oliver and Anna have gathered with Kate and Samantha. "I'll join you in a few minutes."

~

"Everything okay with Cliff?" Leo asks as Julie turns to face him. "The old man seems to be a little out of sorts tonight."

"I don't know what you mean, Leo. He seems perfectly fine to me." She resists the urge to tell him what she really thinks about him. "But I want you to do me a favour."

"If I can."

Julie takes a deep breath to temper her anger. "I want you to behave yourself tonight. Understand?"

"Me?"

She can't tell if he's legitimately shocked by what she's saying or if he's pretending to be innocent. She hates his games.

"Yes." She nods. "You. We get it that things aren't good between you and Carly right now, but I don't want you to bring any crap into this house and ruin this party for everyone, especially for your wife and babies."

"I don't know what you mean."

Julie raises her right hand in a signal for him stop. "Just don't, okay? Let's just get through one night without any arguments or drama.

Whatever is going on between you and Carly is best left in the family. Am I making myself clear?"

His complexion is turning blood red. "I don't know what you're talking about, but I'll do my part."

It seems to her that she may have just insulted Leo, but she doesn't care. Her first instinct is to shelter her daughter and granddaughters from him. "Just do it. Please hear me and understand."

"And, of course, you think it's all my fault."

"I'm not going to argue with you, Leo," Julie snaps. "Just behave yourself."

He exhales. "I got it loud and clear."

"Okay, then," she says. "Carly and the girls are in the kitchen. Cara and Cassie will be happy to see you."

"And Carly? Will she be happy to see me?"

"I don't know, Leo."

Julie hears the doorbell ring. Turning from her son-in-law, she adds, "That's something you'll have to ask her for yourself."

"Fine. I'll do that."

Fine, Julie thinks. *But you may not like what you hear.*

~

"Can you believe that guy?" Cliff asks as he joins his wife at the front door. "What fucking nerve showing up here a couple of hours late and acting like everything is alright. He's got some set of balls on him."

"Cliff. Please keep it down. Not with guests here."

He lowers his voice to a whisper. "I didn't realize I was being so loud. Blame it on the beer and that asshole. He brings out the worst in me."

"I know, Cliff. But try harder."

"Right." He sighs and opens the front door.

He finds doctors Charlie and Rebecca Webster and their young son, Liam, standing on the front doorstep, the quickly falling snow turning them white.

"Sorry we're late." Charlie extends his hand to Cliff. "Took longer to shovel out the car than I had thought it would."

"No worries." Cliff shakes the doctor's hand. "We're just happy that you made it."

"Hi, Liam." Julie greets their younger guest. "Why don't you take off your coat and boots and go find Lauren?" She nods toward the kitchen. "She's in there with our granddaughters. I'm sure she'll be happy to see you."

"Can I?" the young boy asks his parents.

"Of course, sweetie." Rebecca's voice is soft, sounding more like a whisper.

"As for you two," Cliff says to the parents, "let me have your coats and you go on into the living room. What can I get you to drink?"

"I'll just have water, please." Rebecca slips out of her navy parka and hands it to Cliff.

Julie takes her slender guest by the arm and leads her away from the men. "I haven't seen you in a while. Let's catch up."

"And you?" Cliff asks Charlie. "What will you have? Please don't tell me you're having water, too."

"God, no." Charlie shrugs out of the vintage brown aviation-style leather jacket that Rebecca and Liam gave him for Christmas. "I'll have a beer, please, but first I want to talk to you about something." He quickly glances around to see if there is anyone within earshot.

"Sure." Cliff hangs the Websters' coats in the entryway closet. "What's up, Doc?"

"I don't want to alarm you, but when I pulled into your driveway, I could have sworn that I saw someone lurking at the corner of your garage. They were just standing there, as if they were looking things over."

"What?" Cliff is startled. "You're kidding."

Charlie shakes his head. "I'm very serious."

"God-damn it. Could you tell who it was?"

"Sorry, but I have no idea. At first, I thought maybe it might be you or one of your guests, but when my headlights lit up the yard, whoever it was darted away into the backyard. That didn't seem normal to me, and I thought you would want to know."

Cliff exhales. "You're absolutely right about that. I'm glad you told me. Could you tell who it was?"

"Afraid not. It happened pretty fast, and I don't think Rebecca or Liam saw anything," Charlie adds. "But it was almost like they were casing out the house. It was all a little creepy."

Cliff reaches into the closet to grab his Canada Goose coat. "I'll just check things out. Why don't you go inside and grab yourself a beer? There's lots in the fridge behind the bar in the den. Oliver and Warren are in there, too."

Charlie nods. "I can do that, but do you want me to come with you? I don't mind."

"No, I'll be fine." Cliff slips into his coat. "But if Julie asks where I am, please don't tell her about this. I don't want her to worry."

Cliff steps onto the front doorstep, closing the door behind him. The snow is now falling steadily, making the surroundings eerily quiet.

He quickly glances around the yard. *You're right about one thing, Charlie. It is creepy out here.*

He immediately notices a gathering of crows perched on the roof of his garage. "Okay, fellas. Now what?" He determines there are still nine in this murder, just like earlier.

"Did you guys see someone out here?" he asks the crows.

He waits a few seconds, almost as if he expects them to answer.

"No? Huh." He shakes his head, thinking that it can't do any harm to ask them for assistance. "Okay, then. At least keep an eye out in case someone is still here, and let me know if you see anything."

The crows remain silent, scanning the surrounding area, their heads constantly turning side to side, as if on a swivel.

Cliff descends the front steps and goes to the corner of the garage where he notices a set of footprints in the fresh snow. It's clear that someone had been standing there for a while, switching from one foot to the other to try to stay warm.

What the hell?

Sliding his cellphone from his pocket and switching on the flashlight mode, Cliff slowly moves into the backyard, trudging through the calf-deep snow that spills in over his ankle-high shoes, making his feet wet and cold. He shines the light around the yard, and his breath catches in his throat as he sees the footprints crossing the backyard.

"Shit," he whispers, a thick cloud of breath hanging in front of his face. "Someone was definitely out here. Jesus Christ. I don't need this."

Who the hell are you and what the hell do you want?

Approaching the edge of his backyard, where the snow-covered lawn meets with the edge of the dense forest that protects his property from encroaching development, Cliff stops. He decides that, even though he can see that the trail leads into the underbrush, it's probably not a good idea for him to venture into the woods by himself.

Who the fuck knows who could be hiding in there?

Scanning the trees with his flashlight, he's nervous. It's a sensation he doesn't often feel, but this situation has suddenly become very serious. His instincts are telling him to retreat.

Backing away from the trees, Cliff decides he should go back inside the house and not push his luck.

He shivers at the cloud of condensation from his breath hanging in the air and at the thoughts of someone lurking around his property.

Backtracking in his own footsteps, Cliff makes a beeline to the house.

Whoever you are, you bastard, I hope you know who you're messing with. I catch anyone snooping around here and I'll knock your fucking head off your shoulders. No questions asked.

He returns to the front steps, pauses, and scans the yard again. He can't shake the feeling that he's being watched, and he isn't counting the crows which are still perched on the garage roof.

It's as if they are maintaining a vigil, he thinks, *but for who?*

But his instincts are telling him this is serious.

"Come on, Cliff." He tells himself, opening the door to slip inside. "Pull your shit together. You've got guests."

23: Memories of the future

"Your friends sure know how to throw a great party," Anna says.

Oliver hands her another glass of Chardonnay and smiles broadly. "They sure do. Julie and Cliff are great people."

"'Authentic' is how I would describe them." Anna takes a sip of Chardonnay and licks her lips suggestively. "Wow. That's very good. You should have some."

"Glad you like it, but I think I will stick to beer. It seems that Julie really knows her wine. I'm sure Cliff is a beer man and probably wouldn't know the difference between a good Chardonnay and Yellow Tail. The man's pretty basic."

"Why, Oliver Lewis." Anna gives him a playful wink. "You never cease to amaze me. Is there anything you don't know? First scones and freshly-ground coffee. Who knew that, on top of everything else that you can do, you are also a wine connoisseur? Colour me impressed."

"Yup. I'm a *bona fide* sommelier, but there's a lot you don't know about me, my dear," he says with a grin. "But we can have a lot of fun while you figure it all out."

"Hmm. I like the sounds of that," she whispers over the rim of the glass of Riesling that Julie had set out for her wine-drinking guests. She takes another sip and closes her eyes, savouring the hints of vanilla and notes of oak from the barrel in which it was aged. "So, you've known these people a long time?"

"A while." Oliver scans the room. "Cliff is a great guy, but for some reason, whenever there is trouble in this town, it seems he's always front and centre. But that's what makes Cliff, Cliff. I like him, a lot. A little rough around the edges, but he's no nonsense and straight to the point. You always know where you stand with him."

"Gotta like that in a person," Anna points out.

"The other thing about Cliff that I learned a long time ago, is that he'll do anything to help anyone who needs a hand. He always seems to have everyone's back."

"I hope someone's got *his* back."

"I think he's good there. He and Warren seem pretty tight."

"Everyone needs a friend like that. I've only heard good things about Cliff and his family since I moved here. He was an RCMP officer, wasn't he?" Anna asks.

Oliver nods and takes a drink of his Alexander Keith's. "He's been retired for a few years, and after that he did some private investigative work. Had his own business for a while, in fact. But I'm not really sure what he does now. I think he's laying low these days."

Anna smiles. "I'd like to get to know him and his wife better before I leave town. Maybe we could have them over for dinner as a way to thank them for inviting us tonight." She pauses, takes a drink of wine. "Actually, we should spend more time with all of your friends. You may not get to see them as often once you move to Halifax."

"You're moving to Halifax? When?" asks a voice that Oliver immediately recognizes.

He had been so consumed in his conversation with Anna he had failed to notice that his young friends, Alex Goodwin and his girlfriend, Bree Hamilton, had come up behind him.

Oliver turns to address the young man, who had been the target of an unusual attack several months ago. He could have died had Oliver not intervened. "How long have you been standing here?"

"Long enough to hear that you're leaving town," Alex answers. "Why am I just hearing about this now? When are you moving?"

It's clear to Oliver that his young friend doesn't want him to see how upset this news has made him.

"I am sorry, Alex." Oliver offers him a warm smile. "I didn't expect for you to find out this way." He takes a deep breath. "But yes, I was going to tell you tonight that I am thinking of moving to Halifax. Anna has been offered a great job at the best psychiatric clinic east of Montreal, and there is talk of me going with her."

"Thinking?" Anna says with surprise. "Forgive me, Oliver, but I thought we had decided that you *were* coming with me. If I am wrong, please enlighten me."

Oliver nods. "Sorry. I meant to say that I *am* moving to Halifax. If you need me, Alex, I'll only be a phone call away. And you can text me anytime."

"It won't be the same thing," Alex replies.

"I know my responsibility and my duty to you, so I'll always answer the call, but if I want to be with Anna, I must move. But, like I said, it wouldn't take me long to get back to Liverpool if you need me. And I hope it won't come to that."

"I'm not so sure about that," Alex tells him.

"What do you mean?"

"I am worried about those nine crows that have suddenly appeared," Alex explains. "They are up to something. I can feel it. And then there are the weird dreams that Bree has been having."

"What dreams?"

"I'm not sure this is really a good time to talk about this," Bree says.

"This is the perfect time," Oliver responds. "Anna is a psychiatrist, one of the best. She's helped me through a lot, so she may be able to help you understand what's going on."

Alex looks to Bree. "Should we tell them?"

"I don't mind," she says. "Maybe Dr. Robbie can help us."

"Tell us about them," Anna says. She keeps her voice low and mellow while at the same time taking on a more professional stance.

"You will think I'm crazy."

Anna shakes her head. "No, I will not and, please, let's not use that word again. It implies something negative or dismissive. Mental health issues are serious business. Putting such labels on people who are suffering from a mental health issue does them a great disservice."

"Sorry. Understood." Bree takes a deep breath. "I call them dreams, but I don't think that's an accurate description of what's going on. I think they are more like messages from the future."

"The future?" The phrase catches Oliver off guard. He suddenly feels vulnerable. "What do you mean?"

"Go on." Alex says to Bree. "You should tell them everything."

"Okay." She exhales forcefully. "I have been having these very vivid dreams about me and Alex in the future. I see that we are married, and we have four children—a boy, who is the youngest, and three little girls, triplets."

"Triplets?" Oliver is stunned.

"Please, Oliver," Anna says, squeezing his arm. "Don't interrupt."

Bree continues, "Our boy's name is Seth, and the three girls are Bailey, Piper and—"

"Sydney." Oliver says. "Am I right?"

"Correct," Bree says. "But how could you possibly know that?"

"Because I, feel like I've met them."

"What the hell, Oliver?" Alex's responsible is predictable.

Anna says sharply, "I thought we had addressed these *visions* you think you've had."

"I really don't understand it myself,"—Oliver looks directly at Alex —"but remember when I was missing for those three days after I fell off the bridge?"

Alex nods. "Everyone thought you were dead. But I didn't."

"That's because I *wasn't* dead. I, uh, went to the future."

"Oliver, my dear," Anna squeezes his arm. "We determined that those delusions were the result of the trauma you suffered from that fall. You hit your head pretty hard and suffered a serious concussion. Remember? You were very confused for a time after that."

"I thought we had." He slowly shakes his head, biting down on his lower lip. "But now, after hearing the details in Bree's dreams, I'm not sure what I believe. How could I know so much about her visions?"

"There is probably a logical explanation for this," Anna says. "We just have to drill down until we find it."

"I know what it is," Alex says. "It's the crows. They did it, just like they do everything else around here." Addressing Oliver, he asks, "Why didn't you tell me about this before now? I thought we had become friends."

"We are friends," Oliver insists. He reaches out to take Alex by the shoulder.

Alex pulls away. "What friend would keep something like this from another friend, especially after we've been through so much together?"

"He wanted to tell you," Anna explains. "But I told him he shouldn't because I honestly believe that he was delusional. We know there's no possible way he could have been transported to the future."

"We don't know that." Alex sucks in a deep breath. "The crows are very powerful, and I believe it is absolutely possible for them to take Oliver to the future if they knew I was in trouble there and needed his help."

"Come on, Alex." Anna is trying hard not to sound condescending. "Please don't make this any worse than it already is by encouraging him. It may have been six months ago, but Oliver is still recovering from those injuries. He's made a lot of progress, so let's not take him backwards."

"I'm fine," Oliver says. "And I'm very sane."

Bree jumps in. "But how he possibly know the name of the baby in my dreams when the only person I have ever told about them was Alex. And I just told him this afternoon."

Anna studies Bree and then glances to Oliver. She sighs. "I agree that is a good question, and right now, I can't answer that, but we will get to the bottom of it. I'm sure there is a logical explanation."

"No need, Dr. Robbie," Alex says. "I think we know what happened."

To Oliver, he asks, "Did you see anything else in the future that I should know about?"

"There's a lot more I could tell you, but apparently what I think happened, didn't really happen." He shakes his head.

"Jesus, Oliver. How far into the future did you go?" Alex asks.

"You mean, how far does he *think* he went," Anna says.

Oliver holds his ground. "I know you don't believe it, Anna, because your logical mind won't allow you to go there, but that's what happened."

Bree says, "If the crows are responsible for this, we need to do something. Maybe we should tell Alex's mom. She knows a lot about crows."

"Telling other people about this will only feed his delusions," Anna says.

"Telling other people will just confuse the issue even more," Oliver says. "How can we prove any of this when even my girlfriend doesn't believe me? Alex, I could tell you more about what I saw and what happens, but you are going to have to bide your time like everybody else until the future arrives. Just be mindful that a threat awaits you in the future."

24: News nobody wants to hear

After getting some refreshments, doctors Charlie and Rebecca Webster make their way into the living room, where they find his sister, Kate, and her wife, Samantha, seated on the sofa near the fireplace.

"I thought I'd find you next to the fire," Charlie says to Kate. "You're al-ways cold."

"Always." Kate rises and hugs her brother and Rebecca. "Glad to see you guys finally made it. We were starting to wonder if you decided to stay home because of the snow."

"I'm not so sure we shouldn't have," Charlie says.

He and Rebecca sit in the plush armchairs that are stationed across from the sofa. A glass-top coffee table stands between them, where they sit their drinks on coasters.

"It's coming down pretty hard. Give it another hour or two and the roads are going to be treacherous. It probably would have been smarter for all of us to have stayed at home."

"That's not a good sign," Samantha says. "The storm wasn't even sup-posed to hit this area until tomorrow morning, so that probably means we're in for a huge mess. The weather forecasts say it's going to be a doozy." She shudders. "Sounds like tomorrow will be good day to hunker down and read a good book."

Charlie shakes his head. "It doesn't sound good and we are probably not going to stay all that long. We're just here to put in an appearance. We knew Cliff and Julie were counting on people showing up, despite the snow and we didn't want to leave them in a lurch."

"We'll see how it goes, Charlie." Rebecca takes a sip of her water. "We're already here, so why don't you try to have a good time?"

"Listen to your wife, Charlie." Kate smiles at her brother. "Just let it go and enjoy yourself. You've got snow tires on your car, haven't you? I'm sure you'll be fine."

"Yeah." Charlie takes a gulp of beer. "Fun. Right."

"Everything all right, Charlie?" Samantha asks. "You look like something is bothering you."

"I'm fine." He twists his lips into a frown. "I'm on call tomorrow at the hospital and I hate to think about having to shovel myself out before I go to work."

"You need to get yourself one of those fancy snowblowers like Cliff has," Samantha says. "Julie tells me that he really loves his machine. I mean, just look at that driveway out there. He's got it pretty freaking clear."

"Are you sure you're just worried about the storm, Charlie?" Kate looks hard at her brother. "I don't recall you ever letting a snowstorm get you so worked up before."

"I'm getting older," Charlie says lightly. He takes another gulp of beer and returns the almost-empty bottle to the coffee table. "Guess worrying about stuff you can't change comes with old age."

"I guess." Kate says. "But I learned a long time ago that you just have to accept things as they come at you, bad weather being one of those things."

"Charlie." Rebecca takes her husband's hand and squeezes gently. "Why don't you go and find Oliver? I'm sure he'd love to see you."

Charlie shakes his head. "I think I'll stay right here. I'm finding it a little cold myself and this fire feels pretty good."

"Okay, Charlie. What's going on?" Kate says. "I can tell when you're worried about something."

Charlie takes a deep breath, exhales but says nothing. Instead, he turns back to the blaze and stares into the fire.

Kate lets it go for now. Instead, she says to Rebecca, "So how have you been? I haven't seen much of you since Thanksgiving."

"I've been busy at work." Rebecca takes another sip of her water. "The current doctor shortages mean people like me and Charlie have to pull down extra shifts at the hospital and it's getting to be a little too much. We're exhausted."

"It must be brutal." Kate studies her sister-in-law. "You guys have to pace yourselves or you'll get run down, and the next thing you know you'll be sick."

"Oh for God's sake, Kate," Charlie suddenly blurts out. "Can you please just let it go? For once in your life, can you just stop prying?"

"What are you talking about?" Kate is caught off-guard. "I'm not prying. I was just talking to Rebecca. If I was prying, you'd know it."

"Come on, Charlie," Rebecca whispers. "Just let it go."

"You know I can't do that." He sighs as tears well in eyes.

Kate says, "I'm sensing that you're hiding something from me, Charlie." She glances at her wife sitting quietly beside her. "From both of us, and I don't like secrets. What's going on?"

"Your intuition is amazing, Kate." Charlie glares at his sister, his upper lip curled up as it always does when he's annoyed. "But then again, you have always been nosy. I guess that's what makes you such a good lawyer, but sometimes your constant probing can be very annoying. "But please just let this go, will you?"

"No," Rebecca says. Her voice is soft and full of despair. It's almost a whisper. "Come on, Charlie. I can't do this anymore. I think it's time that you tell your family what's really going on."

"I don't think this is the right time or place." Charlie lowers his head. "We are supposed to be at a party."

"There's never going to be a good time or a good place for this news." She smiles softly at him. "Just tell Kate and Samantha. If you can't do it, I will, because I can't stand the tension any longer."

"You would do that?" He looks at his wife, hurt that she would break their confidence. "Even though I said that I think we should wait?"

"Don't you think we've waited long enough?" She touches his cheek. The gesture melts his heart. "This is as good a time as any, and they have a right to know."

Charlie takes a deep breath and exhales. "I guess they do, but I don't want to ruin the party for them."

Kate reaches for her wife's hand and squeezes it tightly. "You know you can tell us anything," she says softly to her brother.

He drops his head and stares at the empty beer bottle on the coffee table. "I know you have always been there for me...for us, and we appreciate all of that."

"It's what families do," Samantha says.

Charlie nods. His eyes fill with tears. "We have some bad news to tell you but..." he turns away, overcome with emotion.

"But," Rebecca picks up the conversation, her voice a little raspy, "we don't want you to make a big deal out of this. But I feel you have a right to know what's going on."

"Suddenly, it doesn't feel much like a celebration." Kate looks into Rebecca's eyes. "This isn't good, is it?"

Rebecca shakes her head. She squeezes Charlie's hand. "I have cancer."

For Kate and Samantha, it's like someone just punched them in their guts.

For Rebecca and Charlie, it's like the genie has just escaped from its bottle. Saying the word out loud to someone else has suddenly made this illness all too real, and they know they can never put that secret back into confinement.

"Cancer?" Samantha finally stutters. "Is it some place where they can treat it?"

"Not really," Rebecca whispers. "There's not much they can do for me. And as a doctor, I know what I'm facing."

"Jesus Christ," Kate says. "How long has this been going on, Charlie? Why didn't you tell us sooner? We could have helped you."

"We really just found out all the particulars," Rebecca answers as her husband is struggling to speak. "Please don't be angry at Charlie. We really were hoping it wasn't all that serious and we'd have better news for you."

"How serious?" Kate says.

Samantha shoots a look at her wife, a silent gesture telling her to calm down.

Rebecca's voice cracks as she speaks. "It's terminal."

Samantha gasps, tears welling in her eyes. "Oh my God. Are you sure?"

Charlie finally speaks up. "We're sure. She's had all the tests and seen the best oncologists in Halifax. This fucking disease is going to kill my wife and there's not a god-damned thing I can do about it."

"How can we help?" Samantha asks.

"Just be there for Charlie and Liam," Rebecca says softly. "I need to know they will be all right."

"Of course, sweetheart." Samantha wipes her eyes. "You know you can count on us. Whatever you need us to do."

Kate suddenly rises from the sofa. "I need a drink. I'll be right back."

"Kate?" Charlie asks as his sister heads toward the den where Cliff has the bar set up.

"No, Charlie." Rebecca pats his knee. "I think your sister needs a minute to digest what she's just heard."

"Rebecca is right," Samantha says. "You know what Kate is like. She will need to find a way to put this news into its proper place in her head, then she'll be able to face it. As she does that, I've always found that the best thing is to give her space to pull herself together."

"That's that lawyer brain of hers," Charlie says. "But we're talking life and death, not some legal briefs. There's no legal strategy that she can use to argue her way out of this."

"Give her time, Charlie," Samantha urges her brother-in-law. "She will come around."

"She always does this." He takes a deep breath. "Whenever there was a problem when we were kids, Kate always avoided it until the very last minute. But this isn't going to go away." He wipes his eyes. "I wish it would."

Samantha rises from the sofa and kneels in front of Charlie and Rebecca. "She'll be there for both of you as will I, but she needs to think her way through this."

"Thank you, Samantha," Rebecca whispers. "I'm not going to lie. This is very hard. I know what this disease is going to do to me, but my biggest worry is what's going to happen to Liam and Charlie."

"You take care of yourself." Samantha squeezes her hand. "Kate and I will take care of Liam and Charlie. We will make sure they will be all right."

"I can't do this." Charlie rises to his feet, his tall, lean body towering over the two women.

"Where are you going?" Rebecca whispers.

"I just need to get some air." He heads toward the front door. "I'll be right back."

"Don't forget your coat," she tells him, but he doesn't answer.

Turning to Samantha, she says, "He and Kate are so much alike."

Samantha nods. "But don't tell either of them that."

~

"Fuck. Fuck. Fuck."

Charlie stands on the front doorstep, the dense snow falling on his dark hair and navy sweater, quickly turning them white. He feels the urge to scream, but he knows that any such commotion will only alert the people inside the house that he's feeling immense despair and hurt.

His heart is breaking for the woman he loves, and it's killing him that, even as a doctor, there is nothing he can do to help her. He doesn't remember ever feeling so helpless—so lost.

"This is so unfair." He glances upwards and watches as the heavy snowflakes plummet to the Earth, not to meet their demise, but to join the hundreds of millions of other snowflakes that are quickly accumulating on the ground to become a major pain in the ass for him in the morning.

I'm a doctor, he thinks. *I'm supposed to be able to help people. I am supposed to know all the cures in the world to help everyone when they're sick so why can't I help my wife?*

He whispers, "Rebecca has helped so many people over the years. She doesn't deserve this."

Charlie knows the prognosis isn't good for his wife. He cringes when he thinks about the journey she faces.

Dear God, what am I going to do, he wonders as the tears continue falling.

The idea of his wife dying soon is tearing him apart, and while he knows he must find a way to come to grips with the total devastation he's feeling, he doesn't believe he can do that.

But I must do it for her sake.

He takes a deep breath and exhales, a cloud of white air immediately forming in front of his face. "How can I let her go?"

His attention is quickly drawn to a sudden movement on the roof of Cliff's garage. "What the…?"

Charlie knows that it's not unusual to see crows hanging around, but he wasn't expecting to see them tonight, in the middle of a major snowstorm. Although he's never had any intimate dealings with the crows, he is aware of others who have, especially his nephew, Alex. The thought causes him to shudder.

"What's up, fellas?" he asks nervously as he does a quick count of the snow-covered crows perched on the roof. He feels his heartbeat quicken. "Nine."

I wish Samantha or Alex were out here right now. They'd know what that means.

As if the crows have heard and understand his words, they turn in tandem and stare at him, eighteen tiny, pellet-like eyes gleaming through the rapidly-falling snow. He can't shake the feeling they are desperately trying to tell him something.

Charlie backs up toward the door. "Easy, guys. I didn't mean to disturb you, so don't freak out."

25: The good stuff

On his way to the kitchen, Leo makes a detour to the den to check out the bottle of Grant's Scotch that Cliff claims he just bought. He is not convinced that Cliff got the good stuff, as he insists that he did.

Admittedly, it has been a while since he's had any of the expensive Scotch that he likes, but he doesn't believe the stuff that Cliff gave him tastes anything like he remembers it. Holding the bottle in front of his face, he studies the distinctive red and white label.

Yup, says right there that it's Grants.

Removing the cap, he sniffs the honey-coloured liquid, and the smell causes him to cringe.

Damn. That's freaking rancid. Ain't no way that's the stuff I remember.

He wonders if it's possible for Scotch to spoil.

I didn't think so but now, I'm just not sure. Oh well. What the hell?

Since the first drink that Cliff got for him is long gone, he shrugs and pours a healthy shot of the whisky into his glass.

Why did I even bother to come here tonight, except to let Carly know who's boss? This party is a fucking waste of time. Carly better 'put out' this time, he thinks, a sneer forming on his lips.

Quickly glancing around to see if anyone is watching him, he fills the glass right to the rim, to the point of almost overflowing. He takes a quick sip and then tops off the glass again. He wrinkles up his nose.

Jesus. That's disgusting.

Then he grins. *What the fuck? A few more of these and it won't really matter how it smells or even how it tastes.*

Full glass in hand, Leo makes a beeline to the kitchen, where he finds Carly and his daughters sitting at the table, playing some kind of board game that he thinks is Candy Land, but he isn't sure as it looks new to him. He decides it was probably a Christmas gift. There are two other older kids at the table whom he doesn't know and doesn't really care to know.

He approaches his wife, bends, and plants a kiss on the top of her head. As he rubs her shoulders, he feels her shiver and pull away.

"Hey, babe. I finally made it. Did you miss me?"

"Sure." She doesn't look at him. "How were the roads?"

"Shitty."

"Leo." Now she looks up, with a glare. "For God's sake. The girls are sitting right here."

He half smirks. "Sorry, but it's nothing they haven't heard before."

"They are like little sponges, and I just don't want them repeating words like that, so please try to restrain yourself." Carly returns her focus to the tiny girls sitting beside her—Cara to her left and Cassie to her right—as they giggle and move their game pieces around the board.

"I don't think they even know I'm here," Leo says. "Which is pretty typical."

"Whose fault is that? But you made it just in time. We're about to finish this game and then I'm taking the girls up to bed. They wanted to see you see you first."

"But I just got here." Leo protests. "I was hoping to spend some time with them."

"Then you should have made sure you were here earlier. They're already off their schedules so it's time for them to go to bed or they'll be in a really bad way tomorrow."

"Well, we wouldn't want that." He takes a large gulp of his drink. "Heaven forbid that they get to spend any time with their father."

"Not tonight, Leo."

"Is quality time with my daughters too much to ask for?"

Carly watches the game progress. "You'll see them in the morning."

"But I want to play with them tonight."

Carly sighs. "Where were you, anyway? I've already kept them up an hour past their bedtimes waiting for you."

"I told you that I had some work to do that couldn't wait."

"You had work to do on New Year's Eve? Must have been really important that it couldn't wait an extra day."

"You know me, babe. I'm always working."

"Oh, I know you all right."

"What's that supposed to mean?"

She applauds as the girls finish their game amid a chorus of tiny giggles. "I'm just saying that you only function on one schedule and that's your own. You never stop to think about how your actions affect anyone else."

"Are you trying to pick a fight, Carly?" Leo feels emboldened by the whisky that's now coursing through his veins.

"Nope." She turns her attention to the older kids sitting at the table, watching the girls play. "Lauren and Liam. It's time for you guys to go back to your moms and dads, as I've got to get these two little snuggle bugs ready for bed." She smiles at them. "But thank you for your help. The girls really enjoyed having you here to play with them."

"I'll get the girls ready for bed," Julie says as she strolls into the kitchen with a handful of empty trays and plates.

"Hey, Mom," Carly replies. "Don't you think you've got enough to do?"

"It's no problem." Julie puts down her load and extends her hands to the girls. "Come on, my little lovelies. I'll get you ready for bed. Mommy and Daddy can tuck you in once you've got your teeth brushed and you're in your jammies."

"You really don't have to do that, Mom. I can handle it."

Julie shakes her head. "You stay here with your husband. I think you guys need to talk. But"—she pauses as her granddaughters slide from their chairs and scramble to take her hands and Liam and Lauren leave the kitchen—"I want you to be civil to each other."

"Right." Leo stares at the liquid in his half-full glass. "Civil. That would be a switch."

"Leo." Julie's voice becomes stern. "I'm warning you. You'd better behave yourself tonight."

"Or what?" His tone is as arrogant as ever. "You'll throw me out in the snow?"

"I won't do that, but I know someone who will be very happy to do it for me. For the sake of your daughters, be on your best behaviour."

He nods. "Yes, ma'am."

"So, you had to work late on New Year's Eve?" Carly asks after her mother and kids have left the room. She returns the game board and pieces back to their box. "What could have possibly been so important that it couldn't wait until after the holiday? You could have at least texted me to let me know you were going to be late."

"I was working on some year-end reports and financial statements." He takes another gulp of the cheap whisky. "Guess I just lost track of time."

"In all the years that we've been together, I've never known you to work late on a holiday before."

"Yeah, well." His voice is hard. "Things are different now."

She nods. "Are you planning to head back home tomorrow?"

"That's my plan. When are you and the girls coming home? You told me you were planning to stay for a few days to help your mother get things in order. How long do you mean, exactly?"

"I'm not sure." She slides the game box to the middle of the table. "But I am going to stay for a while. I need time and space to think about a few things."

"What kind of things? Us?"

"Especially us." Carly moves to the counter. She begins scraping scraps of bread, meats, crackers, and sweets off plates into the green bin.

"What's really going on?" Leo takes a seat at the kitchen table. He watches his wife as she cleans up the mess that has been accumulating. "I'm getting the feeling that there's more to do this."

"Nope. Just want to be with Mom and Dad. They keep me grounded and I need that right now."

"Don't you want to be with me?"

Carly sighs and places her hands on the counter, palms down, her back to him. "Not right now, Leo. I just can't."

"Jesus Christ. What the hell are you saying, Carly?"

"Please don't get angry, Leo." She pauses. "But I just can't go back to Halifax and pretend like nothing has happened."

"This again?" His anger is rising. "I apologized to you and promised that it will never happen again. I thought we had put this all behind us."

"It is not that easy. I can't just pretend like nothing has happened." Her anger and disappointment are evident in her words. "When you cheated on me you hurt me really bad. and, honestly, I don't feel that I can trust you anymore."

"So, what are you really saying?" He gulps down the last of the whisky in his glass. "That you want a divorce?"

Carly turns to look her husband in the eyes. "Yes, Leo, that is what I'm saying. I can no longer be with you."

"But I still love you." He snuffles as the tears begin to flow down his face. "And I want to be with you."

"The thing is, Leo, I still love you too. Very much, in fact. But I don't like you anymore. When you cheated on me, you destroyed what we had. You took my love for you and drove a knife right down the middle of it—straight through my heart. So no, Leo"—she wipes her eyes—"I can't be with you anymore."

"Yes, you can," he cries. "I don't understand. I admit I made a mistake, but it won't happen again."

"How can I ever be sure?"

"Because I am telling you it won't."

"I have to do what's best for me and for the girls."

"And you think divorcing their father is what's best for the girls?" Shaking off his sorrow, he adds, "What if I don't agree to this?"

"Let's just keep this simple and cordial for everyone's sake."

"Cordial?" His anger rushes to the surface. He rises from his chair and glares at his wife. "I won't let you keep me away from my girls."

"I would never do that."

He moves forward, closing the physical distance between them. He hears the breath catch in her throat, but she speaks calmly, "I know you love our daughters, and they love you very much, but sometimes love just isn't enough. For a relationship to work, there also must be mutual trust, and you broke that trust."

Leo shakes his head. "I won't make this easy for you. Why do you insist on destroying everything we have?"

"*Me* destroy everything? How dare you? I didn't climb into bed with someone else. I'm not the one who cheated. It wasn't me who hit the woman he claims to love. That's all on you, Leo. You did this."

He takes several long strides across the kitchen and comes within several inches of his wife. "I know what I did, but did you ever think you're the one who drove me to do it?"

"Don't. You. Dare. Touch. Me." She backs away from her husband. "Just stay away from me."

"Don't worry, princess." Spit foams at the corners of his mouth; his words are like venom. "I am not going to hit you. I wouldn't want you to go running to your daddy."

"Everything all right in here?"

Spinning around, Leo is surprised to see his father-in-law has entered the kitchen. "Yes," he sputters, hoping Cliff hadn't heard that last comment. "Everything is perfectly fine in here." He moves away from Carly. "We're all hunky-dory."

"Doesn't look fine." Cliff moves closer to his daughter. "What are you doing, Leo?"

"Your daughter and I were just talking."

"Looks like it was more than talk," Cliff says.

"No, Daddy," Carly speaks up. "Leo is right. We were just talking."

"Did you want something, Cliff?" Leo asks.

Cliff shakes his head. "This is my kitchen and my house. I can go anywhere I want to go, and I don't need a reason or anyone's permission, especially not from you."

Cliff is a big man, and the size differential intimidates Leo. "I know this is your house, Cliff, and I know when I'm not wanted."

Cliff shakes his head. "I don't think you do."

Leo scowls at Cliff and then turns to Carly. "Fine, I'm going to leave."

"You can't go right now," she tells him. "The roads are too bad to be on them, and you've had too much to drink. Think of your children. You are going to stay the night and then we'll figure all of this out in the morning."

"As much as I would like to see your sorry ass heading out the door right now, you should listen to her, Leo," Cliff says.

"You don't want me here, Cliff."

"You're right about that. But there's no way I can let you go out on those roads in your condition. Stay the night, but come tomorrow morning, you can take your sorry ass back to Halifax and then I don't want to see you around here ever again."

"Daddy," Carly says through her tears. "You can't banish him altogether. The girls are going to be staying here for a while and I want them to see their father."

"We'll see what happens. But I'll be watching you, Leo, so don't do anything more stupid than you've already done."

Leo inhales deeply and waves his glass at his father-in-law as if Cliff is his servant. "I need another drink."

Cliff visibly bristles. "So get it. You know where the bar is. That good stuff out there has your name all over it, but remember what I said. You'd better behave yourself."

~

After Leo has left the kitchen, Carly takes hold of her father's arm. "Oh, Daddy, what am I going to do?"

"Just breathe, honey." He pulls her in close for a hug. "You've got to take this one day at a time, but I promise that you'll get through it. You know your mother and I will be with you every step of the way."

Tears trickle down her face. "I can't shake the feeling that something bad is about to happen."

"Everything will be fine. You can't let Leo get to you like this."

"No. It's more than that. It has something to do with those weird things that have been happening to me all day. I can just feel it."

Cliff hugs his daughter tightly. "I wish I could make all of this go away for you. But whatever is going on, we will face this together."

26: Be on your toes

"Motherfucker," Cliff whispers.

He's pissed, and it's taking every ounce of self-control he can muster to refrain from completely losing his temper and making a spectacle of himself in front of a houseful of guests, people he loves and respects. But he would like nothing better than to rip into his son-in-law and then, once he had put him in his place, show him the road.

He'd like to punch something, but he hears Julie's cautionary words ringing in his ears. "Violence only leads to more violence," she's warned him many times. "And it usually creates more problems than it solves. Think with your brain, not with your fists."

She's a wise woman.

Sliding behind the bar to grab himself another beer from the fridge, he quickly glances around in hopes that no one else has noticed his rage.

He mumbles, "You little piece of shit. If only you knew how much I really hate you and how much I really want to hurt you—"

"Something bothering you, Brother?" Warren interrupts.

"Hey, Brother." Cliff is relieved when his best friend slides up to the bar and passes him an empty bottle. "Gonna have another?"

"You know it. Please and thank you very much."

Cliff hands him a fresh bottle. "Drink up, buddy. There's lots more back here. By the way, how's the mood tonight? Doesn't seem like I've had much time to chat with folks. Too many distractions, if you catch my drift. I hope everyone is having a good time."

"Haven't heard any complaints. You and Julie have really outdone yourselves this year, in spite of any distractions." Warren takes a quick gulp of his beer. "So, what's going on?"

"What do you mean?"

"You look like you could chew tacks and spit nails. Clearly, you're pissed at something."

"Is it really that obvious?"

Warren takes another drink. "Discreet is not a word I would use to describe you right now. You're not exactly trying to hide your feelings."

"Yeah, well." Cliff takes a deep breath. "I've got good reason to be pissed."

"Let me guess. Your creepy son-in-law? I ran into Leo right after he arrived. Guy's a piece of work."

Cliff looks at him, his silence speaking volumes.

"So, tell me what's up. Is there anything I can do to help?"

Cliff shakes his head. "Not with this, unless you want to slap the little shit around for me. But thanks for asking."

Warren's eyes narrow. "Talking about it might help."

"Maybe."

Warren remains quiet.

"I just walked in on that little prick giving Carly a hard time." Cliff opens a new bottle of beer for himself, gulps down a mouthful and sets the bottle on the bar. "I really wanted to throw his sorry ass out in the fucking snow, but Carly and Julie wouldn't want me to do that, so I'm letting the little prick stay, but only for tonight. Come the morning, I want that motherfucker out of our lives once and for all."

"You're a good man, Cliff Graham," Warren says. "I'm not sure I could have held myself back."

"At least Carly finally told him she wants a divorce, so that's a good thing. Maybe she can finally move on and find someone who will treat her with the respect she deserves."

"Let's hope so." Warren raises his beer towards his friend in a salute. "I'll drink to that."

"Me, too." Cliff swallows half his beer in one gulp. "But, enough about that little shit. If you have a minute, though, there is something else I want to talk to you about."

Warren nods. "What's up?"

"Well, that's just the thing." Cliff shrugs. "I really don't know what's up."

"I don't follow."

"Remember how I told you that it seemed like someone was following me around the liquor store this morning, and then there was someone spying on me this afternoon through the garage window?"

"Creepy as hell. Maybe it's the cop in me, but it still freaks me out when I think of it. Something is definitely going on around here."

"Yeah well, it's starting to freak me out too," Cliff admits.

"Well, here's something else that will freak you out even more," Warren says. "When I stopped at Kate and Samantha's to pick up Bree, I spotted someone lurking around their house."

"Seriously? Any idea who it was or what they wanted?"

Warren shakes his head. "I haven't told Kate and Samantha yet because I didn't want to worry them, but I guess I should, shouldn't I? What do you think, Cliff?"

"I don't know." Cliff shrugs again. "It could be nothing, I suppose, and you wouldn't want to scare them over nothing. But then again, it could be something because it doesn't stop there."

"What do you mean?"

"I mean that whoever has been lurking around here all day, was back a little while ago. When Charlie and Rebecca arrived, he told me he had seen someone hanging around out by the garage, so I quickly went outside and had a look, but I didn't see anyone."

"Do you think the person I spotted is connected to what's been happening with you today?"

Cliff exhales. "I don't know, Brother, but it's pretty freaking weird. There's a good chance it's all related. Some stranger lurking around our two properties on the same day seems like too much of a coincidence."

"I don't like this."

"At first, I really didn't think it was anything to worry about. But now I am getting worried that there's something more serious going on."

Warren takes a gulp of his beer. "But what?"

"Could be anything. What about the missing Pittmann girl? Think that's related, too?"

Warren shakes his head. "Maybe, but I don't see how she could get here in one day all the way from Oakville, Ontario, unless she had the money for a plane ticket. But she just got out of jail, so is that even possible? I'm sure that's the first thing parole officials would have checked once they realized she was missing."

"Oh, my friend," Cliff replies. "If I've learned one thing over all these years, it's that I should never dismiss anything because even when it seems impossible, it can turn out to be very possible."

"I guess you are right about that." Warren pauses and considers the incidents that happened today. "So now what do we do?"

"I'm not sure if there's anything we *can* do. But I know we have to be on our toes." Cliff gulps down another drink of beer. "I will admit this to you, and only you, my friend: I'm a little on edge this evening. Between the hell that my idiot son-in-law is putting my daughter through and all this sneaking around by some mysterious person, my spider senses are on high alert."

"Mine too," Warren agrees. "Do you think anyone is in danger?"

Cliff shrugs, his eyes narrowing as he thinks. "I think we have to assume that everyone could be in danger." He pauses, glances around to make sure no one else is listening. "There is one more thing that's more than a little worrisome."

"Jesus. What else?"

Cliff lowers his voice to a whisper. "Crows. Those black birds freak me out more than anything else that's happened today."

"Right." Warren gulps down the last of the beer in his bottle. "About the crows. I've seen them, too."

Cliff takes the empty from his friend and reaches into the fridge to get him a fresh one. "I'm not surprised to hear that. I believe they are trying to tell me something, but I have never been able to communicate with them, not like some people I know."

"Yeah, I've been picking up strange vibes from them all day as well. How many are you seeing?"

Cliff leans in closer. "There are nine crows in this particular murder."

"I saw them, too. What does that even mean, anyway?"

"In spite of everything I've seen over the years, I know very little about those birds, but according to Samantha, the legend says it's nine crows for kiss."

"For a *kiss*?"

"That's what Samantha tells me, but I have no idea what it means."

"What are we supposed to do with that?" Warren asks. "Not much of a clue to go on."

"According to Samantha, you can't always look for a literal meaning in the numbers of crows. When you think it means one thing, it usually means something completely different."

"Seems like they like to play games."

"And sometimes it's a pretty serious game," Cliff says.

27: What friends are for

Oliver leans in and gives Anna a quick kiss.

"Your glass is almost empty," he says. "Drink up and I'll get you another Chardonnay."

"I know what you're doing, Oliver Lewis." She winks at him.

"You see right through me." He smiles.

"And don't you forget it, mister."

"Oh, trust me," he whispers as he nuzzles her neck. "I know the kind of woman I'm dealing with, and you know what? I like it."

"Here's an idea: How about I go get myself a Chardonnay and you go find Charlie?" Anna rubs his arm, her touch sending goosebumps up his spine. "Didn't you tell me you were going to talk to him tonight about your decision to move?"

"Right." Oliver pops a stuffed mushroom in his mouth, savouring the cheesy taste. He offers her one. "These are delicious. You should try them. I have to remember to tell Julie how impressed I am. Her food is always great, but she has really outdone herself this year."

"Maybe later. I'm not hungry right now." She studies him. "Are you changing your mind about coming to Halifax with me?"

He shakes his head, pops the last stuffed mushroom in his mouth and places the empty plate on a nearby table. "What makes you think that?"

"I just get the feeling, Oliver, that since you talked to Alex, you've been acting differently. I'm wondering if maybe your young friend said something that got to you, and now you are having second thoughts."

He shakes his head again. "If I'm having second thoughts, I'm not conscious of them. I'm sorry if it seems that way. You should know by now how I feel about you."

"Well then, darling"—Anna swirls the last of her wine in the bottom of her glass—"Then I think you should go find Charlie. You need to tell him what's happening before he hears it from someone else. That wouldn't be fair to your best friend, and Alex seemed pretty upset when he overheard our conversation. He may tell someone about your plans. You know how quickly secrets can spread."

Oliver shrugs. "Who would he tell?"

"His mother, for one. And since she is married to Charlie's sister, the word is certain to get back to him. You and Charlie are pretty close, and I think he should hear this news from you."

Oliver rubs the back of his head for a moment. "Of course, you're right. He'd be very upset if he heard the news from anyone else but me. I owe him that much."

"Exactly." She wraps her arms around his waist and gives him a gentle squeeze. "So, you go find your friend and I will go get some more wine."

"Okay, I'm going." Oliver gives her another quick kiss before heading to the living room, the last place he had seen his best friend.

Man, oh man. He scans the room looking for Charlie. *That is one amazing woman. How did I get so lucky? It must be fate. All I know is that I can't do anything to mess this up.*

Even though he's happy to be building a new future with Anna, he dreads breaking the news to his best friend. Even though he doesn't see Charlie as often as he'd like, he knows they will always have each other's backs, no matter what. He hopes that would never change, even if he's not living close by.

All of that aside, however, he knows that he must have this conversation and he's sure Charlie will be happy for him. Oliver smiles. *I am sure I love that woman and I am sure this is the right thing to do. It's time that I do something for myself.*

He sighs. It will be hard to leave behind everything he's built up here, especially his business and his circle of friends.

Especially my friends. I hate to see Alex so upset, but I hope he will understand that I have to do this. I just can't put my life on hold any longer, waiting for the crows to beckon me. Besides, I'm not even leaving the province, so it won't take me long to get back here if he needs me.

Noticing Charlie enter the house through the front door, Oliver waves for him to come over.

The two men embrace. Charlie says, "It seems like I haven't seen you in forever. How's it going?"

"Oh, you know. It's going." Oliver quickly pulls away from his friend, who still has snow in his brown hair. "Sheesh. You're all wet, buddy."

"Right." Charlie shakes his head like a wet dog. "It's starting to get pretty wild out there. The snow is really coming down now and it's building up quickly. If anyone is planning on going home tonight, they may want to be on their way pretty soon, and when I say *pretty soon*, I mean right now. I'm gonna let Rebecca know that we should get ready to head out."

"You just got here. Oliver looks around the room and observes the party goers as they enjoy the food, drinks, and conversation. "Everyone is having a good time. I don't think anyone looks like they're in a rush to go anywhere just yet."

"Appearances can be deceiving."

"What do you mean?" Oliver studies the man he considers to be more like a brother to him than a friend. He picks up some very strong vibes that Charlie is upset. "What's wrong?"

"Nothing."

"Don't do that."

"Do what?"

"I have known you for a very long time, my friend, and I know when something is bothering you. Let's go get you a beer, and then you can tell me about it."

"Thanks, but I don't want a beer."

"Come with me anyway."

Oliver takes Charlie by the arm and leads him into the empty kitchen. He's sure Cliff and Julie won't mind if they find some privacy in here. "Something's got you upset, so spill it. I'm all ears."

Charlie takes a deep breath. "It's hard to talk about, because when I say it out loud, it makes it real."

"What becomes real? Let me help you."

Charlie shakes his head. "You can't help me." He pauses and swallows. "We've had some terrible news." His words are so soft, Oliver has to lean in closer to hear them.

"What is it?" Oliver has never seen Charlie show such emotion before. "What's so bad?"

Charlie squeezes his eyes shut. Tears roll down his cheeks. "Rebecca is dying." He almost chokes on his words.

Oliver feels like someone has just punched him in the gut. "Dying? What are you talking about?"

"It's true." Charlie wipes the tears away with the back of his right hand. "She's been diagnosed with pancreatic cancer and there's no cure."

Oliver feels his knees go weak. "Oh, my God." He clears his throat. "How long have you known?"

"A few days now." Charlie takes a deep breath and exhales. "The cancer is very aggressive and it's moving quickly."

Oliver's heart is breaking for his friend. "You say it's terminal? Are the doctors sure?"

"They are positive."

"So how long, then? How many years are we talking?"

"We're not talking years." Charlie's voice trembles. "We're talking months, maybe weeks. And it's such a hideous and painful death."

He bends forward and places his hands on his knees. Oliver can see he is trying to regain his composure. He straightens up and stares into Oliver's eyes. "Oh my God, what am I going to do? I don't want to lose her." He sobs. "I can't lose her."

"Maybe it won't come to that." Oliver takes on a soothing tone in hopes of calming his friend's nerves.

"I'm a doctor, and I know there's nothing they can do for her, except to treat her pain." Charlie trembles as he speaks. "We've seen the specialists and they've given us their prognosis. And I know they are right. Becca knows this, too."

"You can't give up. Fifteen years ago, when I was really sick, everyone said there was nothing they could do for me. I remember that when they told me I had brain cancer, I thought it was the end of the road for me but look at me now. Here I am, still going strong. I'm living proof that miracles can happen, but you have to have hope. You have to believe it."

"Oh, my friend, like I've told you many times, as a doctor, I don't know how you're still with us. But I am glad that you are."

Charlie forces a smile which, to Oliver, seems more like a grimace.

Charlie continues, "I am praying for a similar miracle for Becca, but I know such miracles are one in a trillion. I see sickness and death every day and I know miracles are rare. Very rare."

He sniffs. "I don't know what I'm going to do if I lose Rebecca. She's my whole world and I don't know how I'll exist without her in it. How will I raise Liam all on my own? She's the parent he needs, not me."

"You won't be alone, and don't sell yourself short. You're a great father. But if you need anything, you know Kate and Samantha will do everything they can to help you. and I will be there for you, every step of the way."

"I can't ask you to give up your life to help me. This is my fight."

Oliver pulls his best friend into a quick embrace. "You know you can count on me for whatever you need. Anything at all."

"What about Anna?" Charlie steps back to look at his friend. "I've heard down at the hospital that she's taking a new job in Halifax. I assume you will be going with her. Will she understand?"

"She will be busy with the move and the new job, which means I'll have more time to spend with you. I want to do this for you and Rebecca."

"Anna will be okay with that?"

"No question about it," Oliver answers without hesitation. "She's a very caring person. She knows you and I are close friends, and she will totally understand that I need to be here to help you. I will be there for you even if it's only to spend time with Liam so you can be with Rebecca."

"You'd do that?"

"Of course. You are my best friend. You don't even have to ask."

Charlie shakes his head. "I don't want this to cause you and Anna any problems."

"Why would it cause problems for us?"

Charlie looks him in the eyes. "If the woman I loved was moving to Halifax, I'd want to go with her."

"She'll understand."

A ghost of a smile flits across Charlie's face. "I have to confess that I'll feel better knowing that you'll be with me through all of this."

"Without question," Oliver tells him. He ignores the sharp pain in the pit of his stomach. "That's what friends are for."

28: Anguish

"How are the girls, Mom?" Carly whispers as she enters the bedroom where her daughters sleep when they visit their grandparents.

It's the room in which Carly spent her childhood, and the décor of various shades of purple, her favourite colour, hasn't changed since she moved out to attend university. That's where she met Leo Watkins. He was the brash, hotshot business major from Calgary who swept her off her feet, made her fall in love with him and changed her life.

Back then, she had no idea he was such a chameleon. Today, he is nothing like the young man she fell in love with. Even though she believes their relationship is now irreversibly broken, in the beginning, he was sweet, generous, and thoughtful, and made her feel like the most important thing in his life.

Not so much anymore, she thinks.

Watching her beautiful daughters as they snuggle under the blankets, her heart is filled with so much love for them that she feels blessed. But at the same time, her heart fills with disdain and resentment for the man who betrayed her trust.

Whatever happened to us? she wonders, even though she knows Leo is the reason their marriage has fallen apart.

She does sometimes wonder if she had done something to drive him into the arms of another woman, but whenever she has such thoughts, she brushes them off because she is certain the responsibility is all his.

There is no excuse for what he did. None.

"They went out like a light." Julie tucks the covers snugly around Cassie's chin. "They fell asleep as soon as their sweet little heads hit their pillows. They had a busy day."

"I can relate." Carly kisses each of her daughters gently on the forehead. "I'm plain tuckered out, too."

"Understandable." Julie takes her daughter's hand and leads her away from the bed so as not to disturb the girls. "There's a lot going on right now, and that kind of emotional turmoil can play you out. Why don't you call it a night and turn in?"

"I can't go to bed when you're having a party downstairs." Carly curls up her nose. "That seems rude."

"Yes, you can. Everyone will understand. If you become worn out, then you could get sick, and we don't want that."

"No, but I can't go to bed and leave Leo unattended. God only knows what he'll do in his current state of mind, especially now that he's got a few drinks in him."

"Don't you worry about Leo, sweetheart. Your father and I will take care of him."

"I appreciate the suggestion, but I wouldn't saddle you and Daddy with that. You have no idea what he's like when he gets wound up, and I suspect, after what I told him, he's off fuming somewhere and getting pie-eyed drunk in the process."

"Oh, Carly, I believe I know him better than you think." Julie rolls her eyes.

"I was glad Daddy showed up when he did, because Leo was pretty upset when I told him I am staying here for a while."

"I imagine he was angry. But your father is down there. He'll keep an eye on him," Julie tries to assure her daughter.

"I'm sure Daddy will know what to do, but if you think Leo was bad before, wait until he's in his newfound state of drunkenness. He becomes a real ass."

"Honey, he's always been more than a little obnoxious when he's drinking."

"True, but lately he's become even more mouthy, and he becomes extremely confrontational and belligerent, which isn't like how he was. I'm afraid he'll push Daddy's buttons the wrong way."

"We don't want that." Julie shakes her head. "The last thing we need tonight is for someone to lose his temper, and I'm not talking about Leo."

"We certainly don't want that," Carly agrees.

"So, you go get into bed and I'll go back down to make sure our husbands are on their best behaviours." Julie takes her daughter by the arm and gently leads her out of the room. "No arguments."

Carly sighs. "Okay, Mom. You win. But I'll only lie down if you'll promise that you'll wake me up about fifteen minutes before midnight. I want to be awake to ring in the New Year."

"Very well. But please don't worry. I know everything may seem hopeless right now, but I promise things will look different in the light of a new year. You'll find your way."

Julie gently nudges her daughter toward the spare bedroom since the girls are in her childhood room. She will worry about where to put Leo later, as she's not letting him anywhere near her daughter tonight. "Now please go lie down before you fall down."

"Do I really look that bad, Mom?"

"Afraid so, dear but even in your current state of exhaustion, you are still very lovely." Julie smiles.

~

Despite her mother's instance that she needs to rest, Carly knows there is no way she will be able to sleep, not while she's worrying about what kind of trouble her husband is causing. She tosses and turns, her mind racing through past events, and she worries about what the future holds for her and her daughters.

Leo would never do anything to hurt us, would he?

Even though he has gotten physical with her in the past, especially when he's been drinking, she doesn't want to believe that he would ever do anything so drastic again.

I know what Mom and Dad think. She stares at the nondescript white ceiling. *They don't think I can ever trust him again. Maybe they are right.*

Thinking about her babies, Carly knows that the decision to leave Leo is for the best. *They don't need to see their mommy and daddy arguing all the time. That's not healthy for them.*

She's sure she's doing the right thing to protect her children, not that she thinks Leo would ever hit the girls.

I'd kill the bastard if he did. It's one thing to take his anger out on me, but my girls are off limits.

Trying to force herself to fall asleep, Carly struggles to keep from crying. *When did life get so hard? All I wanted was to have a happy marriage and to raise my babies and watch them grow into beautiful young women. What happened?*

She exhales. It feels like the room is spinning and the walls are closing in on her. *It's over. Everything I ever wanted and hoped for, everything I ever dreamed of, has gone to shit and now I have to start all over. Only this time, things are different.*

For Carly, there is nothing any more important than the safety and wellbeing of her daughters, and she will do everything in her power to protect them and to give them the life she believes they deserve. Everything else, including her own wellbeing, takes a backseat. For that reason alone, she knows she must get away from Leo.

Oh, there is no question that he loves his babies. Carly closes her eyes tightly as the tears begin to flow more steadily. *But only when it's convenient for him.*

"It's the right thing to do," she whispers. "Time to move on," she says as sleep finally catches up to her and she drifts off.

~

"Carly."

She has no idea how long she's been sleeping when she hears a voice calling to her through a thick, white veil. The sweet, gentle voice, coming from somewhere far off, sounds as though it is lilting on the air.

"My sweet Carly, come and sit right here beside me."

As the image gradually comes into view, Carly recognizes the small-featured, elderly woman with the wrinkled face and her snow-white hair pulled back on the top of her head in a tight bun. Even though they never met, she has seen pictures of her great-grandmother Mae, and she is certain this is her. Sitting in her rocking chair, basking in the bright sunlight that's spilling down around her, the woman looks like an angel.

"Grandma Mae? But how? How did you get here? You've been dead for a long time."

"It's not important how I got here, my dear. The important thing is that I am here for you."

"I don't understand."

"You don't need to understand it, sweetheart. All you must do is embrace it."

"I'm confused, Grandma. Am I dying? I cannot leave my babies."

"Heavens no, my sweet girl. But I am here to give you a warning."

"About what?"

"That death is nearby. It's lurking in the cold shadows. The darkness is ready to pounce like a caged beast."

"Who is going to die? Please tell me it is not someone I love."

"That is not for me to say, my dear. All I can do is warn you to prepare for what is about to happen."

"What's going to happen, Grandma? Please tell me."

"Be ready, Carly," the woman whispers as the imagine slowly fades into the bleak darkness. *"Be ready ..."*

~

Carly screams as her eyes snap open. "Shit. What the hell was that all about?" She shakes her head. "Was I dreaming?"

She sits up on the bed and wipes her eyes. "What is going on?"

"I think you were having a dream."

"Leo?" She gasps as he emerges from the shadows. "Why aren't you downstairs at the party?"

"I'm not in the mood to be around your parents and their friends." He approaches the bed. "And why does it matter? This is my bedroom too, isn't it? Or have you already kicked me out of your bed?"

"It's just that you startled me," Carly stutters. "I didn't know anyone else was in the room."

"Just brought my bag up." He takes a large gulp of the drink he's holding. "When I saw your mother come back down, I knew you were up here all alone." He smirks. "I thought maybe we could ring in the New Year a little bit early. I figured you'd be as horny as I am. I can always make you wet."

"Jesus, Leo." She detests how vulgar he has become. "Do you have to be so disgusting all the time? Get away from me." She pulls the sheet up to her chin and clutches it tightly to her chest. Her heart is beating so fast she can hear the thumping in her ears.

"Look at this," he commands, pulling his pants down to show her his erect penis. "This is what you really need."

Carly almost gags. *How could I ever think I still love him?*

He stands over her, pulling on himself slowly, his lips curled down as he stares in her face. "You're still my wife and I have needs. Show me how much you love me and then we can go back downstairs to celebrate with everyone else. Come on. Open your mouth."

She quickly rolls to the other side of the bed and stands up. "Stay away from me. Didn't you hear what I said earlier? We're done, so there's no more *fun* to be had with me. And I don't know where you're sleeping tonight, but you aren't sleeping in here with me."

His eyes narrow to tiny slits. "I know you don't mean that, Carly. That's just the booze talking."

"Well, that's where you're wrong. I haven't had anything to drink. Not one drop."

"There you go," he snaps. "That's your problem. What you need is a little drink to loosen you up."

"I'm loose enough, Leo." She shoots back. "Now, please just leave me alone. And put that ugly prick back in your pants before I vomit."

"Come on, Carly." He darts to her side of the bed. "Just touch it. Let's just have a little quickie. It will make you feel better to work off a little of that stress."

He reaches for her, but she slaps his hand away. "I said I don't feel like it." The mere thought of his touch repulses her. "Now, leave me alone before you do something that you'll regret."

"What are you going to do? Call your daddy? See if I care. He doesn't intimidate me."

She decides it's best to take a softer tone instead of risking a confrontation between him and her father, especially when there's booze involved. "Let's just go back to the party. I'm suddenly feeling very hungry. I think I need something to eat, or I might be sick."

"No, you don't. You're just trying to get rid of me. Well, I have a message for you, sweetheart." He steps towards her, still clutching himself. "I'm not going away that easily. If you think you can push me out of your life and I'm just going to let you do it, then you have another thought coming."

She resists the urge to slap his face. "Do you really want to fight tonight?"

"I'm going back to Halifax tomorrow and, apparently, you're staying here, so when are we going to do this?"

"When you're sober."

"Oh, honey, I am not drunk," he says. "I'm just getting started."

"Then you can stay here and argue with yourself, whack yourself off, or whatever you want to do, but I'm going downstairs before I vomit."

She moves toward the bedroom door.

He grabs her by her arm and pulls her to him. "You're pretty brave in your daddy's house," he sneers. "You're not this brave at home, are you? And I'm not done yet."

She tries pushing him away, but she feels his grip tightening. She knows she'll have another bruise by morning. "Let go of me right now. You're a sick pervert forcing me to do things with you that disgust me. Let go of me or I will scream."

"You owe your husband a favour," he whines. "That's all I ask."

"Stop it, Leo," she cries as his grip tightens on her forearms. "You disgust me."

He twists her arm and tries forcing her to her knees. "Let's see if I can really disgust you with this." He grabs her by the jaw and tries to force it open.

Finding a sudden surge of strength, she breaks loose and pushes him away. "You bastard. Don't you ever touch me again or I'll cut your balls off." She fights back the tears.

"You think you're so tough, you little bitch. I need you to do this."

"I don't give a shit what you need." She glares at him. "I'm going downstairs. My advice to you is to stay right here and think about what you're doing. Maybe even have a quick nap, because you don't want to come down there and cause a scene. Daddy will throw you out, and then what will you do?"

"Fuck your daddy," Leo fires back, fumbling with his zipper. "I won't go easily."

"He'd like nothing better than to throw you out in the snow, especially when I've told him what you just did." Carly heads to the bedroom door.

"Come on, Carly," Leo stutters. "I still love you very much. What am I ever going to do without you?"

"You don't get to say that to me. Not ever again."

In the doorway she turns to look at him knowing hatred must be radiating from her. "This is all your doing, Leo. You will have to live with the consequences."

29: Vodka and 7-Up

"Hey, Sam." Cliff smiles as his guest sits her empty glass on the bar. "Are you having a good time?"

She nods. "I was until a few minutes ago."

"Looks like you could use a refill." She seems upset to him. "Tell me again what you're drinking, and I'll take care of that for you."

She leans in and rests her elbows on the bar. "I was drinking wine, but I think I need something a bit stronger. I'll take a vodka and Sprite if you have any."

"Sorry, I don't have Sprite, but how's about 7-Up?"

"That'll work. I just need something to dull this pounding in my skull."

Cliff grabs a bottle of Polar Ice from the shelf behind the bar and pours her a double shot of vodka. "This will fix you right up."

He adds two ice cubes, tops off the glass with 7-Up and slides the drink towards the woman he's grown to respect and admire since he arrived in Liverpool almost thirty years ago.

"If you don't mind me asking, Sam, what's wrong?" When she doesn't answer, he persists. "You don't look so well. Everything okay?"

She takes a large gulp of the vodka drink. He can see tears well in her eyes. She quickly rubs them away.

"Everything's wrong, Cliff." Her voice cracks as she speaks. "I just received some devastating news that's tearing me apart. I feel completely gutted."

"Anything you can talk about? I'm not trying to be nosy, but you know I'm always here to talk to if you need someone to listen. Things always seem more manageable once you talk about them."

She frowns. "I wish I could, but I'm not sure this information is public yet."

"That's okay." He offers her a smile that he hopes will lighten the mood. "I totally understand. You've always been there for me whenever I've needed a hand, so if you need anything, you just say the word."

"Thank you for that." She takes another drink. "I appreciate you being here very much and I'm sure we'll have the opportunity to talk about it very soon." She smiles but Cliff can see that it's a fake gesture. "This just isn't the time or place."

"Well, since you're here, do you feel up to talking with me about something else?" His eyebrows rise as he asks the question.

She nods. "Anything to help get my mind off what I just heard." She closes her eyes for a second and swallows, as if she's pushing her pain deep below the surface. "What can I help you with?"

Cliff glances around to see if anyone else is listening to their conversation. He's almost afraid to say the word out loud for fear of invoking some sort of ancient curse or evil spirits. He leans in closer to her and whispers, "It's the crows."

He can see she's surprised. Her eyes squint. "Are they still bothering you?"

"I'm afraid so."

He grabs himself another beer, pops off the cap and gulps down nearly half the bottle. "The problem is, I really have no idea what they want from me."

"Tell me what's going on."

Certain that his other guests are not listening to him and Samantha, he continues. "As I mentioned to you earlier, I've noticed that nine crows have been hanging around here all day and I think they've also been following me. I can't shake the feeling that they are trying to tell me something. I've been around this town long enough to know how this works with them."

"Maybe it's a warning." She takes another sip of her drink and stares at her glass as she swooshes around the clear liquid, careful not to slosh it over the sides. "That would be like them to try to warn you about something that's going to happen."

His eyes narrow to skinny slots. "Do you think? It kind of feels that way, and then there's the other thing."

"What other thing?"

He wonders now if maybe he should not be telling her about seeing someone lurking around his property and following him around the liquor store because it's clear she has a lot on her mind and maybe he shouldn't be adding anything to her stress. "Oh, nothing really. It's not all that important."

"Oh no, Cliff Graham. You can't drop something like that into the conversation and then just try to change the subject. That's not going to work with me. I've known you long enough to know when something is bothering you, so I am not letting you off the hook that easily." She squints at him again. "What's really going on here?"

Clearly, he thinks, *I should have engaged my brain before opening my mouth but as usual, I've put my foot into it once again. Julie is so right about me. I always speak before I think.*

"What is it? You know I'm not going to let you off the hook so tell me everything."

He accepts that there's no getting out of this. "Like I said, I have noticed the nine crows following me around all day, and they've really freaked me out, but on top of that, I have also noticed that someone is spying on me."

He can see the news hits her like a club.

"What are you talking about?"

He takes a gulp of beer. "I know it sounds a little over the top, but I first noticed it when I was in the liquor store this morning and I saw a woman watching me. It seemed like she was doing surveillance on me."

"Really? Or are you just being paranoid?"

"No way." He shakes his head. "I have been a cop for more than thirty years, Samantha, and I know what surveillance looks like. I'm telling you that someone was watching me this morning."

"I believe you, Cliff." She takes a drink. "This can't be good."

"Nope. Not at all."

"Any idea who it might be?"

"Not a clue. Normally, I don't let this kind of stuff get to me and so at first, I just kind of shrugged it off, but this afternoon I caught someone watching me through the garage window and then this evening, Charlie told me that when he and Rebecca got here, he noticed someone lurking around outside by the garage. I went out and looked around but couldn't see anyone. It's clear though that someone was out there. I found lots of footprints."

"That's creepy."

"It sure is."

"Any idea why someone would be stalking you?"

"I have no idea, but I have to tell you, it's got me more than a little on edge."

"I'm sure you are, and I understand why. What are you going to do now?"

He decides not to tell her that Warren also saw someone lurking around her and Kate's house until he can get both women together with

Warren. "I get the feeling that the crows and this person, whoever it is, are somehow connected. I'm just not sure how or why, but the cop in me is telling me to be on alert."

"I can see why you're on edge. What can I do?"

"You can tell me whatever you know about the crows."

"You would think that I would know a lot about those black birds by now," she says. "But the truth is, I know very little about them or why they do the things they do. The crows are very mysterious creatures, but I can tell you, that when they are on a mission, they can be relentless. You've seen them in action, Cliff. You know what I'm talking about."

"I certainly do. They're like little heat-seeking missiles aimed at their targets. I think maybe that's why I'm so worried about what's going on around here."

She downs the last of the vodka and slides the empty glass toward her friend. "I would be worried too. I'll have another of those, please, if you don't mind."

"I don't mind at all." Cliff grabs the Polar Ice and 7-Up to replenish her drink. He sets in the bottles in front of her. "If you want more when that's gone, just help yourself. Now, tell me again what it means when you see nine crows."

She welcomes the fresh drink. "It's nine crows for a kiss."

"Since I'm not feeling very romantic right now, I don't think it's anything like that. What else could it mean?"

"The crows' meaning is not always clear so you cannot look for the literal explanation around the numbers. I've found that their mission can often seem obscure. Nothing the crows do will ever seem immediately obvious. I've learned that lesson the hard way."

"I have no idea what to do with any of this. But I have to tell you, Sam, that it feels like the other shoe is about to drop."

"I must admit I'm feeling more than a little anxious myself. Based upon what you've just told me, I would say there is definitely something going on around here and whatever it is, the crows clearly know about it."

Cliff takes another drink. "That's what I'm afraid of."

"The question is, are they the instigators or are they trying to warn you about something? That could be very difficult to discern."

"Hell if I know." Cliff shakes his head.

"I wish I could be more helpful, but I do have one piece of advice for you."

"What's that?"

"Don't be fooled by the crows." Her warning is filled with genuine concern for her friend. "They aren't always a bad thing. In fact, I have discovered that the crows are often more protective of residents of this town than they are harmful, so instead of shying away from them, try to embrace them. Maybe the crows will find a way to connect with you and then you'll be better able to understand what they are up to."

"You think?"

She smiles. "I don't know. You're a hard nut to crack, Cliff Graham, but I do know that eventually, the truth will be revealed, and you'll say, 'Holy shit, so that's what the crows were trying to tell me.' Happens to me all the time. Keep an open mind about them and pay attention to what they're doing."

"Well, I hope they soon give me some answers because I don't like mysteries or playing games."

"I don't think it's a game. Just open yourself to the crows. Let them show you the way, but don't let them intimidate you."

Cliff nods. "Appreciate the advice. I knew you were the right person to talk to about this."

"The truth is, Alex knows a lot more about them than I do. You might be better off talking to him."

"He is a smart young man so I may just do that."

Cliff senses that their conversation has run its course. "And listen, I don't know what's going on with you but let me know if you ever need to talk."

She rises from the bar stool, smiles and takes her drink. "Thanks. I appreciate that."

From the corner of his eye, Cliff notices Carly coming down the stairs. "I see Carly over there and she looks pretty upset. I better go and see what's going on."

"By all means. I should be getting back to Kate anyway."

~

"Hey, honey." Cliff wraps his large arms around his daughter. She seems more rigid than he's used to experiencing with her. "What's wrong?"

"Nothing."

"Come on, Carly. You can't lie to me. So, I'll ask again, what's wrong?"

"It's just more of Leo's crap. There's nothing to worry about."

"What did he do now?"

"More of the same, but I handled it."

"Where is the little prick now?"

"Please, Daddy. This is hard enough for me. Don't make an issue out of this."

"Did he do something to you? Did he hurt you?"

"It's okay, Daddy." She starts to cry. "It was nothing."

"Stop protecting him." Cliff's anger is getting the best of him. "Where is he, Carly?"

"He's upstairs. I told him to lie down and have a nap. I'm hoping that if he sleeps it off, he won't bother anyone else tonight."

He notices the red handprints on her forearms where Leo grabbed her. He also zeros in on the red marks in the shape of fingertips on either side of her jaw.

His temper boils over. "He did hurt you. That son-of-a-bitch. I'll kick his god-damned ass all the way back to Halifax."

She grabs him by the arm. "Please don't go up there and cause a fight. The girls are sleeping and you'll wake them up. Just let it go for tonight."

"Stop defending him, Carly. He doesn't deserve it." He starts up the stairs.

"He's probably asleep by now so let him sleep it off. He'll be leaving in the morning. Just let it go, please."

"Not a chance." Cliff huffs as he sprints up toward the second floor.

"If you go up there, Daddy, I'm going to get Mom."

"Do whatever you have to do, Carly. Just don't come up here."

30: A matter of perspective

Her drink in hand, Samantha approaches her wife. Kate is sitting on the sofa, staring blankly at the flames as they dance in the fireplace while a small billow of smoke escapes up the chimney. She thinks it would be a cozy setting if not for the bleak thoughts that are consuming her brain.

"Hey, you." Her voice cracks with emotion. She sits beside Kate, places her drink on the coffee table, takes her wife's hand and offers her a warm smile. "How are you doing now?"

Kate is slow to respond, and Samantha doesn't push the issue. She knows her wife needs time to assimilate the devastating news she just heard about her brother's wife.

"Honestly, not very well," she finally whispers. "I feel like I was just hit in the head with a two-by-four."

"I know what you mean." Wanting to be the rock she believes her wife needs right now, Samantha digs deep for any hidden reserve of courage she can muster. "I feel the same way. My head is spinning so fast that it feels like it's on a swivel. It's a lot to digest."

"Should we leave?"

Samantha shrugs. "I don't know what to do."

"It is snowing pretty hard out there, so we can always blame it on the storm and road conditions."

"Maybe we should stick around until after midnight?" Samantha's response is more like a question than a comment. "I know it's difficult to be here right now, but I don't want to offend Cliff and Julie by leaving early. They've put a lot of work into organizing this function and, honestly, what are we going to do at home besides cry into our wine? It's probably better to be here in case Charlie and Rebecca need support."

Kate pushes the tears from her eyes with the back of her right hand. "Rebecca doesn't deserve this."

"No one deserves this."

"She is so young, and I feel so helpless." Kate cries. "I don't know what to do, or even what to say. I don't know how to help her."

"It's natural that you feel that way." Samantha knows that, no matter how much her wife's heart is breaking, there is nothing either of them can do to help Rebecca and Charlie, except to be available when they need support. "There really is no easy way to process news like this except to take things one day at a time and try to move forward."

"Poor Liam." Kate faces her wife. "Charlie is a great dad, but the boy needs his mother."

"You know Rebecca will be there for him as much as she can be, no matter what, and so will we."

Tears trickle from Kate's eyes. "Rebecca and Liam are very close. They've got a special relationship that I've always envied and wished we would have had with our sons. We will never be able to replace her."

"Let's hope they have lots of time left to be together, but we won't even try to replace Rebecca because we never could in Liam's eyes," Samantha says. "We'll be there for Liam and for Charlie to lean on."

"For sure. This is gut wrenching, Samantha. Never in my wildest dreams would I have ever imaged that our family would be facing something like this right now."

"Just when you think things are going well, something will come along to kick you in the ass and turn your world upside down." Samantha glances around the room. "Where did Charlie and Rebecca get to?"

"The last time I saw Charlie, he was heading into the kitchen with Oliver," Kate says. "I'm glad they connected tonight because he needs his best friend right now. And I think I saw Rebecca going into the little playroom down the hall with Liam and Lauren. Julie set up an entertainment centre for the young kids in there with a bunch of throw pillows, where they could watch movies. I think Rebecca wanted to make sure they were settled down."

"She is an amazing mom. And smart thinking on Julie's part to think of the younger kids. She's quite the savvy hostess."

"Indeed. I would never have thought of doing something like that, not that we entertain that much."

Samantha says, "Speaking of being a good host, I see your drink is gone. Want another?"

Kate shakes her head. "I don't really feel much like drinking right now. I'll drive us home, so you don't have to worry about that."

"And you don't have to worry about driving either. I'll get Hunter or maybe Lisa to drive us home." Samantha winks at her wife, a signal that she's got it handled. "We can leave our car here and get it tomorrow, so if you want another drink, go for it."

"No thanks. I'm good."

Kate spies their oldest son, Hunter, and his girlfriend, Ally, moving in their direction. "Speaking of Hunter, it looks like we've got incoming, and brace yourself because, based upon the pep in his step, I would say he's on a mission."

"He does look hot to trot." Samantha chuckles. "Wonder what he's up to?"

"Hey, guys," Hunter says as he and Ally sit in the plush chairs at either end of the sofa. "Great party. If you haven't tried any of that hot crab dip, I would highly recommend that you have some. It's freaking awesome."

"It's one of my favourites, too." Samantha glances from one to the other. Hunter seems fidgety to her, and she knows it's a sign that he's nervous over something. Ally, on the other hand, sits quietly, as if waiting for something. "What have you guys been up to?"

"We were just in the living room with Alex and Bree." Hunter answers quickly. "We were hoping to hang with Carly and Leo for a while, but we can't find them anywhere. We had so much fun with them last year, but they seem to be avoiding us this time around."

"It's not you, Hunter." Samantha touches her son's knee. "They are having some—let's just say—issues right now. Don't expect to see much of them this evening."

"What kind of issues?"

"Nothing that concerns us." Kate speaks up. "But I'm glad you took the time to hang with your brother. I wish you two would spend more time together. There's going to come a time when you'll regret that you weren't closer to each other."

Hunter rolls his eyes at her. "You want to bring that up in the middle of a party?"

"I'm just saying that you two are the only siblings you have so please make the most of each other." Kate takes a deep breath. "Besides, you'll be going back to university in a few days, so you won't see much of him for a while. You may not believe it, but Alex really misses you when you're gone."

"That's just the thing," Hunter says. He reaches as if to take Ally's hand, but the distance between the chairs is too great. "There is some-thing we want to talk to you about."

"Careful, Hunter." Samantha warns. She has no idea where this conver-sation is going, but she can tell he is bursting to tell them something very serious. She has always had the uncanny ability to read her oldest son from the day they adopted him, when he was just a year old. "You may want to choose your next words very carefully, young man."

"I'm not a child, Mom. I am an adult, and I have made some decisions that I know you guys are not going to like."

"That's not any way to instill confidence in us," Samantha replies.

Kate says, "If you're going to tell us what I think you're going to tell us, do you really think this is a good time for it? As you just pointed out, we are at a party and there are other people around."

Hunter throws a quick glance at Ally. "I'm not really worried about any of that. It's as good as time as any." He takes a deep breath. "Besides, there's a never a good time to talk to you two because you are never together."

"That's not true," Kate rebuts. "We're always together. But okay." She quickly looks around the room to see if anyone else is close enough to hear them. "I can tell that you need to get this off your chest so whatever it is, just tell us."

With that, Hunter just blurts it out. "Ally is pregnant and I'm quitting university." He quickly throws up his left hand, a gesture to stop them before they have a chance to light into him. "And before either of you say anything, yes, I've thought this through and yes, this is what I want to do."

"Hunter!" Samantha is flabbergasted. "For God's sake. What are you thinking?"

Hunter shakes his head. "Please don't lecture me about my life choices and my future. I love Ally very much. We are going to have a baby and we are going raise our child together. I want to stay at home and take care of the baby while Ally gets her degree so she can become a teacher, like she's always wanted to do."

He gestures as if he is pulling a zipper across his mouth. "That's it. End of story."

Kate shakes her head. "Not end of story. You've just lobbed quite a bomb at us, mister. Two, in fact."

"I understand you are shocked, but I hope you will trust that I know what I'm doing. I need you to respect my decisions."

"These decisions are going to have major implications for you in the future." Kate tries to remain calm. "We have to talk about this."

"There's nothing to talk about." He smiles at Ally who has remained silent to this point.

"My God, Hunter." Samantha exhales. "We knew you guys were sexually active, but I thought you were both smart enough to use protection."

"We did use protection. Always, but I guess I've got strong swimmers."

"Jokes, Hunter?" Samantha says. "At a time like this?"

"Jeez." He grimaces. "Just trying to lighten the mood."

"We are not laughing, mister."

"I can see that."

"He's right, Ms. Henderson," Ally pipes up. "We were always very careful."

"Apparently not careful enough." Samantha directs her eyes at the young woman her son obviously cares for. "You guys are way too young to take on this huge responsibility. This is going to ruin your lives."

"That's a matter of perspective," Hunter says. "Where you see this as something negative, we see it as something positive for us. You see it your way, we'll see it our way."

"But you've put so much effort into your studies." Kate maintains an even voice. "You only have another year and a half to go to get your degree. Why not stick with your studies? It will put you in a better position for a good job."

"Will it?' He squints at Kate. "I'm not worried about that. In fact, if I'm really being honest, I hate university. Didn't like it from day one. I've only been going to classes because I knew that's what you guys wanted."

"Oh my." Samantha closes her eyes and presses her fingertips to her temples to relieve the tension that has suddenly taken up residence behind her eyeballs. "This is the last thing we need, on top of everything else."

"What are you talking about?" Hunter is confused. "What else is going on?"

"I am not going to get into details with you right now"—she looks at him sharply—"but this is a bad time for us. We just found out your Aunt Rebecca is sick."

"How sick?"

"Very sick," Kate answers.

"That's too bad." Hunter relaxes his rigid posture, now that he's told his parents the major news. "I'm sorry to hear that. She's a wonderful person and I hope she will be okay, but that doesn't change anything as far Ally and I are concerned. We are having the baby and I'm quitting university to get a job and to raise it. End of story."

Samantha shakes her head. "Not end of story." She focuses on the young woman again. "How does your mother feel about this, Ally?"

Ally casts her eyes to the floor. "The thing is, Ms. Henderson, I haven't told her yet."

"I see." Samantha's eyes narrow. "Don't you think you should tell her?"

Ally nods. "And I will, but we wanted to you tell you guys first. I know she will be angry with me. She believes good girls should remain chaste until they are married."

"Do you have any idea what it to takes to care for a baby?" Samantha tries to maintain a reasoned approach. "It will change your whole life. Are you prepared for that?"

"I think so." Ally nods slowly. "Or at least I hope so."

"Knowing you can do it and hoping you can do it are two completely different things," Samantha observes. "If you are going to have this baby, then you better be one hundred percent positive that it's what you want. Once you have that baby in your arms, there is no going back."

"We've talked about it, Mom," Hunter says. "And we know what we are doing. Please don't be angry with Ally. She has done nothing wrong."

Samantha turns to him. "I'm not angry with Ally or with you. However, I am disappointed in you both."

"Come on, Mom," he snaps. "Don't be so old-fashioned."

"If I'm old fashioned, it's because I love you and want what's best for you." She grits her teeth. "I'm older than you and I've learned a thing or two about life."

"Why can't you just be happy for us?"

"I know you are not that naive, Hunter," Kate says. "You can't believe that we were just going to accept this news without questioning your judgment."

"There is nothing wrong with my judgment." Now he's getting miffed. "You guys have always taught me to take responsibility for my actions so that's what I'm doing. It's my fault that Ally is pregnant and I'm going to do the right thing—even if it is the hardest thing I ever do. I am going to be a good father."

"Dear God in Heaven." Samantha throws her hands up. "Now you're throwing our own words back at us?" She's almost proud of her son for throwing this little twist at them. She turns to her wife. "What are we going to do?"

"What can we do? Sounds to me like he's got his mind made up."

Hunter speaks up. "Ally and I are not looking for your approval. Our minds *are* made up about this, so nothing you can say will change anything." He offers them a gentle smile. "I know you want me to finish university, and I love you for that, but honestly, that is not what I want. I want to be a good father to my son or daughter and, when the time is right, Ally and I are getting married. What we would really love is to have your blessings."

"Okay, Hunter." Kate says after a few seconds of awkward silence. "We understand your perspective and respect your commitment to doing the right thing, and we love you for wanting to shoulder a burden that is your responsibility, but we will have to discuss this further."

Samantha adds, "While we love you and Ally, and we'll most certainly love the baby, there are other ways to handle this situation, ways that don't include you dropping out of university and messing up your future."

"That's the future *you* want for me," he interrupts. "It's not the future I want for me."

"You are so close to earning your degree. You should stick with it, and we will help you do that," Kate says. "You just have to let us help."

Hunter bites his lower lip as he's always done whenever he's thinking or angry, an idiosyncrasy he's had since he was a child. "I love you both for wanting to help, but I hope you will understand that I must do this my way. If we let you guys help us, then you will want to control everything, and I can't have that." He stands, moves closer to Ally and takes her hand. "I appreciate your offers to help, but we've got this. We are going to do this our way."

31: The watchers

They wait in the darkness. They are destined to be here; compelled by a force beyond their compression.

Despite the blustering snow and strong winds, the chill so cold it cuts to their bones, the nine hold strong. They are the first and last line of defence.

The crows, perched silently in the towering pine trees that surround the Graham property, remain at their posts, refusing to give in to the storm that grows more severe by the second.

They will not leave. They cannot leave. It's as though they are tethered to their branches.

Watching. Observing.

They are steadfast in their commitment to protect those inside the well-lit house, the humans who are oblivious to the threat that hangs over them.

While the threat is not yet clear, the crows know something is brewing as the universe feels off kilter to them. With their sharp senses of sight, smell and hearing on extreme alert, the large and powerful birds can feel it.

The danger is palpable. They will intervene when necessary.

The nine silent sentinels dutifully scout out the property, moving only when necessary, but constantly watching for anything that might be a threat. They preserve their body heat and their strength. They will only react to neutralize the threat.

They are one, brothers and sisters in the cause. As a sudden movement in the Graham backyard, near the tree line where the lawn meets the alders, attracts their attention, their heads move in unison, their eighteen pellet-like eyes focusing on a dark figure.

Someone approaches.

A stranger.

The nine watch quietly as the figure, cloaked in darkness, moves slowly and stealthily through the backyard, making their way through the knee-deep snow toward the back of the house. Remaining in the shadows, this stranger, of average build and height, wants to avoid detection.

But the crows know. The crows see the stranger.

As the snow falls steadily, covering the earth in a thick and pristine blanket of pure white, the crows are on high alert, their senses firing on all cylinders. This person—whoever it is—does not belong here.

The danger has arrived.

32: Shadows in the snow

"I have to say, Julie, you have really outdone yourself this year." Lisa Hamilton smiles while trying to chew discretely.

She chases the comment with a sip of wine and then another nibble of her sausage roll. "What did you put in these things? I've had sausage rolls before, but I don't remember them ever tasting this good."

Julie leans closer to her friend and whispers, as if she's about to divulge a tightly held state secret, "It's the Worcestershire sauce."

"Really? I never would have guessed, but it works."

Lisa turns to Dr. Anna Robbie, who quickly bonded with these two women after she started dating Oliver Lewis a few months earlier. "Have you tried these yet? If you haven't, you ought to." She licks her lips. "They are amazing."

Anna shakes her head. "I've been too busy enjoying the Chardonnay." She playfully waives the half-full glass in front on her friends. "But after three of these babies, I think I should have something to eat or else."

"Or else what?" Julie smirks. "Oliver will have a wild vixen on his hands when you get him home tonight?"

"Oh, my dear ladies." Anna laughs, her eyes sparkling with devilish intent. "You have no idea what this stuff does to me. Oliver is in a for a wild ride."

"You're one lucky woman." Lisa sighs, almost wistfully. "That Oliver Lewis is one fine looking hunk of a man."

"Lisa Hamilton." Julie pretends to be surprised. "What would your husband say if he heard you talk like that?"

"Who cares what he says?" Lisa's answer is sharp. "It's not like I'm in the market for another man." She pauses. "Although there are times..."

"Really?" Julie's tone takes on a more serious edge. "Everything alright with you and Warren?"

"Oh yes." Lisa sighs. "Yes, indeed."

Julie probes. "You don't sound convinced."

"Quite sure." Lisa's mood visibly becomes more stoic. "I'm just tired, that's all."

"Been there, done that." Julie takes a deep breath. "I remember when Cliff was still on the force. It was brutal at times. The constant stress is a lot to handle. Between holding down the fort at home with the kids and worrying about him every moment he was on duty, I was lucky if I got any more than an hour or two of sleep most nights. You do that for a few years, and it wears you down. Only people who work in policing or have a loved one who is a police officer can understand what it's like."

"Well, I think it's a thankless job," Anna says. "Those brave police officers lay their lives on the line every single time they put on their uniforms, and they usually do it for very little pay but often a whole lot of grief from people who don't understand what it's like to serve the public in such a dangerous profession. It takes a very special kind of person to do that job. And a very special family support unit to keep them going."

She nods knowingly at the two other women. "Your husbands are amazing for what they do, but so are you guys. You don't get enough credit. You really are the strong ones in your families."

"That's very kind of you to say." Julie smiles and raises her glass in a toast. "To all the women and men who support our police officers." She winks. "Those guys in uniform owe it all to us."

"I'll drink to that." Lisa giggles before she takes a sip of her wine. "Oh my God. That is so freaking good, but this better be my last one because I have to drive tonight. This is Warren's night for a blowout. He's had a tough stretch of it lately, so he's earned the right to party, and he loves hanging with Cliff, so I'm sure he's having a good time."

Julie laughs. "Whenever those two are together, you can be sure trouble will follow." She quickly glances around the room. "I wonder what they're up to?"

Lisa also scouts out the room. "I see Warren over there talking to Anna's fine specimen of male human flesh. But I don't see Cliff anywhere."

"I wonder where he's gotten to and what he's up to."

"I can tell you what he's up to, Mom." Carly suddenly appears. She struggles to quiet her breathing. "He's up to beating the crap out of my husband, that's what."

Julie takes Carly by the shoulders. "What are you talking about?"

"He's going to kill him, Mom." Carly sobs. "He's really angry and he says he's going to throw Leo out tonight. You have to stop him."

"Okay." Julie pulls her daughter in for a hug and addresses the other women. "Sorry, but I've got to go and find my husband before he kills my idiot son-in-law."

"Do you want me to get Warren?" Lisa asks. "Maybe he can help."

"No." Julie shakes her head. "I think it's best if I handle this one on my own. Sometimes, if you add more people to the mix, it only makes things worse."

~

Julie leads her daughter up the stairs. "You pop in and check on the girls." Reaching the closed door of the guest bedroom, she stops and listens. "I don't hear anything, so that's a good sign." She doesn't really believe what she's saying but she remains hopeful. "Maybe your father and Leo are talking it out."

"Wouldn't that be nice?" Carly whispers. She disappears into the bedroom where the girls are sleeping.

Julie takes a deep breath and gingerly turns the knob, carefully opening the door a crack as a sudden loud thud from inside the room gives her pause. The blood quickly rushes to her heart.

"Cliff?" She's almost afraid of the answer. "Are you in here? Are you okay?"

"Yes," Cliff quickly answers. "Come in."

Julie steps into the room. She is surprised, but relieved, to find Cliff is alone. He is sitting on the edge of the bed, staring down at his hands.

"What's wrong?"

"Nothing." He nods toward the hole in the wall next to the door. "I was just so pissed off when I got here, and Leo was gone that I punched the wall. I didn't mean to, but I just snapped."

"Oh my God. Are you alright?" She notices Leo's overnight bag on the floor near the dresser. "Where's Leo?" She hesitates, afraid to upset her husband. "Did you do something to him?"

Cliff shakes his head and glances up at his wife. "I wanted to break his fucking neck, but when I got here, the room was empty."

"That doesn't make any sense. How did he get downstairs without any of us seeing him? There's only one staircase."

"I have no idea. But it's freaking weird because I came up right after Carly told me that Leo got physical with her. I can't explain it but the little fucker is slippery so who knows where he's gone."

Recalling the run-ins Carly has had with forerunners over the past twenty-four hours, Julie shivers. "Carly is going to freak out if we can't figure out where Leo has gotten to. Do you think he's a danger to any-one?"

"I'd like to say no." Cliff looks sharply into his wife's eyes. "But I don't know anything for sure when it comes to him. According to Carly, he's been drinking a lot. If he's feeling like his back is against the wall, he might snap and then God knows what he'll do."

"He wouldn't have driven off somewhere, would he?"

"I doubt it." Cliff rises from the bed and extends his hand to his wife. "He's an asshole but he's not stupid. He knows that he's too drunk to drive, or at least I hope he knows that."

Julie takes her husband's hand, rises from the bed, and stands beside him. "He thinks he's invincible or immortal, and never makes mistakes."

"Sorry, honey, but when I get my hands on him, he's going to learn the hard way that he's made one major fuck-up tonight," Cliff says.

"I know you're angry." Julie squeezes his hand. "I'm angry, too, and I want him stopped, but please promise me you won't do anything drastic."

"I can't promise you that."

"When you find him, please don't hit him," Julie pleads. "That won't help anything."

"He deserves it after everything he's done, the little prick."

"Am I going to have to ask Warren to keep you in order?"

"Go ahead." He lets her hand go. "He's on my side."

"Of course, he is." Julie's response is sharp. "I wouldn't expect anything else from him."

Cliff glares at his wife, then looks away. "Let's go find that prick so we can get back to our guests. I don't want to be dealing with Leo's sorry ass when the clock strikes midnight. That's not how I want to ring in the New Year."

Julie takes a deep breath and then exhales. "Okay, Cliff. Do things your way, but please think of your daughter and your granddaughters before you do something stupid that you might regret."

His eyes narrow to tiny slits. "Why do you think I'm so pissed right now? The idea that he would put his hands on his wife while his little girls are sleeping just down the hall and might hear everything, makes me want to punch his face in. And you want to know something? I think he tried to rape her."

Julie closes her eyes. Hard. "It makes me angry, too, but you have to control yourself. Having you going off the deep end will not make Carly happy. She has enough to worry about right now. Leo will pay a price for what he's done. We'll figure this out."

"Just a second." Cliff raises his right hand. "I want to check on something."

He goes to the bedroom window that looks out over the front yard and the driveway to see if any vehicles have left the yard.

He pulls back the curtains and peers through the window. The winds have pelted the snow against the glass and nearly obscured the view. Holding his breath to keep from fogging up the glass, he peers out into the night.

"Man." He exhales. "It is really coming down. I don't think our guests are going anywhere for a while. I hope they all brought their PJs."

"Is it that bad, Cliff?" Julie joins him near the window and peers into the snow-filled yard. "I can't see anything out there. It's coming down so hard that even the outside lights aren't helping very much."

Cliff scans the snow-covered vehicles parked in the yard. "All the cars are accounted for, at least by my count, and I don't see any tire tracks, which means the bastard's in here somewhere. He knows he fucked up, so he's probably hiding from us."

"Wait a minute." Julie's eyes are drawn to a sudden movement. "What's that out by the front corner of the garage?" She whispers, "Is that someone out there? Do you think it's Leo?"

"Where?"

"Right there." She points. "See it? There is someone out there."

"Fucking Christ," Cliff blurts out. He makes a beeline to the bedroom door. "There sure as hell is."

"Where are you going?"

"I'm going to see who the fuck that is out there. You stay in the house."

"Wait," Julie calls as he disappears through the bedroom door. "You can't go out there alone."

33: Flickering lights

Dr. Charlie Webster has tried to enjoy the party, but the prospect of losing his wife sometime in the coming months has dominated his thoughts throughout the evening, pushing out any happiness he had hoped to find in the festivities.

How can I possibly celebrate the New Year when that future promises to be such a dark and bleak period for me and my family? he wonders. Whenever he thinks about a future without his wife beside him, it feels like someone has reached down his throat, pulled out of his heart and squeezed the life out of it.

He finds Rebecca in the den, sitting in a large armchair stationed near the fireplace, her long legs pulled up under her slender, frail frame. She is staring into the flames.

He kneels in front of her and takes her hands into his. "How are you doing, honey?" His voice is soft and gentle. "Can I get you anything? Need more water?"

"I'm alright." She forces a smile.

He can tell she's lying.

He gently rubs the backs of her hand with his fingertips. "I'm going to find Liam, and then we're leaving."

"Don't you want to ring in the New Year with your sister and all the others?" Her sunken eyes with the dark rings around them convey her current state of discomfort.

He shakes his head. "It's time to get you home and tucked back into bed so you can rest. Besides, it's almost time for your meds."

"I'm okay, Charlie." Her protest is feeble.

"No, you aren't. Give me a few minutes to get Liam geared up. Then I'm going out to start the car and get the snow cleaned off it. Stay in here where it's warm, and I'll come and get you when we're ready to head out."

"How is Kate doing? You need to talk to her before we leave."

"You're the one who's sick and in pain and you're asking me how Kate is doing?" He shrugs. "I'm sure she's upset. Why wouldn't she be? But I'm not really worried about my sister right now. I want to get you home, where we should have stayed. If you remember, I didn't want to come here in the first place."

"Please, honey." Her voice is raspy. "Don't lecture me."

"I'm not lecturing you, Becca." He looks lovingly at her. "But I regret that I didn't stand my ground when I suggested that we should stay home."

"This could be the last time that I get to see all of these people together in one spot, so please don't ruin it for me." Tears well in her eyes. "Let's just wait until after midnight. If you look in my purse, you'll find some Tramadol."

Charlie finds the brown plastic bottle and hands her two long white pills that may look like Tylenol but are considerably stronger and better for masking pain. She pops them in her mouth and chases them with a sip of water.

"Need anything else?"

"Thank you." She closes her eyes and leans her head back against the chair. "I'll be fine once that Tramadol kicks in."

He shakes his head. "Nothing's ever going to be fine again."

"You can do this, Charlie." She opens her eyes and stares into his face, trying to force a smile. She rubs her long, bony fingers through his thick, dark hair. "We can both do this."

"Oh, Rebecca." His eyes become misty as tears form and trickle down his cheeks. "I don't believe I can."

"I promise everything will be all right."

"Nothing will ever be all right again."

The lights in the den suddenly flicker several times.

"Damn it." Charlie rises to his feet. "The last thing we need is for the power to go off."

~

The playroom is far enough from the party that Lauren and Liam can't hear the ruckus the grownups are making while they enjoy their movie.

Lisa finds her daughter, Lauren, there, along with Liam, Charlie and Rebecca's son, each perched on a faux-leather, vintage-style beanbag chair that looks like it came right out of the 1970s. They are enjoying a bowl of Tostitos and salsa. "What's that you're watching?"

"It's a great movie." Lauren's eyes remain fixated to the TV screen.

"What's it called?" Lisa asks.

"*We Have a Ghost.*" The tone in the young girl's voice conveys her displeasure at having her movie interrupted by an intrusive adult. "Now, can you please stop talking so we can hear the movie? It's almost over."

"Just one more question."

"Okay Mom." Lauren turns to her and sighs. "What is it?"

"What's it about?"

"It's about a boy who moves into a new home with his family only to discover that it's already occupied by a ghost named Ernest," Liam says. "He makes a video of Ernest and when his video goes viral, they end up in the government's crosshairs. That's when the fun begins. It's really good."

"Ghosts? Huh." She smiles at Liam. "Do you believe in ghosts?"

"Don't know." The young boy shrugs. "I never really thought about it before."

Lisa says, "Can I watch it with you guys for a bit or have I been expelled from the kid's club?"

"Only if you stop talking." Lauren throws her hands up and glares at her mother. "We only have a little more to watch and we'd really like to hear it."

"Roger that." Lisa pulls her hand across her mouth as if she's closing an invisible zipper.

Planking her butt on the floor between the two beanbag chairs, Lisa turns her focus to the TV screen.

Ten minutes later, as the credits start to roll, Lauren presses the off button on the remote and the television blinks to black. "Okay, Mom," she says. "What did you want?"

"I just wanted to see how you're doing. Need anything?"

Lauren shakes her head. "All good here."

"Okay, then." Lisa sighs and pulls her body up to her knees while groaning as only an adult can. "Then I guess I should be getting back to the party."

"Okay, Mom." Lauren smiles but to Lisa it looked more like a grimace.

"Just one more thing, Lauren," she says. "How are you feeling?"

"I'm doing okay."

"Not feeling too tired?"

Lauren shakes her head. "I'm okay. Really. Please stop worrying about me."

"I'm your mother. It's my job to worry about you."

As Lisa gets to her feet, the lights flicker.

"Is the power going to go off, Mrs. Hamilton?" Liam immediately asks.

"I don't know, but I certainly hope not too."

"I hate it when the power goes off." A tinge of nervous apprehension is audible in the young boy's voice.

Lisa nods. "I think everyone hates it, especially us grownups."

"I don't hate it," Lauren says. "I love snuggling under a pile of blankets and reading a book by flashlight. It's a lot of fun."

"Yeah, that can be fun," Lisa says.

The lights flicker twice more and then stabilize, keeping the darkness at bay—for the time being, at least.

~

Approaching Oliver from behind, Anna wraps her arms tightly around his trim waist and gives him a hug.

"Here you are, mister." She laughs, rubbing her hands up his tight stomach. "Thought I'd find you near the bar."

"Where else would I be?" He playfully pushes his butt back against her slender body.

She stretches on her toes and kisses him on the back of his neck. "With all these horny women watching you, I thought you might be in a bedroom somewhere upstairs. Apparently, you're the hottest ticket in town."

He turns to face her, pulls her close and kisses her on the lips. "I know Kate and Samantha aren't interested and all the other women are tied up with their husbands who just happen to be cops, so what horny women are you talking about?"

"Me." She smiles up at him while sliding her hands down his back to grab his bum cheeks.

"You better behave yourself, Dr. Robbie."

"Or what?"

He laughs. "Or I may have to ask Cliff or Julie if I can borrow a bedroom for a short minute."

"For just a minute?" She squeezes his bum even harder, driving her fingernails into his jeans. "I think you're going to need it for longer than a minute. Let's excuse ourselves and go home."

"Don't you want to ring in the New Year with all of our friends?"

"Not really." Standing on her tiptoes she whispers into his ear, "No offence to them, darling, but all I want to do is get you home and strip you naked so I can use my tongue to ravish your body from head to toe." Pulling back, she adds, "Are you saying you'd rather stay here instead?"

"Well, when you put it like that…I'll find our hosts and make our excuses. You get our coats and I will meet you at the front door."

"Deal." She plants a light kiss on his lips just as the lights flicker. "That can't be good."

Oliver pulls away. "No. Maybe we better hang on for just a few minutes to see how this turns out."

~

Hunter holds Ally's hand as they stand at the living room window, watching the snow fall. He speaks softly. "Well, that went a little better than I thought it would."

"Do you really think so?" Her voice cracks with emotion. "From where I was sitting, it didn't seem that they took the news very well."

"They didn't scream or shout or tell me I shouldn't see you anymore, so I see all of that as a good thing."

"They didn't exactly jump for joy either."

"No, they didn't. But they will come around. They just need some time to let the news sink in."

"Don't be so naïve, Hunter. Your mothers are both very smart women. What if they are right? What if having this baby ruins our lives? What then?"

"I know you are scared, Ally. The idea of being a parent is also scary to me, but don't let them get into your head." He takes a deep breath. "Talking in circles and lecturing, especially their own children, is what they do best. They will find a way to manipulate you and you won't ever know it's happening."

"Come on, Hunter. They aren't like that."

"Oh yes they are. Once you let them into your head space, they'll live there. It happened to me many times when I was growing up."

"I just don't want us to do anything that we are going to regret."

"We won't," he assures her. "I promise you that everything will work out just fine. You'll see."

"I think I want to go home now."

"Can we wait just a while longer? I promised my parents that I would drive them home." He waits for her to answer and, when she doesn't, he adds, "They could both be drinking now and shouldn't drive. They're counting on me."

"I suppose."

Just then, the lights flicker several times.

"Please. Please. Please, power," she says. "Please don't go off. I hate it when we lose electricity in the middle of a storm."

He hugs her tight. "I'd say there's a pretty good chance that the town will lose power before this night is out."

"Oh, no. I really hope not." Ally exhales. "That is never a good thing."

~

"Hey, ladies." Warren joins Kate Webster and Samantha Henderson in the living room. He has decided it's time to tell them about the stranger he and Bree saw lurking around their house.

"Hi, Warren." They smile and answer in unison.

"Is it okay if I join you? I don't want to interrupt anything but if you have a minute, there is something I would like to talk to you about."

Kate nods. "I need something to distract to me. What's on your mind, Warren?"

"Before you start, it isn't anything too serious, is it?" Samantha asks.

"Not exactly good news, Mayor Henderson." Warren shrugs. "First, as far as I know there is still no news on the whereabouts of Gwen Pittmann." He decides that leading with this update is the best strategy.

"Her probation officer promised to call me if they found her," Kate tells him. "But since I haven't heard anything, I am guessing that means Gwen is still MIA."

"I wish I had better news on that front, but I do think that if she's any-where in Nova Scotia the police are going to spot her. We've got everyone looking for her."

"In this weather?" Samantha asks. "Come on Warren. That isn't very likely, is it?"

"Well." He stalls. "Probably not right now in the middle of a blizzard."

"Is that the urgent matter you wanted to discuss with us?" Kate asks.

He shakes his head. "But it could be related."

The lights flicker.

"Damn it," Samantha says. "Looks like this god-damn storm's going to take out the power." She turns to Kate. "We should head home?"

"Just a second, Mayor," Warren says. "The reason I brought up Gwen Pitt—"

"Warren. Good, I've found you." Julie joins the trio. "I need you to come with me right away."

He spins around and sees she is distraught. "What's wrong?"

"It's Cliff." The fear in her words is palpable. "I think he might be in trouble, and he needs you for back up."

34: Alex's vision

"Holy crap, Bree." Alex says. "I don't like the looks of this."

He stares intently at the three-by-six-inch screen on the new iPhone his parents gave him for a Christmas present. They may have said they gave it to him because they wanted him to always keep in touch, but he knows they had an ulterior motive—keeping tabs on him.

Even though he's already turned seventeen, he shrugs it off. He knows his parents mean well. Considering everything he's gone through in recent years, he understands why they worry about him but, on top of that, he was in serious need of an updated model.

He just smiled on Christmas morning and said, "Thank you very much."

On the Weather Network app, he points to a map of the Maritimes that shows the region completely covered by the large storm system that has settled over the three provinces. "This freaking storm is massive. We're going to get clobbered. I have never seen anything like it before."

Bree cranks her neck, trying to get a glimpse of the small screen that has so entranced her boyfriend. "Let me see."

He turns the phone so she can get a better look. "It looks like two storm fronts have converged. They say it's going to be stalled over us for at least the next twenty-four to thirty hours."

"It sounds really bad. But who are *they*?" Bree smiles. "Are *they* the weather gods?"

Alex chuckles. He knows what she's trying to do. "They are predicting upwards of one hundred and fifty centimetres, maybe even as much as two hundred in some places. I don't ever remember that much snow all at once, do you?"

She shakes her head. "Too bad it isn't a school night. If they had to cancel school tomorrow, I'd be up for that. Do you think they'll give us a day in lieu of? Like when Christmas falls on a weekend?"

"You think?" His eyebrows rise as he laughs. "With that much snow, they'd probably have to cancel school for the next two or three days. Maybe even a week."

Bree brushes the phone aside. "Let's go find Hunter and Ally. It's New Year's Eve, remember? I'd like to be with them when the clock strikes midnight."

"If you really want to. I guess they'd be better to hang out with than the old folks."

"You better not let your mothers hear you call them that," she warns him.

Alex shakes his head. "They would not be too impressed, that's for sure." He smirks. "But seriously, you and Ally seem to be getting along quite well. I'm glad about that. I like her very much."

"Me, too. And do you find that Hunter has changed over the past six months? It's like he's, I don't know, more grown up or something. More mature."

Alex shakes his head. "I don't know what you see, but he's still an ass to me most of the time."

"No, he isn't. He's usually just having fun with you, but you always take it the wrong way."

"You're sticking up for my brother?" Alex is surprised. "If there's a way for him to piss me off, then he'll always find it. He seems to take great pleasure in making me unhappy."

"I know it seems that way to you, Alex." She sighs. "But did you ever think that if you didn't give him that reaction, maybe he wouldn't pick on you so much?"

"Like I said, he's just an ass," Alex counters. "There's really no way to sugar coat the truth." He pauses. "But, yes, I agree that Ally seems to be good for him."

"If he knows what's good for him, he better hang onto her." Bree says. "Think they'll get married some day?"

"God, Bree." He squints at her, wondering why she would even bring that up. "You're kind of getting ahead of yourself, aren't you? My parents will insist that he finish university first, so anything like marriage for them will have to wait."

She shrugs. "I know a few married couples who still go to university and it seems to be working for them. It's not so rare. Anyhow, let's go see what they're doing."

Alex suddenly staggers backwards as if he's stepped on a spinning disk and lost his balance. "Jesus." He reaches out to grab Bree's arm. "What the hell was that?"

"What the hell *was* what?" Bree guides him to a nearby chair. "Sit here for a minute." She stands back and looks him over. "Are you alright, Alex?"

"I think so."

"What happened?"

"I just suddenly felt really dizzy, like I couldn't keep my balance. It felt like my legs were spaghetti and my feet wanted to do their own thing. And there was a flashing light all around me. It was very strange."

"Are you feeling better now?"

"A little." He keeps his head down, his eyes closed.

"Maybe I should get your mother," Bree suggests.

He shakes his head. "Please don't bother her." He looks up at her. "I'm okay."

Bree observes him closely. "I can tell something is wrong. Your eyes are glazed over and you look flushed. You're really white, pasty like."

"Probably something I ate."

"It's definitely more than something you ate."

Alex sighs. "Okay, Bree." He motions for her to come closer as he wants to speak quietly. "If you must know. I just had a vision."

She kneels in front of him. "A vision?"

"It just popped into my head and it lasted just a few seconds but I'm sure that's what it was."

"You haven't had one of those in a while."

He shakes his head. "Not since last summer, before all hell broke loose."

"Could it be related to that?"

"I don't think so. It was different than what happened before. It was like a light going on and off. It was gone as quickly as it came."

"Could you see anything?"

"I don't have a lot of details."

"So, tell me what you do know."

He takes another deep breath and holds it for several seconds before exhaling. "I was in a small, dark place, like maybe a basement, an attic or an outside shed of some kind."

"Any idea where this place is?"

"Not a freaking clue. It was too dark, and it went by so quickly, but I'm pretty sure that it wasn't any place I've ever been because I didn't recognize anything."

She takes his hand into her hands and squeezes them, gently. "Go on, please."

"This is the worst part, Bree."

"That bad?"

"Very bad." He swallows. "I saw a man hanging by his neck and ..." his voice trails off.

"And?"

Looking into Bree's eyes, he blinks back tears. "And I'm sure he was dead."

"Could you see who the man was?"

"I don't know." He maintains his stoic posture "But there was something about him that made me think I knew him."

"I think you should tell your mother," Bree says. "She's usually very good about your visions. I'm going to get her."

"No." Alex becomes stern. He squeezes her hands, his grip getting tighter. "I don't want you to do that. If I tell my mother about this, she'll just get all worked up, and that won't help anything."

"What if it's a warning, and you're supposed to do something to help this man?"

He looks her in the eyes. "What if I just imagined it? What if I cause everyone to panic over nothing?"

Bree sighs. "The last time you kept secrets from your mother, it didn't work out so well."

"I really don't want to have to deal with her tonight. I already have a headache and it will only get worse with her asking question after question after question. You know what she's like. She'll think she's helping but she won't be."

Bree pulls away and stands straight. "Alright Alex. I won't say anything. But you have to promise me that if this happens again you will tell your mother about it."

He nods. "I promise."

"Can I believe you?"

"You can." He rises from the chair and reaches for her arm. "Now, let's find Hunter and Ally. It's time to banish all evil spirits back to whatever hell from whence they came and where they belong. Isn't that what they say about ringing in the New Year?"

"Really, Alex? You're trying to be funny after what you just experienced?"

"I'm certainly not going to cry over it."

"It's nothing to laugh about, mister."

"No. Someone could be dead, or about to die. There is nothing funny about that."

35: Grounded

Cliff slips quietly out the front door so as not to disturb the party guests. He stands on the front steps, his insulated combat-style boots planted firmly on the snow-covered Wolmanized planks.

He sucks in a mouthful of cold air, letting the ice crystals assault his airway and lungs, then slowly exhales, deliberately surveying the yard and driveway. His eyes focus on the corner of the garage where he and Julie saw someone lurking

"Okay, you motherfucker, where the fuck did you get to?" Even though he's alone, he hopes his words find their way to the prowler.

He pulls his black knitted toque down over his ears to protect them from the biting cold wind that's throwing gusts of snow in his face, and slowly makes his way down the steps and across the driveway. The snow pelts his exposed skin as he trudges cautiously through the thigh-deep drifts. His watering eyes quickly dart from one direction to the next as if he's anticipating a blindside attack from someone hiding in the shadows.

"Easy, Cliff." He wills himself not to panic. As a police officer with more than thirty years' experience, he's been in many situations where he's felt vulnerable, but somehow this feels different. Personal.

He moves stealth-like through the snow. When he was just a rookie and in situations such as this, he remembers one of his training officers telling him that when you are exposed in the open, you must have eyes in the back of your head.

"You must always expect that you are the target," the training officer's voice rings in his ears. "Anticipate the attack before it happens."

"Fuck me." He cringes and exhales. *You're an old son-of-a-bitch, Cliff Graham.*

Pushing on through the deep snow, his head moves quickly to the left and then to the right. *That was a long time ago,* he thinks, *but still good advice, nonetheless.*

Feeling a mixture of anger, apprehension and even fear from not knowing what he could be walking into, Cliff trudges onward toward the garage.

"You choose the wrong person to fuck with, asshole." He's not sure if the prowler can hear his words, but venting makes him feel better.

Reaching the corner of the garage, he's frustrated to find that the storm has erased any signs of an intruder.

Now what? he wonders.

As the wind howls around his head, Cliff hears a loud banging sound coming from somewhere at the back of the garage.

"God-damn it. Now what the fuck's going on?"

The tiny hairs in his nose have long since frozen into minuscule icicles. He hunches his shoulders and lowers his head into his coat, hoping to avoid as much of nature's assault as possible.

Bang! Bang! Bang!

He can't figure out where the noise can be coming from.

Following the banging noise, Cliff pushes his way through the piles of snow. Some drifts are almost as deep as his waist where the wind has banked it in against the side of the building.

Reaching the back of the garage, he's alarmed to find the door is wide open, swinging wildly in the wind and pounding against the inside wall as the blustering snow piles up inside on the cement floor.

"For fuck's sake."

He's sure the door was closed and locked up tight when he left earlier this afternoon, so he can't stop thinking this could be a trap. He takes a deep breath and cautiously enters the garage. He quickly scans the interior, scouring every dark corner and lingering on every shadow. He is relieved to find no one inside. He's also relieved that, on first glance, everything appears in order. He can rule out theft or vandalism as the stalker's reason for being here.

Unable to figure out what is going on, he feels like the proverbial fly trapped in the spider's web. He hates this feeling of being played and manipulated, as he's used to being the one in control.

Come on, Cliff. You've been in worse spots than this before. Stay focused.

If it's not theft or vandalism that brought the intruder to his place of solitude, they might want to cause him or his family harm, or at least scare them.

If someone is coming after his family then that changes the water on the beans, as his father would often say in tricky situations. If the stalker has their sights set on someone he loves, they will have to go through him first.

He's seething at the mere thought of someone having the balls to stalk his family. He carefully scans the garage again, looking into every corner and crevasse, every nook and cranny. He shivers. He is not used to being in this position and he hates feeling so vulnerable. It's the not knowing the identity of this mysterious prowler that bugs him the most.

"So much for a party." He turns to face the pile of snow that's banked around the open door, grabs a snow shovel that's standing in the corner near his workbench and begins cleaning up the mess.

I know I locked that door. He digs into the pile of snow, then freezes as a sudden movement to the left side of the garage catches his attention. He sees a large figure approaching the open door.

He stands firm and steels his nerves, snow shovel in hand as a make-shift weapon.

"Come on you, motherfucker." He raises the shovel over his head.

"Whoa there, Brother; it's me."

Cliff recognizes the voice. His heart skips a beat. "Fuck me."

Warren emerges from the darkness. "I wasn't trying to sneak up on you. Julie asked me to see if you need help."

He stops in the open doorway and surveys the mess, and his buddy holding his shovel like a club. "What's going on, Cliff?"

"I don't really know, but I'm pretty sure it's connected to whoever has been following me around all day."

"Seriously?"

"Julie and I saw them out here a few minutes ago. I was hoping that she wouldn't find out about this, at least not tonight, but that plan has shit to bed. She's freaking out."

"This is getting pretty serious," Warren says. "We should call in a unit and have them do a sweep of the area. You and I aren't equipped to do that right now, not in our condition."

Cliff brandishes the snow shovel. "I'm good to go. I'll bash the mother-fucker's head in if I find them."

"Let's get some officers over here for backup who haven't had so many beers. The last thing we need is for you to get tangled up with someone who's motives aren't clear. They could be dangerous, Cliff. Maybe even have a gun."

Cliff leans on the shove and sighs. "All right, Brother. You've made your point. Go ahead and call them."

~

Warren pulls out his cellphone and punches in a backdoor number that will connect him to the local detachment. This number is only to be used for emergency calls and, right now, he's not sure this situation isn't an emergency.

"Hello."

He recognizes the voice as Constable Nolan Shaw, one of the two rookie recruits who joined the detachment in the summer.

"Hey, Nolan. Happy New Year," Warren says. "You alone right now?"

"Happy New Year, Warren. No, the others are also here. They're all in the lunchroom. Someone dropped off a tray of goodies for us to enjoy so we're just having a coffee. What's up?"

"Think you could grab one of the others and the two of you can swing by Corporal Cliff Graham's place? I think you should know his address."

"I do."

"I need you to do a patrol of the area. Someone's been lurking around here all day and we're afraid they're up to something."

"No can do," the rookie constable responds.

"What do you mean?"

"I mean we're all grounded," Nolan explains. "Headquarters has ordered all vehicles off the road until the storm passes. Everything is at a standstill. The only way we're permitted to head out tonight is if it's life or death."

Warren sighs. "Are you freaking kidding me right now?"

"No, sir. They've even pulled the snowplows off the roads," Constable Shaw answers. "I'm sorry."

"For fuck's sake," Warren snaps. "We don't know if this situation is life or death because we have no idea who's snooping around or what they want. Are we supposed to wait until someone is dead before we can get a cruiser out here?"

"Sorry sir," Nolan replies. "Just following orders."

"I guess it's not your fault." Warren pauses, considering the options. "Cliff and I will figure it out."

"Be careful, sir," the constable says.

"We're going to try." Frowning at Cliff, Warren says to the young officer on the phone, "Well, I will let you go, Nolan. I'm guessing you're getting a lot of calls tonight."

"You have no idea."

"Oh, I think I do. See you in a few days."

Warren ends the call. He turns to his best friend and shrugs. "Looks like you and me are going to have to handle this on our own. We shouldn't be expecting reinforcements tonight."

~

"Seriously?" Cliff is incredulous. "Young bucks can't handle a little snow?"

"'Looks that way." Warren slips his cellphone back into his coat pocket. "Headquarters has ordered all vehicles off the roads, so everyone is grounded."

"Shit. That's not good." Cliff shakes his head. "I can only ever remember one other time when the fleet was grounded around here because of a storm, and was a few years ago now."

Warren nods. "And the worst part about this, Cliff, is that if the roads are closed to emergency vehicles, it's probably not a good idea for your guests to leave here for a while. How do you think they're going to feel about that?"

"I can guarantee you that there will be a few unhappy people in there."

"Can you accommodate everyone?"

"We'll find a way," Cliff says. "We may not have enough beds for everyone, but we've got lots of sleeping bags, blankets, and couches. As for food, we have enough to last an army at least a week. We always stock up this time of year."

"Jesus, man." Warren chuckles. "I love you like a brother, but I don't want to spend a whole week with you cooped up in your house. No offence, but that's not my idea of a good time."

Cliff smirks. "Let's hope it doesn't come to that." He hands his friend another snow shovel. "Help me clean this shit out of here and then we'll go inside and break the news to everyone."

"It's almost midnight, Cliff." Warren attacks the pile of snow. "We better make sure we're back in there before the magic hour, or our wives will string us up. I don't know about you, pal, but I value my balls."

"For sure." Cliff scoops a large mound of snow onto his shovel. "So, I guess you better get your ass in gear, Brother, and shovel quickly."

"I'm on it." Warren drives his shovel into the pile of snow for a second scoop. He chuckles. "This is going to cost you."

"How much?" Cliff laughs.

"Another beer. I come pretty cheap."

"That's what I hear, but no worries. I've got you covered."

They dig into the pile of snow, but both freeze when a blood-curdling cackling sound reverberates through the night, and echoes throughout the garage.

Warren quickly glances at his companion. "What the hell was that?"

"Crows." Cliff steps outside and scans the yard and trees. "What do you suppose they want?"

"Could it be a warning?"

Cliff shakes his head. "We better hurry up and get our asses back inside just in case they have something else on their minds."

Warren stops shovelling. "Like what?"

"I have no idea. But we don't want to find out."

36: At the stroke of midnight

Cliff and Julie Graham hug each other tightly as their guests cram into the living room, waiting for the clock to strike midnight so they can officially kiss the old year goodbye. While they are happy to be putting the past twelve months behind them, the weight of the current situation weighs heavily on their minds.

Where could Leo have gotten to? Who has been sneaking around the house? Could the family be in danger? they wonder. *How will our friends deal with the news that the storm has cut us off from the rest of the town?*

With drinks in hand, they step in front of their family and friends. Ready to toast the arrival of the New Year, they paint on happy faces and lean on each other for support.

"We can do this, honey." Cliff pulls his wife closer and gives her a quick kiss on the forehead. "Love you. Forever and for always."

With a grin, she answers, "Right back at you, stud."

Smiling, Cliff clears his throat. "Hey, everyone. Can I please have your attention? My better half has something she wants to say."

"First of all." Julie says, "Cliff and I want to thank you all for showing up this evening. We know that with this crazy storm, some of you were a little timid about coming out, but we appreciate you being here as it's important to be with family and friends on special occasions."

She locks eyes with her daughter, who she knows is in panic mode because no one can find her husband. She hasn't told Carly, but she's afraid that Leo may have stumbled off into the blizzard. If he's done that, God only knows where he has gotten to, especially being so drunk.

She and Cliff will resume their search once they mark this important milestone with their loved ones.

She takes a deep breath and continues her speech. "We always look forward to this night with great anticipation. This party is important to Cliff and me—to all of us, we hope—as it gives us the opportunity to celebrate the good things in our lives while also basking in the joy of the people we love."

"Hear, hear." Warren raises his beer in a toast to his friends. "And thank you both for welcoming all of us into your home again this year."

He smiles to the others gathered around the room. "You guys always go out of your way to make this night special for all of us. This party is always one of the highlights of my holidays."

"Shush." Lisa takes her husband's arm and pulls him close, as if scolding a child. "Just be quiet and let them talk."

Julie smiles. "Thank you, Warren. We're always glad to do it. Now, as the clock ticks closer to midnight, Cliff and I would like you all to grab a drink, if you don't already have one, and join us in a toast to ring in the New Year."

"But first"—Cliff interrupts and takes his wife's hand. He gently squeezes, letting her know that he has decided to go off script—"There's something I have to tell you all."

Julie leans closer to him and says quietly, "You are going to ruin the mood."

"They have a right to know." He turns to their guests. "So, here's the thing: you can see that the storm has gotten a whole lot worse. It's really bad out there. Worse than anyone could have ever predicted."

"They did predict it," Julie murmurs. "But someone wouldn't listen."

"How bad?" Samantha asks

"So bad," Cliff says, "that they've shut down all of the roads. None of you are going anywhere for a while."

Kate locks arms with her wife. "What exactly are you saying, Cliff?"

"Nothing is moving right now, not even emergency crews. The entire province is at a standstill until this thing passes."

"Shit," Samantha says. "So, you're saying we're stranded?"

"That's what I'm saying." Cliff nods.

She exhales. "I'm surprised I haven't heard an alert. They know to call me when there's an emergency."

"I don't know what to tell you, Sam. I can only pass along what we've heard."

Kate asks, "So we're stuck here, Cliff?"

He nods. "That is exactly what I'm saying. But we don't want anyone to panic. We have plenty of room and there's lots of food. We'll be okay even if we're stuck here for a few days."

"No," Dr. Charlie Webster says. "I appreciate what you're saying Cliff, but we can't stay here. I have to get Rebecca back to our place."

Cliff shakes his head. "Sorry, but you can't take a chance on those roads, especially in the dark. They've pulled the snowplows because the snow is coming down so fast that they can't keep up with it, so you won't get far. You need to stay put, for your own good."

Charlie's desperation is obvious. "It's important that we get back to our house."

"I don't see how that's going to be possible, Dr. Webster." Warren jumps in to deflect questions from his friend. "Cliff is right. I need everyone to hear me on this. It's not safe for anyone to be out there."

Alex has joined his girlfriend and they are standing close to his parents. He leans in close to Bree. "What did I tell you? If they think it's bad now, it's only just started. Just wait. It's going to get wild."

Bree shivers, her voice trembles. "Are we going to be okay?"

"We're all safe together in a warm house. What could possibly happen?"

Charlie persists. "It is imperative that Rebecca and I get out of here. Tonight."

"I'd like to help you, Doc, but I don't see it happening," Cliff says. "What's so important that you have to leave right away?"

"It's okay, honey." Rebecca takes Charlie's arm. "I'll be alright."

Charlie shakes his head. He says quietly, urgently, "You need your medications."

"I'm sure I can make it without them for a few hours."

"Is there anything I can do to help?" Dr. Anna Robbie approaches the doctors.

"I wish." Charlie throws his head back and closes his eyes. "But unless you've got a magical dog sled and a team of huskies with rockets up their asses, I don't see how."

Maybe it's the wine talking but Anna fires back. "I don't know what's wrong, Charlie, but please don't take it out on me."

"No. I'm sorry, Anna." Rebecca immediately replies, forcing a smile. "Charlie's just a little on edge because of this sudden change of plans."

"I get it." Anna smiles. Oliver, standing beside her, bites his lower lip. "He feels trapped and his baser instinct is telling him to escape. Some people can cope with these situations better than others."

Oliver says, "I've known Charlie for a long time. He is usually a very calm person, even in the tensest situations."

"I totally understand." Anna studies her new friends. "I don't like this much myself so please let me know if there's anything I can do to help your predicament."

"Come with me, Charlie." Oliver takes him by the shoulders. "I'm sure we can figure something out."

"How?" Charlie snaps. "What are we going to do? Rebecca needs her medication."

Oliver pulls his friend aside from the crowd. "If Rebecca needs it right away, I'll go get it."

Charlie looks him directly in the eyes. "If anyone has to go out in this storm, then I'll be the one to go."

Oliver shakes his head. "You'll need to stay here with Rebecca. So, be honest with me, does she need this medication tonight?"

"The meds are mostly for pain so it will be a rough night for her if she doesn't have them." Charlie struggles to keep his emotions in check.

"We'll figure something out." Oliver squeezes his shoulder.

"Hey everyone." Samantha calls out, as only a politician can. "First, let's show some gratitude to our wonderful hosts for opening their home to us. I know none of us were planning on spending the night here, but it is what it is, so let's just try to make the most of it. Once the sun comes up, we can all figure out what we're doing."

"Thank you, Samantha," Julie says. "Once we toast the New Year, I will draw up a plan for sleeping arrangements. If anyone has any special requests, please just let me know."

"Okay everyone." Cliff calls out. "We've got about ten seconds to the New Year. Please raise your glass and let's count down together."

"Ten, nine, eight, seven"—Skipping six, Cliff takes a quick sip of his beer—"Five, four three, two ..."

Suddenly the house is plunged into complete darkness. The power has gone off.

"Mommy," the young Liam Webster cries out. "What's happening?"

"It's all right, sweetie," Rebecca pulls her son close. "The power has gone off."

"I want to go home," the boy cries.

She speaks softly in hopes of soothing his fear. "Mommy and Daddy are right here. Everything is going to be all right."

"God-damned it to hell." Cliff cusses. Remembering there are children present, he bites his tongue. "Don't panic, anyone. We're all good. I've got two generators in the garage and gas to last us a few days. We'll have light once I get them fired up and there's lots of heat from the fireplace in the den. I suggest we move this party into that room."

"Holy shit." A voice suddenly cuts through the darkness.

Cliff squints, trying to see. "What's wrong? Is everyone okay?"

"It's just me," Alex Goodwin says. "Sorry. I just hit my knee on a table."

"Are you hurt?" Samantha asks, turning to her son.

"No. I'm alright."

Alex pulls Bree toward him and whispers, "Remember that vision I had?"

Bree nods. "Why? Did you see the power going out in that vision?"

"No, not that. But I think I just realized who I saw hanging from the rafters."

"Who?" Bree leans in close to her boyfriend so no one else can hear their conversation.

"Do you think this place has an attic?"

"I would think so," Bree says. "Why?"

"Because I think that's where the man is hanging."

"Do you think it's time to share this with your mother?"

Alex nods. "I need to tell her about this."

37: Don't panic

Outside the Graham house, the nine crows defy the elements, silently holding fast to their snow-covered perches, clinging desperately to the branches, knowing that the winds would pick them up and toss them about as if they were specks of dust. Despite the threat to their very lives, the birds refuse to abandon their posts.

They know where they could find a safe haven to weather this storm, but the nine crows in this murder will make the ultimate sacrifice, if it comes to that. They will protect those in their charge, throwing down their own lives to save the lives of these humans. That is their mandate and nothing, not even a killer snowstorm, will stand in their way.

Instead, with their senses firing on all cylinders, they are stoked, remaining on high alert, ready to spring into action when the threat becomes real. Danger is close; they can feel it.

~

Inside the house, Cliff springs into action. His instinct to take control in an emergency kicks in.

He reviews the priorities necessary to protect those under his roof—shelter, heat, light, and food.

Check to all the above.

Even though most of his guests are adults and can fend for themselves, Cliff still believes it is his responsibility to ensure that everyone is safe and secure. After all, he reasons, these people are trapped here because they came to his house.

He takes a deep breath. *When Julie wanted to cancel the party, I should have agreed. Now, look at the mess I've made.*

He starts to execute the emergency plan he's just devised. *There's no time to think about who is to blame. We can do that after the storm moves off.*

"Okay, everyone," he calls out as his guests assemble in the den, where a blaze crackles in the fireplace. "Please listen up, and we'll get through this together. I would like the younger men to keep the fire burning while we get ourselves organized."

He zeroes in on Hunter. "That job is yours, and your brother can help. Once the wood in the box is gone, there is more in the basement. Keep it going so everyone can stay warm."

"On it." Hunter searches the gathering of guests for his younger brother. "You can count on me, Mr. Graham, although I have no idea where Alex is."

"I saw him in the living room with your parents," Ally says. "Bree is with them, and it looked they were having a pretty intense conversation."

"Knowing my brother, it's probably just more drama," Hunter says.

Cliff continues. "Julie, can you please take care of the sleeping arrangements? As for food, well"—he smiles at his wife—"you've already got that handled."

"We'll be fine, Cliff," She tries to assure him. "Don't worry so much. We've all survived power outages before, so I'm sure everyone will be okay."

Cliff nods. "But we don't have any idea how long this storm is going to last, and I'd like to be prepared."

"I understand." She offers her husband a reassuring smile. "Don't you worry about us, Corporal. You just worry about getting those generators working."

"On it." Cliff motions to Warren to join him. "We'll have power on in no time."

Warren says, "What do you need me to do, Brother?"

"You and I are going to get the generators fired up. There's nothing like a little light to make everyone relax."

Warren nods. "I'm ready whenever you are."

"Just a second." Cliff moves closer to Oliver, whom he's gotten to know as a straight-shooting, no-nonsense kind of guy. He leans in and whispers, "Is our friend, the doctor, going to be okay? He seems pretty worked up over something."

Oliver whispers back, "He is worried about his wife so that's probably why he's so on edge."

"What's wrong with her?"

Oliver hesitates, then says, "It's just that she's not feeling well."

"Okay." Cliff senses that Oliver is holding something back, but he lets it slide. "Do you think we can count on the doctor to remain calm? It's not good to have someone agitated in these situations."

"I'm sure he will be fine, but I'll keep a close watch over him."

Cliff nods. "Warren and I have to go deal with the generators. I don't want to have to worry about what's happening in here as well."

"I'll make sure he remains calm."

~

Samantha and Kate, with Alex and Bree in tow, find Julie in the kids' play-room, pulling spare pillows and blankets from a storage closet.

"Julie." Samantha's tone is serious. "I know you are really busy, but can you give us a second? This can't wait."

"Take these." Julie hands Samantha a pile of pillows. "What's up?"

Samantha passes the pillows to Bree. "I don't know if you understand how special Alex really is."

Julie looks at the young man and smiles. "Only what I've heard from other people, but I just ignore most of that stuff as small-town rumours and idle gossip. I figured if you guys wanted me to know anything about your son, you would tell me when you're ready."

Kate says, "The thing is that he possesses special abilities."

"I'm afraid I don't understand."

Samantha takes Alex's hand. "He has a special connection to the crows that gather in this town."

Julie shakes her head. "I still don't get it."

"Alex has the ability to talk to the crows," Samantha says.

"I see." Julie sounds skeptical.

"I know it sounds far-fetched, but Alex can communicate with the crows and sometimes they send him visions," Samantha explains.

The skepticism is now more evident in Julie's voice. "Such as?"

Samantha says, "Such as the one he had tonight that he believes in-volves your family."

"How would it involve my family?"

"Where is Carly?" Samantha asks.

"Why? Has something happened to Carly?"

Samantha shakes her head. "It's not your daughter but does your house have an attic?"

Julie nods. "A pretty good sized one. We use it for storage. There is an access door at the furthest end of the upstairs hallway, but we always keep the door locked because we don't want our granddaughters to go up there. You know how curious young kids can be."

She looks hard at Samantha. "Why are you worried about the attic?"

Alex suddenly says, "Because I saw someone hanging from the rafters up there."

Julie takes a step back. "There's no one in my attic."

"Are you sure?" Kate asks.

Alex says, "I didn't even know you had an attic, but I'm pretty sure it was yours, and that the man I saw was dead."

Samantha takes her son's hand. "Please let me handle this."

"There's a dead man hanging in my attic?" Julie cries. "That can't be true."

"We don't know anything for sure." Samantha hopes she can lessen the impact of Alex's sudden proclamation. "But we think you should check the attic just to make sure. Should we get Cliff?"

Julie shakes her head. "God, no. He's got enough on his hands right now."

"I will go up with you to check things out," Kate says.

"I'll go, too." Alex offers. "You might need some help."

Julie shakes her head. "Samantha, you and Kate take care of getting the bedding to the living room and den so people can have them when they need them. I will check the attic."

"Not by yourself," Samantha says.

""I'm going to get Oliver to come with me, just in case."

"Just in case what, Mrs. Graham?" Alex asks. "You don't believe what I saw?"

"I'm just saying that I need to make sure," Julie says.

38: Jellybean

With her phone on flashlight mode, Carly quietly enters the darkened room where her two daughters are sleeping.

Cautiously pulling the door closed to keep out the noise from the party downstairs, she creeps through the darkness, being careful not to make any noise. The last thing she wants to do right now is to wake her children. She knows they would be terrified by the current predicament, because she's terrified.

Can't say I'd blame them. A major storm trapping everyone here indefinitely. No power. Their father missing. Carly shivers. *I wish I could go to sleep and forget all of this.*

She's relieved to see her daughters are sleeping soundly, snugly under the covers. If it gets too cold in the upstairs bedrooms with the power being off, she will have to bring them downstairs so they can be warm next to the fireplace, but, for right now, they seem to be fine.

She is thankful that, in their innocence, the young girls are oblivious to the blizzard ragging outside and to the mayhem that threatens to tear apart their family. She vows to protect her babies at all costs, everything else be damned.

If there's one good thing that has come out of her relationship with Leo, it's Cara and Cassie. Her daughters offer her hope for a brighter future.

She gingerly takes a seat in the white wicker chair next to the bed. She may have many regrets about her relationship with Leo, but having these babies is not among them.

Even though Leo is the one who cheated on her, and even though he is the one who physically assaulted her, Carly wonders if, in some way, she contributed to the deterioration of their relationship.

What did I do wrong? she wonders. *Did I not show him enough love and affection? Did I neglect him? Or was I so caught up in my own world that I was tuned out to his needs? Should I have been more accommodat-*

ing to his weird fetishes?

She takes a deep breath and, with images of past confrontations quickly flashing through her mind, considers past events.

Or is he just too needy? Too demanding. Too into his own perverted desires to consider what I feel?

When she recalls some of the disgusting things that he wanted her to do, it makes her skin crawl as if someone was pouring ice-cold water down her back. *Maybe I should have been more willing to participate in his weird sexual games.*

She cringes at the idea.

But he crossed the line. I just couldn't bring myself to do some of those weird things that he wanted me to do. I wonder how he got turned onto all that weird stuff in the first place? He wasn't like that when we first met.

She sighs and wipes tears from her eyes.

Bondage? Asphyxiation? Total submission?

The idea creeps her out. *I will never be that submissive to anyone, not even my husband. No way I was going to render myself helpless to him so he would be free to do whatever he wanted...And God knows what that would have been.*

The thought causes her head to spin. She is torn between love and hatred for Leo. Love for what they once shared; hatred for the monster he has become.

What pushed him into those dark places? She shakes her head. *It says a lot when you no longer feel comfortable—or safe—around your own husband.*

She takes a deep breath. *No. This isn't on me.*

Something changed in Leo. He became a monster out to please only himself.

She leans toward the bed and watches her daughters sleeping, the blankets slowly rising and falling as they breathe. She draws upon their energy for strength. They seem so peaceful, and she is glad for that. Youthful ignorance is bliss, she tells herself.

She takes a deep breath and exhales.

What happened to you Leo? Where did we go wrong?

And now, she wonders, *where the hell are you?*

No matter what happened in their relationship, she would never want anything bad to happen to the father of her children. And, on some level, she still has feelings for him, even if he does repulse her at times.

Jesus, Leo, she thinks. *What have you done? Even if you're pissed at me, please think of our babies. They still love you very much and even if we can no longer be together, they will always need you.*

Leaning back in the wicker chair, Carly closes her eyes, tight, and tries to imagine what her life will look like moving forward but try as she might, she can't get past the present.

I'm so confused.

As tears trickle down her cheeks, she suddenly hears a voice.

"Follow your heart, my dear," it says.

What the hell? Carly wonders. *Who said that?*

"You are living in dark times. It is okay to be scared, but you must let your feelings guide you," a woman whispers. "But do not allow false loyalties to cloud your judgment."

Carly does not recognize the voice.

"You are about to be tested in ways you cannot begin to imagine, but you must be strong, Jellybean. Dig deep. Find your anchor, hang on and never let go."

Jesus. Who said that?

Her eyes snap open. Carly squints in the darkness, searching the room. She is positive she heard a woman speaking to her, but she also knows she is alone except for the two little girls asleep in the bed.

Swallowing the little bit of spit that remains in her mouth, she almost chokes as the saliva feels like tiny shards of broken glass on its way down her constricted throat. Slowly rising from the chair, she searches the darkness.

Am I going crazy?

She shakes her head.

I know I heard someone talking to me.

"I know I did." She tries to swallow again, but her mouth and throat are too dry.

She replays the words in her mind. "Jellybean. No one has ever called me Jellybean."

Where have I heard that before?

As the wind pelts gusts of snow against the window, Carly shakes. Cold chills tingle along her spine, sending shockwaves through her body as a realization suddenly pops into her head.

"Great-grandmother Mae," she says softly. "Oh, my God. Is that you?"

Her breath catches in her throat as she recalls her earlier dream that Leo interrupted.

Jellybean, she thinks. *Isn't that what she used to call my mother?*

Her voice is barely a whisper. "Is that you, great-grandmother?"

Clearly, I'm losing my mind, she tells herself. *I'm more freaked out than*

I thought I was.

A sudden shuffle in the hallway just outside the bedroom door causes her heart to skip a beat.

"What is that?" she whispers.

She holds her breath, opens the door just a crack and peers outside. She has no idea what she expected to see but is relieved to find her mother and Oliver in the hallway. Both have flashlights.

"Mom? What are you doing out here?"

"Sorry, honey. Just go back with the girls," her mother whispers. "We have to pop up to the attic to check something out."

"The attic," Carly says with surprise. "What for?"

Julie shakes her head. "There's nothing to worry about."

"They are asleep and don't even know I'm here." Carly studies her mother's face. "If you're going to the attic, I'm coming with you."

Julie sighs. "We could all be stuck here for a while, so we're getting some extra blankets."

Carly senses her mother is holding something back. "I don't ever recall seeing any blankets up there."

"Well, there are."

"Julie." Oliver speaks up. He seems anxious. "If we're going to do this, can we please just do it? The longer we're up here, the more people will become suspicious that something is wrong."

Julie nods. "You're right, Oliver. We should just do this and get back to the others." She takes a deep breath and exhales. "Okay, Carly, you win. Come with us."

39: Big drifts, deep trouble

The snow is almost to their waists, much deeper now than it was less than a half an hour ago when Cliff and Warren were in the garage.

"This is ridiculous," Warren complains. "I hate this fucking stuff. Who in their right mind would wish for this shit?"

"Come on, Warren. Suck it up." Cliff pushes his tall, bulky body through the drifts, his blue coat quickly turning white from the driving snow.

Warren huffs. "I know I can't change anything, but it makes me feel better to say it out loud. You sound just like Lisa. She hates it when I complain about the weather. 'Get over it.' She doesn't understand. If I could *get over it,* I would."

Cliff trudges on, carefully choosing where he places his feet. "Let's just get to the garage and fire up those generators. Everyone back in the house will feel a whole lot better once the power is flowing again and the lights are on."

"How much gas do you have?" Warren follows in his friend's footsteps.

"Enough to get us through a couple of days."

Pushing toward the garage door, Cliff scans the snow-covered surroundings. He glances around the yard, peers into the shadows, and looks for signs of an intruder. He's not sure if he's really expecting to see anyone in such extreme conditions, but he is mindful that someone has been watching him all day.

"Keep your eyes open, Warren." He glances back over his shoulder. "I get the feeling someone is watching us."

"Or something?"

Cliff considers his friend's suggestion. "Yes. Crows, maybe."

"Out here in this shit? Wouldn't they go somewhere safe to escape this fucking storm? These winds would probably tear them apart, wouldn't they?"

"You'd think." Cliff knows that when it comes to the crows, nothing is as simple as it seems. "But I get the feeling these nine crows could find a way to somehow survive this storm. I bet they are close by and watching us right now."

"Way to creep out a brother." Warren instinctively glances over his shoulder. "Do you think the crows we've seen hanging around all day are connected to whoever has been stalking you?"

Cliff shivers not so much from the cold, but because of his friend's suggestion. "I get the feeling the crows have been watching over me. Anyhow, we're here."

He is looking forward to a respite in the garage from the relentless snow that's been assaulting them ever since they left the safety of his house.

"Thank Jesus." Warren pushes closer to his friend. "I thought I was in pretty good shape, but it's freaking hard going through all of this shit. It's really kicking the snot out of me."

Cliff rounds the corner and approaches the garage door. He stops abruptly. "For fuck's sake."

"What's wrong?" Warren peers over Cliff's shoulder. "Did you see someone?"

Cliff shakes his head. "Didn't we close this door when we were out here before?"

Warren nods. "We sure as hell did. I double-checked the lock."

Cliff feels his heart pounding in his chest as he inches closer to the door. "Looks like someone has broken in again."

"Careful, buddy." Warren cautions. "You can't just barge in there."

"The hell I can't."

"Go easy, Cliff. You don't know if someone is still inside."

Wishing that he had his RCMP issue Smith & Wesson 5946 in his hand, the one he had to give up when he retired, Cliff cautiously steps inside the garage. Pushing through the knee-deep pile of snow that has blustered inside, he surveys the interior.

"Fucking Christ." He exhales. His nostrils flare in anger. "Who did this?"

"See anything?" Warren slowly follows his friend inside.

Cliff shakes his head. "Do you smell that?"

Warren takes a deep breath and coughs. "Gasoline."

"And a lot of it." Cliff puts his right hand over his nose and quickly moves toward the corner of the garage where he stores the generators and spare jugs of gasoline. "Jesus. Jesus. Jesus."

Warren keeps an eye on his friend. "Be careful, Cliff."

"Careful went out the fucking door the minute I smelled that gas."

Cliff apprehensively approaches the generators. "God-damn it."

He can't believe what he's seeing. "Every fucking gas jug has been emptied."

Warren surveys the damage. "Who would do something like this?"

"I have no idea." Cliff feels defeated. He gasps for air. It feels like someone has reached through his chest and is slowly squeezing the life out of his heart. "But we have no fuel for the generators, so no power for the house."

"It's also dangerous in here." Warren pulls him towards the open door. "Come on, Brother. If there's even one tiny spark from anything in here, this whole place is going to go up like fireworks on the first of July."

Cliff pulls away. He knows his friend is right, but the idea of losing all his machines—his toys—causes him great angst. "I've got to do something. All my gear is in this building."

"There's nothing you can do. Think of Julie and your family. If you die tonight, what will they do without you?"

Cliff surveys the damage. "Who would do this, Warren? And why?"

"Those are both good questions." Warren grabs his arm again. "But we've got to make sure we live long enough to answer them."

"Of course. You're right. I'm right behind you." Cliff's head is fuzzy from the gas fumes. "We're in deep trouble here, my friend." He gasps for air. "Deep, deep trouble."

40: Characters in a mystery novel

Samantha hands several fleece blankets to Bree and Ally, who are huddled up with sleeping bags on the floor in front of the fireplace, snuggled along with the two younger children, Lauren and Liam.

She's happy that her boys have each found someone they care for. She likes both young women very much and she knows how important it is to find the right partner to share your life with. She hopes both Alex and Hunter are as happy in their lives as she and Kate have been.

She kneels beside the makeshift beds. "You guys look comfy. Everything okay?"

Ally nods. "I think we're all good for now."

She spreads the blankets over the children. "Thanks for these. We'll be all nice and toasty, especially with the boys doing such a great job keeping the fire going."

Samantha smiles. "I'm sure Cliff and Warren will have those generators up and running in no time, so we'll soon have power again. The children will be able to watch a movie or something if they wish. We may need to keep them occupied if this storm lasts for long."

Ally gestures to the young children. "Bree and I told them to pretend they are on a camping trip, and they loved that idea. I think they've both fallen asleep."

Samantha nods. "Where did the boys get to?"

"They went down to the basement to get some more wood," Bree says. "They said they don't want to run out." She is sitting on the floor, with Lauren's head resting in her lap. She gently strokes her younger sister's hair. "I don't know about Liam, but Lauren went out like a light as soon as she lay down."

"He's asleep too." Ally says. "I think they were exhausted by all the excitement and confusion."

"Well, you too are doing a great job with them," Samantha assures the young women. "I'm sure their parents appreciate your help."

Ally nods. "I enjoy spending time with children. That's why I'm going to be a teacher."

Samantha hesitates and then says, "And, Ally, I don't want you to think that I'm afraid you won't be a good mother."

"I don't think that."

"I think you will be an exceptional mother when the time is right." Samantha nods, trying to emphasize her point. "I just think you and Hunter are too young to be parents right now. There will be lots of time for babies in the future."

"I will be honest, Ms. Henderson, I am scared about the idea, but Hunter and I have talked about it, and we feel we are ready for this baby." Ally's cheeks glow, the light from the flames in the hearth reflecting a bright orange and yellow hue. "We have decided that we really want to do this, and we hope you and Ms. Webster will support our decision."

Samantha looks at the young woman, takes a deep breath and exhales. "I know that right now you think you want this baby, but it's the idea of being a mom that you love. Things will look a whole lot different once you are holding that baby in your arms. It is a massive responsibility."

Bree, who has been quietly listening to this exchange, finally speaks up. "Oh, my God, Ally. Are you pregnant?" She doesn't try to hide her excitement. "Why didn't you tell me?"

"I just did a home test a few hours ago and the only people that we've told are Hunter's parents," Ally whispers. "It's not public yet. I want to tell my mom and dad before the news gets out. My mother is going to be mad enough when she hears that I'm pregnant. I don't need her finding out about it second hand."

"No worries," Bree assures her. "Who am I going to tell? But I'm very happy for you guys. You are going to be a great mother. What does Hunter think about this?"

"He's actually very happy with the idea." Ally beams when she speaks.

"He *thinks* he's happy with the idea," Samantha points out. "I am sorry Ally. I didn't mean for that to sound the way it came out. I guess I'm just trying to wrap my head around the idea of my son being a parent when he sometimes still behaves like a child himself. I'm not so sure he's ready to be a father."

"I understand some of what you're saying, Ms. Henderson, considering Hunter's past behaviour." Ally speaks softly but firmly. "However, I really think you should try to give him a chance. He may surprise you. He has really changed, and I think he will rise to the occasion."

Samantha fears that she's already said too much. She studies Ally's face. "Well, girls, I guess I should go and see if anyone needs anything."

Bree watches as Samantha moves to the couch where Kate is sitting with Rebecca and Charlie. "So, Ally. What do you really think? Is she happy for you and Hunter? I honestly couldn't tell."

Ally's voice is hardly a whisper. "I'm really not sure. That woman is difficult to read most of the time."

~

"So, the guys are both busy," Anna says to Lisa while pulling the fleece blanket around her shoulders. They are sitting in plush easy chairs that they had moved closer to the fireplace. "I wonder if there's anything we can do. I feel helpless just sitting around twiddling my thumbs."

Lisa nods. "This doing nothing will drive me nuts. If I was home, I could find lots to do."

"Me too. I could kill a few hours if I had a book to read." Anna stares into the fire. "Give me a bottle of wine—Sauvignon Blanc or Spanish Verdejo, if you please—and a suspenseful book, and I'm good for the night."

"I could handle that, but I don't seem to get much time to read these days." Lisa enjoys the fire's glow, especially as it warms up her face. "What do you like to read?"

"Oh me? I like a good mystery. A lot of people think I'm weird, but I like books about murderers and serial killers. The darker and more twisted, the better I like them. I especially love the suspense and the thrill of trying to figure out who did it. I'm a huge fan of Patricia Cornwell. I have read every one of her Kay Scarpetta series. They are amazing. I love her style and how she keeps you in suspense right until the end. Ever read anything by her?"

Lisa shakes her head. "I'm more of a biography or romance reader myself, but with such a ringing endorsement, maybe I should check her out at the library."

Anna nods. "I don't believe you'd be disappointed. I also think you'll be surprised at how much some of her stories remind you of this town."

"Really?" Lisa frowns. "How?"

"I've only lived here a few years, but I've heard of several mysterious events that remind me of some of Cornwell's writings," Anna explains. "You know. All the deaths. The suspense. The intrigue. The *who* done it?"

"You think?" Lisa considers her friend's suggestion. "Maybe we're all characters in a mystery novel."

Anna nods. "The question is, who is going to die?"

"Jesus, woman. That's a morbid thought." Lisa pauses. "Does someone have to die?"

"Someone always has to die in a mystery novel." Anna smirks. "And the killer is always someone you would never expect."

"You're starting to scare me." Lisa chuckles. "Does Oliver have any idea what he's getting into with you?" She turns her gaze upon the small-featured woman in the armchair next to her. "Does he know what you really think about when you go to bed at night?"

Anna throws her head back and laughs. "Maybe not. I like to keep a little mystery in our relationship. If you give away too much, you ruin the suspense."

Lisa smiles. "We wouldn't want that, would we?"

~

"How are you feeling, Rebecca?" Kate kneels beside the sofa where her sister-in-law is resting. "Do you need anything? Can I get you some water, maybe?"

Rebecca smiles. "No, thank you, Kate. I am alright. Charlie is taking really good care of me."

Kate glances at her brother who is sitting on the edge of the sofa, next to his wife's feet. He seems to be lost in his own head. "He's good at taking care of people. That's why he makes such a good doctor."

"He sure does." Rebecca nods slightly.

It's clear to Kate that her brother's thoughts are elsewhere, and he isn't listening to their conversation. "I knew early on that Charlie was going to be a doctor. In fact, I think I knew it before he did."

"Really? How?"

"Because he was always taking care of other people and putting their needs ahead of his own." Kate recalls their childhood. "Our parents both worked, so Charlie and I were left on our own from a very young age. He was always looking out for me, protecting me, defending me."

"He doesn't talk much about his childhood," Rebecca says. "He's very protective of his past. Did something bad happen to him when you were children?"

"It did." Kate cringes. "I'm not surprised that Charlie hasn't told you much about it, because it was very painful for both of us. He and I both tend to keep our pain bottled up. I'll give you the Cole's Notes version, but you should ask him for more details."

"You don't have to tell me if you don't want to."

"It's okay," Kate says. "The trauma has never gone away, but I've learned to live with it." She takes a deep breath. "When I was eleven, Charlie walked into our living room as our uncle was trying to molest me. I was a scrawny little kid, and our uncle was a big brute—a real monster of a man. I hate to think about what would have happened if Charlie hadn't saved me."

"You don't have to say anything more if it's too painful."

"The uncle was our father's brother, and he was a real pervert." Kate's voice is nothing more than a whisper. "I never did like him, but our father always kept the door open to him and I guess our uncle felt that invitation gave him permission to assault his niece."

"What did Charlie do?"

Again, Kate studies her brother to see if he is listening to her conversation. She sees that he has completely tuned them out. She wonders where his mind has gone. She turns her attention back to Rebecca. "When he saw what our uncle was trying to do, Charlie picked up a large crystal figurine that our mother had on one of the end tables and hit the bastard over the head with it. The damn thing shattered into a million pieces."

"What was it?" Rebecca asks. "The figurine, I mean."

"An angel." Kate shudders. "Charlie hit the pervert with an angel. Wasn't that ironic, or fortuitous at the very least. Our mother had those damned things all over the house. All shapes and sizes and colours. For some reason, she liked angel figurines. Me? I don't collect anything like that."

"Me neither." Rebecca sighs. "Who has time to dust them?"

Kate nods. "Our housekeeper did that for our mother. She couldn't be bothered to do menial house chores. They were beneath her."

"Was your uncle hurt? I hope he was. Did your parents throw his sorry ass out of the house?"

"He had a little cut on his head, but nothing serious. And no. Our parents allowed him to stay around because our father didn't believe me and Charlie when we told them what the prick did to me. I think our mother believed us, but she would never go against her husband. Our father was a special kind of stupid when it came to his children. His rejection hurt us badly, both me and Charlie. Why would we make up something like that?"

"Seriously? No wonder you guys don't like to talk about it."

Kate nods. "After that, Charlie never spoke of it again and I always made sure that I was never alone in any room with my uncle. He's dead now. Had a massive heart attack and dropped dead in the middle of his kitchen. Wish I could say I was sorry, but I'm not. I'm sure he's the reason that I put so much effort into helping victims of assault, so at least something positive came from it. I can identify with the victims."

"You've helped a lot of people over the years and I'm proud of you for what you do."

"Thanks." Kate smiles. "I'm proud of you, too." She takes a depth breath and exhales. "Are you in any pain?"

Rebecca shakes her head. "The pain meds are still working, so I'm all right for now."

"Okay, then." Kate pulls the blanket up over her sister-in-law. "Let's keep you warm. This could be a long night."

~

"What do you think, little brother?" Hunter glances at Alex as the two young men place slabs of firewood into the carrier.

"About the idea of you being a father?"

"Yes, Alex." Hunter sighs. "About me and Ally having a baby."

"I'm not sure."

"Well, *I'm* sure." Hunter pumps up his chest. His pride is obvious. "I'm going to be a great dad."

"I'm sure you will be."

"Why can't you just be happy for me for a change?"

"I *am* happy for you, if that's what you want."

Alex suddenly feels light-headed and dizzy as an image flashes through his head. "Fire," he mumbles, stumbling backwards as if he's about to fall.

"What?" Hunter is confused by his brother's sudden proclamation.

"Shit." Alex reaches out to grab Hunter's arm but falls hard to the basement floor, hitting the cement on his knees.

"Jesus, Alex." Hunter takes him by the arm and pulls him to his feet. "Are you okay?"

"Yes. Yes. I'm okay." Alex stutters and shakes the images from his head. "I must have just slipped."

"On what?" Hunter shines the flashlight at the floor. "There's nothing there for you to slip on."

"I just lost my balance then. It's nothing, really."

"You're sure? I can get mom if something is wrong."

"There's no need to worry them. I'm good." Alex glances around the pitch-black basement. "But do you feel that?"

"I do." Hunter shivers, shining the light around the basement. "That's some powerful draft. I wonder where it's coming from?"

"Over there." Alex points as the light falls on the shattered remains of the basement window. "Looks like Cliff has a broken window."

Hunter surveys the damage and the pile of snow that's accumulating on the concrete floor. "I wonder how long it's been broken?"

"Must have just happened or there would be more snow on the floor." Alex suggests.

He moves closer to the window opening and notices shards of glass on the floor as they reflect the beam of the flashlight. "And do you see this, Hunter?"

"Looks to me like the window was broken from the outside."

"How?" Alex asks.

Hunter shakes his head. "Maybe a branch went through it. That's a pretty powerful wind out there and I could see that happening."

"I guess. But if the wind threw a branch through the window, wouldn't it be here on the floor somewhere?"

"Yes." Hunter shines the light around the basement.

"Well then," Alex asks, "where is it?"

41: Secrets in the attic

Julie motions for Carly and Oliver to wait. She approaches the attic door. "We keep it locked now that there are little kids in the house again. We don't want curious little explorers to get up there and hurt themselves."

"I can't imagine the girls ever going up there, Mom," Carly says. "They'd be too afraid of that dark, scary place."

"You'd be surprised what little kids will do." Julie smiles. "I seem to remember one curious and very active little girl getting herself into a whole heap of trouble by going into places she wasn't supposed to go."

"I can't imagine who you're talking about," Carly says with a grin. "I was your sweet little angel."

"Sweet? Yes. Angel? Not so much."

"Come on, Mom." Carly rolls her eyes. "Don't give away all my secrets."

"Speaking of secrets"—Julie stretches on her tiptoes and runs her hand along the right side of the door casing—"the key to this door is right...wait a minute." She feels her heart sink into her belly. "It's not here."

"Maybe you put it someplace else?" Oliver says.

Julie shakes her head. "No, I'm sure I hung it back up there on the hook after I brought up the last of the Christmas decorations and put them away."

"Who else knows about the key?" Oliver asks.

"Just me and Cliff."

"And me. I know about it," Carly says. "And—"

"Come to think of it, so does your husband." Julie cuts off her daughter. "He and I were up here last week when he helped me bring down the girls' Christmas presents from Santa. He saw where I hid the key."

She presses the latch and watches the door swing open. She turns to Carly. "Do you suppose this is where Leo's been hiding?"

"I would never have thought about checking the attic," Carly says. "But I guess it's starting to look that way."

"What would Leo be doing up there?" Oliver asks.

Julie shakes her head. "Honestly, there's nothing to do up there."

Oliver knows about Alex's vision, and he knows about Alex's abilities better than anyone. If, as Julie has told him, Alex has seen something horrific, he's inclined to believe him.

"Julie," he says, "I think you and Carly should stay down here for now. I'll go up first and check on Leo. He may not even be up there, but if he is and he's not in a good mood, having a crowd suddenly show up to confront him may not be such a smart move."

"I don't think so, Oliver." Carly tires to push past her mother and Oliver. "He is my husband. I should be the one to talk to him."

Oliver takes a position in front of the doorway. "Think about it, Carly. If Leo's upset over something between you and him, then I don't think it's such a good idea that you go up. If he's really angry at you, there's no telling what he might do, especially if he's been drinking."

"Which he has been." Julie takes her daughter by the shoulders. "Listen to him, Carly. I know you are worried about Leo, but I think Oliver is right about this. You said yourself that sometimes Leo loses control when he's drinking. If he's in one of those states, I don't want him flying into you. God only knows what he might do."

"But he's hurting, Mom," Carly cries. "He's done some bad things, but I still want what's best for him. I hate to see him suffering."

"I know, honey." Julie pulls her daughter close and hugs her tightly. "Okay, Oliver. Go ahead and see what's going on with him, if he's even there. Once you tell us the coast is clear, we'll come up."

Oliver cautiously takes the stairs one at a time, bracing for what he may find up in the attic. Julie has told him about Alex's vision and if there's one thing he has come to appreciate in recent months, it's the powers that this extraordinary young man seems to possess.

"Leo?" He keeps his voice low and suppresses the feeling that's building in his gut. "You don't know me all that well, but I'm Oliver Lewis. We've met several times, and I ran into you earlier at the bar. Remember?"

There is only silence from the attic. The wind howls outside, reminding Oliver of the monster storm that's churning around the house.

"We chatted about your love for expensive Scotch, and I told you I was more of a beer man myself. You laughed when I told you that I didn't care much for the taste of Scotch." His anxiety level rises. "I said it reminded me of perfume."

He slowly climbs the stairs, his eyes darting back and forth in the narrow beam of light that his phone-flashlight is throwing in front of him.

"Are you okay Leo?" he calls again. "Are you up here?"

Past experiences have taught him that if you rush someone who is in emotional distress, the situation can quickly escalate and, the next thing you know, you've got a lot of trouble on your hands. *And I don't want any trouble right now.*

He finds the complete silence from the upper level more than a little disconcerting. Reaching the top floor, he takes a deep breath, holds it for a few seconds and then exhales. *I don't like this. Something doesn't feel right here.*

He shines his light around the attic. "If something is wrong, Leo, let's just talk about it. Carly is down there, and she is really worried about you. She just wants to know that you're doing okay."

He swallows, feeling the spit go directly to the pit of his stomach. His head swims with thoughts he'd rather not entertain. Oliver moves slowly around the attic looking for any sign that the young man is up here. "I just want to—"

In an instant, he feels his heart stop. His light falls on a lifeless body hanging at the end of a yellow rope that's tied to a rafter.

Oliver takes a step back as the breath catches in his throat. He struggles to maintain his balance. "Holy shit."

He knows he's just found Leo.

He grabs the lifeless body around the waist and lifts the dead weight in hopes of relieving the tension on the man's throat. "God-damn it, Leo. What the fuck have you done?"

He's positive Leo isn't breathing.

"Oliver?" Julie says. She has come about halfway up the stairs. "Did you find Leo?"

"Don't come any further."

"Why? What's wrong?" Her words are filled with fear and apprehension.

"I need you to go and get Charlie," Oliver says.

Julie advances further up the stairs. "Did you find Leo or not?"

"I did." Oliver is reluctant to tell her too much. "Listen to me, Julie. Get Charlie or ask Carly to go and get him."

"Oh my God, Oliver," she cries. "What's happened? What's going on up there?"

Oliver understands human emotions and knows that Julie will be persistent. "Leo needs a doctor right away."

42: Dark games

"Help me get him down from here and lay him on the floor so I can get a better look at him." Dr. Charlie Webster grabs onto the body to relieve some of his friend's burden.

Oliver has been holding onto the lifeless man since he asked Julie to get the doctor. He has been trying to keep the man's airway unobstructed, but it has been a challenge. Even though Leo Watkins is not a large man, Oliver has struggled as the body has been deadweight.

"Is he dead?" he asks.

"I'm not sure." Charlie cuts the rope and grabs the man's legs. "But it doesn't look good for him."

Oliver holds the lifeless man under the shoulders to bear most of the weight as he and Charlie manoeuvre the body. "That's what I'm afraid of."

Charlie asks, "Do you think this was intentional?"

"I don't know. I just found him hanging here a few minutes ago. I tried to bring him around, but he was unresponsive. I couldn't hear any breathing so I'm really worried."

"If he's dead, we shouldn't disturb the body until the police have done their investigation, but I need to be sure. I'll deal with any blowback. Just focus the light on his chest."

Oliver follows his friend's instructions.

Charlie takes Leo's wrist. "This isn't good." He grimaces. "He's not breathing, and I can't find a pulse."

"So, he's dead?"

Charlie places his hand on Leo's chest. "I think it's too late. His body has already gone cold."

Oliver keeps his voice to a whisper. "This is going to destroy Carly. I have no idea what was going between them, but I don't think things were going well in their marriage."

"I think you're right about that. It's really sad to see people so young fall apart like this." Charlie pauses. "We need to get this body to the hospital as quickly as possible. They'll need to do a full examination to determine a cause of death."

"Did you happen to notice that his pants are open?"

"What?" Oliver is shocked by the question. "Not to sound too flippant, Charlie, but I was too busy trying to keep the man alive to look at his crotch. Is that important?"

"Could be." Charlie shrugs. He shines his light around the attic as if searching for something.

"Are you saying he was up here jacking off as he died? And what are you looking for?"

"Oh, my friend, it happens more than you know." Charlie chooses his words carefully. "It's a real thing." He pauses. "And to answer your question, I'm looking for a pill bottle."

"No way." Oliver isn't a prude, but he still finds the idea repugnant. He joins the search. "You mean like one of those brown bottles that your prescriptions come in?"

"Yes way. It's called auto asphyxiation or auto-erotic asphyxiation. We see it more often than we care to. Think about it. If he came up here to kill himself, why would his pants be open to expose his manhood? And yes. One of those prescription bottles."

Oliver is shocked by this information. "Does it mean he got his jollies by jacking off while he's choking to death?"

"I don't want to be crude," Charlie answers, "but yes, that's exactly what happens. For those who engage in that type of sexual activity, it gives them a certain level of euphoria when the air finally returns to the lungs after someone has literally been chocking the life out of them. For the ultimate gratification, the key is to push it to the very last second, and sometimes, people take it too far. That's when we see problems like this."

"Who would do that?"

"A lot of people do it. More than you would think, but it's not recommended that you do it alone. It's very dangerous, so if you are excited by these games, you should always do it with an experienced partner. Even then, though, people still get hurt and some of them die. When you try to do it alone, there is no safety net. It's even more risky when you add drugs and alcohol to the mix."

"Jesus. So, that's why you're looking for a pill bottle?"

"Precisely."

Oliver shakes his head. "It's a weird freaking world out there." He looks at the dead man lying on the floorboards, his manhood on full display. "So, this could have been an accident?"

"Don't know, but maybe. But from what I understand, he was pretty drunk, and because I don't know his sexual practices, I can't really say for sure. Maybe it was an accident, maybe it wasn't. That's best left for the authorities to figure out. I would just like to get him out of here so there can be a proper examination, and I'm sure the police will want an autopsy."

Oliver nods. "It will be harder on the family the longer the body remains here."

He scans his light around the area where he found the body hanging. "There." He points toward a brown plastic bottle.

"I don't want to involve Cliff, since we're talking about his son-in-law, but maybe Warren can help us," Charlie suggests. "Can you see if you can find him?"

Oliver nods. "Are you going to be okay here by yourself while I go to get him?" He motions toward the bottle. "What kind of medication is that?"

"I'll go down to where Anna and Julie are talking to Carly," Charlie says. "I will close the door so that no one can get up here. It's best not to disturb the scene any more than we already did. The police will have to do their investigation before anyone else can come up here."

He bends down to examine the label on the bottle without touching it. "This may explain a lot of things, Oliver. It's a prescription for Leo Watkins. It's Paroxetine."

"What is that?"

"It's an antidepressant and it can make you hypersexual. It's a pretty powerful medication and, mixed with alcohol it could throw you into a major tailspin."

"So, this could be the reason he was looking for sexual release."

Charlie nods. "Could be, but we definitely need an autopsy to see if he ingested any of this stuff and if so, how much he took."

"Okay, Charlie." Oliver pauses at the head of the stairs. "This is really weird, isn't it?"

"It is. But you and I both know that we should never be surprised when anything weird happens in this town."

"I suppose." Oliver becomes pensive. "I can't quite put my finger on it, but something just seems off to me."

"How so?"

"Don't know." He shakes his head. "Just off. Like something major is brewing."

Charlie sighs. "So it's not just me. I've been feeling that way all evening. In fact, when we got here, I noticed someone lurking around the garage. I told Cliff about it, and he went and checked it out. I never heard anything from him about it, so I assumed everything was okay."

"You don't suppose this could be related to that, do you?" Oliver poses the question, not really wanting an answer.

Charlie shrugs. "But you and I both know anything is possible. Are you thinking someone may have killed Leo? Is that even another option?"

"In this town, Charlie?" Oliver looks directly into his friend's face. "Come on. You know the answer to that question even before you ask it."

"True enough." Charlie shivers. "You better go find Warren. We need to lock this down as quickly as possible."

~

Julie knows there is no consoling her daughter. Instead, she embraces her tightly. "Don't hold back, honey," she whispers into her daughter's ear. "When you're hurting like this, it's better just to let it out."

Carly sobs. "Why would Leo do something like this?"

"I don't know. Maybe it was an accident."

"How could you accidentally hang yourself?"

"There's nothing to suggest that Leo was suicidal, was there? We don't know what really happened, so let's not jump to conclusions."

"Your mother is right, Carly." Dr. Anna Robbie had accompanied Dr. Charlie Webster upstairs when Oliver asked for him, in case she was needed. "Accidents like this happen more than you would think."

Carly sniffs back her tears, pulls away from her mother and turns to face the doctor. "How could anyone accidentally hang himself?"

Anna looks to Julie for support. "Do you think your daughter can handle the truth?"

"I guess that depends on what the truth is." Julie holds Carly tightly, refusing to let her go as she fears if Carly has the chance, she will bolt up to the attic.

"I can't really say for sure what happened to your husband, Carly." Anna says. "But suicide by hanging is only one option."

Carly throws her head back. "Now you think someone dragged him up in the attic and hanged him? That is really the stupidest thing I've heard in a while. Leo would have fought back, and we would have heard something."

"I'm not saying that, either." Anna remains calm and speaks softly.

"Well, then, what *are* you saying?" Carly shoots back.

"Come on, sweetheart." Julie strokes the loose strands of fly-away hair from her daughter's face. "Let Dr. Robbie speak."

"Sorry, Dr. Robbie." Carly struggles to maintain her composure. "I don't mean to take this out on you but it's just too much to deal with. And I've got to check on my babies. They don't need to see or hear any of this."

"It's okay," Julie says. "Lisa took the girls downstairs. They are in front of the fire with Ally and Bree and the other kids. I promise that they are fine."

"Okay, Mom." Carly turns to Anna. "Could it have been an accident?"

"I might be in a better position to answer that if you don't mind answering a question from me. But I must warn you, it is a very personal question?"

"How personal?" Carly squints her eyes.

"About your sex life."

Carly plants her head into her mother's shoulder and sobs.

"Just take a deep breath." Julie slowly rubs her hands over her daughter's back. "You can tell Anna whatever it is. It won't go any further. We can trust her, and no one is going to judge you, I promise."

"It was awful, Mom," Carly cries. "He wanted me to do some terrible things that I wasn't into, and when I wouldn't do them, he would get mad at me, and sometimes he'd hurt me. I hated him for that. I loved him so much in the beginning, but he drove me away."

"Sweetheart, I'm so sorry you had to go through all of that." Julie struggles to make sense out of what her daughter has just said. "I had no idea."

"You wouldn't." Anna directs her comments at Carly. "The thing about sexual deviants is that they know how to keep a secret, and it sounds to me like Leo knew what he was doing."

"He only got into the weird stuff about three years ago, right after Cassie was born." Carly sniffs back her tears. "He wasn't like that when we first got married or I would have never stayed with him. It was awful. I hated every minute of it, and I didn't do much of it with him. I refused him as much as possible. It made me sick when he tried to force me to do that weird stuff."

"Did he cheat on you?" Anna asks.

Carly nods slowly. "Is that important?"

"Perhaps." Anna smiles gently. "His penchant for deviant sexual pleasure may be the reason he cheated on you."

Silence grips the upstairs of the Graham house as, outside, the wind-driven snow pelts the structure, reminding everyone of the blizzard that keeps them trapped here.

"So maybe it wasn't me?" Carly finally whispers.

"God no." Anna's tone becomes stern yet comforting. "This is all on Leo. In all likelihood, he was playing his games with other people long before you ever found out."

"This is so twisted." Julie takes Carly by the hand and guides her to a nearby bedroom. "Thank you for your help, Dr. Robbie, but I think my daughter has had enough to deal with for one night. She needs to rest now."

Anna nods. "I understand. No offence taken."

"Just a second, Mom. There's something I need to know." Carly stands firm and faces the doctor. "Are you saying that Leo could have accidentally killed himself while he was engaged in one of his weird sexual fetishes?"

"Yes, Carly. That's exactly what I'm saying."

43: The protectors

How on earth can so many bad things happen in one night? Constable Warren Hamilton wonders as he dials the backdoor number to the local RCMP detachment.

A massive storm that cripples everything. No power. Stalkers. Intruders. Vandalism. And now an apparent suicide or something maybe even worse, he thinks. *I don't even want to go there.*

"Hello. You've reached the Liverpool RCMP. Constable Shaw here. How can I help you?"

"Nolan?" Warren quickly replies. "It's Warren. I need your help."

"I was just going to call you."

"You were? Why?"

"I have some news for you about that young woman you were looking for," the constable answers.

"Gwen Pittmann?"

"That's the one. A member from the Oakville detachment called to tell us they had located her. I thought you would want to know that she's dead."

"What? Did they say what happened to her?"

"Apparently, she died of an overdose, at a known drug house. She had no identification on her, but when they ran her prints, they learned her identity and that we had issued a bulletin about her."

Warren is shocked. "Guess we don't have to worry about her anymore."

"So, what can I do for you, Warren?"

"Are any of the roads opened yet?"

"No, sir. The latest I've heard is that we shouldn't expect any traffic to be moving until morning at the earliest," the constable explains. "They aren't letting the plows back on the roads until daybreak because the visibility is so poor right now. Why? Do you need something?"

"I need everything," Warren says. "It's extremely urgent. I need an ambulance, the fire department and some of you guys to get out to Corporal Cliff Graham's place as fast as you can."

"I'll call dispatch, but honestly, sir, I wouldn't expect them anytime soon. Are you going to be okay if we can't get to you right away?"

"I'm not worried about me," Warren tells the rookie. "We have already had one death, and there's someone lurking around the property, causing extensive damage. I am afraid this is going to escalate."

"What happened that someone died?"

"That's still to be determined."

"Are you in danger?"

"I think we are all in danger."

"Okay, Warren," Nolan says. "Stand by and I'll call you back."

"Thanks." Warren terminates the call. He knows he shouldn't blame the young officer, as Nolan is only following orders, but he's frustrated and angry at being stranded out here with only himself and Cliff to handle whatever is happening.

He heads to the basement to help Cliff cover up the broken window. Warren can't shake the feeling that all of the people in this house—including his family—are potential targets. He feels helpless to protect them.

~

"Any luck?" Cliff asks as Warren appears. "Are they sending anyone?"

"We shouldn't expect them right away." Warren's answer is blunt. "But they'll try to get someone mobilized as quickly as they can." He exhales. "Probably not before daybreak."

"May be too late."

"That's what I'm afraid of." Warren understands it's impossible to mount an effective defence when they don't know their adversary or what is motivating them. "How are you making out with the window?"

"I've found some plywood that I had stuck down here when I was fixing the wood box. It should do the trick." Cliff slides a piece of plywood over a portion of the shattered window. "Just hold it right here while I screw it into place."

"Got it. I did find out some interesting news."

"Oh yeah?" Cliff sinks the first screw into place.

"The Oakville detachment is reporting that the Pittmann girl is dead."

"What?" Cliff stops the screwdriver. "Seriously?"

"Drug overdose."

"Frig." Cliff sighs and starts the screwdriver again. "I guess that rules her out as our lurker. We have to tell Samantha and Kate. They'll be shocked, for sure, but I'm guessing they will also be relieved. The idea of that girl showing up here really had them freaked out."

"Were you really thinking it could have been her?"

"Actually, I was. And I wish it had been her, because at least we would have known who we're dealing with. But now we have no idea who is responsible for all of this or what they want from us."

"And by all of this, you mean this broken window, too?"

Cliff nods and sinks the next screw into the plywood, sealing it tightly against the window casing. "If the wind had thrown something through the glass, I would have found it in here, but there's nothing."

"What are we going to do, Cliff? I feel like we're trapped."

Cliff nods. "But let's not panic. Whoever is doing this will show themselves eventually and we'll just have to be ready for them when they do."

"Pass me that other piece of plywood and we'll finish up here."

"Then what?"

"Then I've got to go up and check on Carly." Cliff pauses. "I know Julie is with her and the doctors have spoken to her, but I need to be with her right now. I'm really worried about what all of this going to do to her."

"There's not a whole lot you can do right now, is there?"

"Not really," Cliff agrees. "But I just want to be with her. This is going to hit her hard. She'll blame herself."

"I'm sure it will."

"So, you checked out the attic?" Cliff looks at his friend. "Could someone have killed Leo?"

"I was up and had a look around," Warren says. "But I couldn't see anything that looked suspicious to me. I suppose it is possible that someone could have killed him and hung him up to make it look like a suicide or something else, but we'll need an autopsy and a more detailed investigation to determine that."

"Well, if the guys ever get here, they can do that."

"Yes, they can," Warren agrees. "But is it even remotely possible that someone could have gotten into your house and done such a thing with all the people around? I'm sure someone would have heard or seen something."

"It's a stretch to imagine something like that," Cliff concedes. "But you and I both know that nothing is impossible. Take this window, for example. Did someone gain access to the house through it? Why else would they break the window?"

"I guess we can't rule anything out, can we?"

Cliff shakes his head. "First rule of police work—always keep an open mind. Second rule of police—consider all the options."

"Third rule of police work," Warren adds. "Stay alive."

"That's the most important rule of them all."

Cliff slides the second piece of plywood over the broken window. He's about to secure it into place when he glances outside.

"Son of a bitch."

Warren takes a position beside his friend and peers out into the driving snow. "What do you see out there?"

Cliff motions towards the garage. "Somebody is standing right over there, looking at the house."

"Do you think they see us?"

Cliff nods. "If I can see them, then I'm sure they can see us."

"Fuck," Warren says under his breath. His senses are firing on all cylinders.

"I've got to find out who that is."

"If you go out there, they are only going to run away again. You'll never catch them in this deep snow."

"I know, but I have to do something."

"No, I don't think you do."

"What do you mean?"

Warren points to the garage, where a murder of crows has gathered on the roof. "Looks like you have some protectors, my friend. How many do you count?"

"Jesus. I see nine."

Warren nods. "Isn't that the same number of crows that we've been seeing around here all day?"

"It is." Cliff watches the crows as they prance around the garage roof. "What do you suppose they are up to?"

"Better still, how are they even able to survive out there in this goddamned storm?"

"I never question the crows," Cliff says. "I feel they are here for a reason."

"On a mission?"

"Exactly."

They see the nine, large black birds suddenly spring from their perches on the garage roof and take flight. Despite the powerful winds, the crows swoop down and begin an aerial assault against the mysterious prowler.

Cliff and Warren can't hear anything through the roaring winds, but the attack looks brutal to them.

The intruder throws up their arms to fend off the attackers and protect their face, then spins around and darts inside the open garage door to escape the crows' furious attack.

"For fuck's sake." Cliff says through clenched teeth. He then makes a beeline for the basement entrance that leads directly to the backyard.

"Wait Cliff." Warren calls. "Where are you going?"

"Out there."

Cliff quickly throws open the basement door. He's immediately greeted by a blast of icy-cold wind and snow.

"It's not safe. If that stalker doesn't get you, those gas fumes will."

"Got no choice." Cliff pushes through the deep snow. "Those crows may be in trouble."

"The *crows* may be in trouble?" Warren says. "What about you? You don't even have your coat."

44: Deflagration

Cliff approaches the open garage door. His heart pounds. He sucks in the cold air through clenched teeth and coughs. His lungs instantly tighten, rebelling against the ice particles that feel like minuscule daggers as they infiltrate the tender tissue. It hurts to breathe yet he gasps for air.

He hears Julie's voice pounding in his head, cautioning him about venturing into the garage alone. *What are you doing, Cliff Graham? You have no idea who this person is or what they will do if you go storming into that building.*

He knows the voice in his head is right. This could very well be a trap. He's seen what people can do if they feel cornered, but, despite the apprehension, he also feels compelled to investigate. He needs to know the identity of this prowler. More importantly, he needs to know what they want.

He carefully places one foot in front of the other, pushing through the deep banks that are blocking his path. The closer he gets to the garage, the more danger he knows he could face.

The strong smell of gasoline wafts through the air, only to be quickly whisked away by the gusting wind. The fumes are potent enough to make him want to vomit. He knows the danger.

"This is so stupid," he whispers. He's alone, but it makes him feel better to say it loud.

Placing his hand over his mouth and nose, he inches toward the open door. He fights the urge to retch, takes a deep breath and slowly steps into the garage. *Julie would be so disappointed in me. I know I probably should have waited for backup.*

But he isn't even sure if Warren is following him, and who else is there?

He scans the interior of the garage, looking for the prowler, but it's pitch-black inside. "Where are you, you motherfucker?" he calls out. "Show your sorry ass and let's get this over with."

He pauses and listens, but there is no sound.

"He moderates his breathing as best he can. "Suit yourself, you stupid bastard, but do you know how dangerous this is? If we cause even one little spark, this whole god-damned building is going to go up in a blaze of glory and kill us both. Is that what you really want?"

He listens but hears only silence.

He feels weaker the deeper he goes into the garage.

"Who the hell are you, anyway?"

He listens again and this time, he's sure he hears movement near the corner where he stores his trusty snowblower. Then the shuffling stops and it becomes eerily quiet again.

Except for the wind howling outside, there is no noise. The silence, as it reverberates in his ears, is deafening. He shivers.

"Who are you?" His eyes quickly dart to the left and then to the right, but the darkness is too thick.

He shudders, thinking it's time to retreat while he can.

Then the prowler's first words cut through the fume-laden air. "You're so smart, Cliff. I'm surprised you haven't figured out who I am."

The soft voice comes from deep within the garage. "You disappoint me. I thought you were smarter than that. Clearly, I gave you way too much credit."

He's sure he's heard this voice somewhere before, but his mind refuses to cooperate, and he can't form a clear picture. He's lost in a haze, most likely the effects of the gas fumes that cling to him like a wet blanket.

Or maybe it's fear of the unknown.

"Have we met before?" Cliff tries hard not to show that he's feeling ill.

"Yes, Cliff, we have met before." The intruder's words are not helping him to regain his memory. "Many times, in fact, but it was a long time ago. It wasn't pleasant for either of us. But you're getting old, Cliff. It's clear you've lost your edge and your memory is getting cloudy."

Cliff pauses. *A long time ago? Who in hell is this?*

"Exactly how long ago?" He inches slowly toward the corner where he believes the intruder is. "*How* did we meet?"

"You were still an active police officer, when we met for the first time," the voice says. "You hadn't become soft and pudgy. You still had an edge."

"Did I arrest you?" His words feel forced as his breathing becomes laboured.

"No. But you wanted to."

Cliff's confusion grows. "For what reason?"

"If I told you that, Cliff, you would know all my secrets. I want you to figure this out all on your own. You are the great Corporal Cliff Graham, after all. You should be able to get this without any help from me."

Cliff plants his feet on the cement floor, his head swimming. "If you want something from me, let's go back to the house and talk." He knows how stupid the idea sounds as soon as the words leave his mouth. "You don't have to sneak around, scaring the shit out of everyone. If I can help you in some way, just ask."

"Oh, I know how helpful you can be, Cliff Graham. You were so helpful to the Goodwins that you drove me out of town."

"The Goodwins?" This statement stuns Cliff. "What do they have to do with this?"

"Everything. They are the reason I came to this town in the first place, and they are the reason I ran away." The prowler's voice grows more intense. "They are also the reason I came back, after all of these years."

"I don't understand," Cliff says. His head is pounding.

"You will soon enough."

Silence, except for the sounds of the wind howling outside the building, fills the garage again. Cliff feels as if he's about to become unglued. His mind races and his body tingles with apprehension.

"Are you still here?" Cliff gasps for air.

He hears movement, like shuffling. Whoever this prowler is, they are now very close to him. He can sense them, but it's too dark to see anything.

"What do you want?" His voice is raspy. His throat is so dry it hurts to speak.

"I want everything that is owed to me, and I want you to help me get it."

These words leave him even more confused.

"Who owes you what?"

"Maybe you aren't as smart and crafty as I've always thought you were."

Cliff peers into the darkness. "These fucking games are getting old. Just tell me what you want and let's get out of here before we both die."

"Oh Cliff. Where's the man I remember? The man with the piss running through his veins and the fire burning in his gut, the grit in his teeth. The man who kicked the ass of every sleazy asshole who crossed the line. Where is he, Cliff? What have you done with him?"

His head is spinning, and eyes are burning. Cliff decides he has no choice but to get out of this building right now.

As he takes a step backwards, the stranger taunts, "Going somewhere Cliff? We're just getting started. I was just about to jog your memory, because clearly your ole noggin's getting a little rusty."

"Just tell me who the fuck you are and what the hell you want from me."

"Okay, but you have to promise me one thing."

"What's that?"

"Promise that you will help me get what belongs to me."

"I can't promise that, because have no idea what you want."

"You will help me, or I will destroy you and everyone inside your house."

The threat causes Cliff to pause. His heart beats faster as if it wants to pop out of his chest.

The prowler continues, "All those people who are important to you. Your family. Your friends. I never had the chance for any of that because you drove me away. That wasn't the plan, you know."

"What plan?"

"Just promise me that you will help me get what is rightfully mine."

"I cannot promise you anything if I don't know what you want."

"I'll get to that, but first, I want to tell you a little story."

"For Christ's sake." Cliff feels the room spinning. "Just tell me what you want."

"Life has been cruel to me, Cliff, since the day I was born. I've struggled for my crappy existence since my druggie mother gave birth to me. I clung to the hope that, someday, I would be free of the hell that I've suffered. I've been abused, raped, used as a punching bag, forced to scrounge for food, been homeless, hid in the shadows."

Cliff knows this person is near ready to snap.

"There is no way that boy should have everything while I have nothing."

Cliff can sense that the intruder is now close to him. "What boy?"

"When I tell you who I am, you will immediately understand everything."

The voice is hardly a whisper now and it's very close to him. But he finally has a clue. "Are you the woman who was watching me in the liquor store?"

"I am."

"Did you follow me home?"

"I did."

"Were you lurking around here all day?"

"Yes. I was looking for information about him, and I know you have it."

"About who?"

"About my nephew, Alex Goodwin. Maybe now he goes by Webster or Henderson. I heard they adopted him."

"Alex?" Cliff feels like someone has hit him in the face with a two-by-four and then smacked him over the head with an iron pipe for good measure.

"What the fuck?" he stutters. "Are you—"

"Yes, Cliff." The woman almost sounds excited. "I am Maggie Collins."

Cliff is stunned. "There's no god-damned way you're Maggie Collins. I thought you were dead."

"Everyone in this town thought I was dead, and for all intents and purposes, I *was* dead, except I wasn't. In fact, my half-brother, Josh Goodwin —who is also my nephew—helped me get away from you. We knew you were close to charging me for the murder of my grandfather, the sick son of a bitch who was also my father. You also blamed me for the deaths of my uncles, but Josh and I figured out a way for me to escape. I have been laying low ever since."

Cliff can't believe what he's hearing. The Goodwin-Collins case is the one file that he could not close before his retirement. It has haunted him all these years, gnawed at him like a cancer.

Her voice is nothing more than a whisper. "I imagine you feel pretty sick right about now. Your stomach is twisted into knots, isn't it?"

He struggles to maintain his footing. "What do you want?"

"I want what is rightfully mine. When Josh helped me get away from here, he took care of me because I couldn't get a job, as we feared you could track me that way."

She moves closer to him. "In order for me to avoid detection, there could be no trace of me anywhere, so it was necessary for me to completely vanish. Josh had provided well for me, and I managed to survive off the money he gave me, even after he died. But that's all gone now, and I've come to claim the rest of my inheritance."

Cliff shakes his head. "What makes you think you deserve anything? You killed people. You are a murderer and should have been rotting in prison."

"Yes, I killed people, but they all deserved it."

"Maybe they did and maybe they didn't." Cliff digs deep and fires back. "But you acted as the judge, jury and executioner. You don't deserve any reward for that. You got what was coming to you. How can you expect to receive any type of reward for that?"

"When the old man died, Josh got everything," she says. "I know it was a considerable fortune. After Josh died, Alex inherited it all, but a good chunk of that money belongs to me. I've come to collect it, one way or the other."

"I don't know anything about that." Cliff's head is swimming. "I don't see how any of that is connected to me or why I should help you."

"You are my leverage. You can help me force Samantha and Kate to give me what's rightfully mine." The woman is close to him. He can feel her presence. "Josh told me Sam and Kate had gotten married. Interesting that Samantha Henderson was the first person I met when I arrived in this town, all these years ago. I liked her a lot."

Cliff nods. "You had everyone fooled with your sweet, lost girl routine. But I could see through your mask. I knew you were cunning and devious and dangerous. But I didn't fall for your act."

"Ah, yes. The intuitive Corporal Graham. The great detective. You were a worthy adversary back then. Because of your interference, I had to run away and hide. You just couldn't leave well enough alone, so now, the way I see it, you owe me."

"You're deranged if you think I will help you." Cliff grits his teeth. "I don't care how you see it, but I don't owe you a god-damned thing. You are a murderer and everything you've done here today just proves to me that you have no remorse or guilt." He turns to leave. "Why would you think that I would side with you? Why do you think I can help you get what you think you deserve?"

"Because people respect you and will listen to you, and because I'm desperate, Cliff. And when desperate people are down and out, they do desperate things." The woman pauses. "If you don't help me to get my money, then I'll kill your family. I'll pick them off one by one."

"You leave my family out of this." Cliff snaps. "You even think about coming after my family and I'll end you."

"Now, Cliff, who's the one threatening who? There is a better way. All you have to do is agree to help me."

Cliff feels the panic level rise in the pit of his gut. "Why didn't you just come and ask for my help?" he stutters, knowing how stupid that sounds as soon as the words leave his mouth.

"Yeah, right," the woman scoffs. "I can just see it now. Me, an accused murderer showing up at the front door of a highly respected cop and asking you to help me get a bunch of money from your friends. That would have gone over well."

"Fair point." Cliff shrugs. "But following me around all day and scaring the shit out of me is no way to get my help. And neither is threatening my family."

"That money belongs to me. I had to do something to get your atten‑tion."

"Oh, you got my attention, all right, and you're going to pay for what you've done."

"I've already paid a high price, and now, so will you."

He feels something suddenly grab him from out of the darkness. He's not sure if it's the woman, but he instinctively jerks his arm away.

"I'm out of here. These gas fumes could explode at any second."

"I'm not leaving," the woman says. "And neither are you."

As the flames suddenly flash around him, Cliff knows it's too late to run.

45: A week later

Julie is relieved when she opens the front door and discovers Warren has finally arrived. Since being released from the hospital two days ago, Cliff has been withdrawn and evasive with her. He doesn't talk much and hardly eats, which isn't at all like him. She's worried and hopes that a visit from Warren will bring him around.

"Oh, God, Warren, I am so happy to see you." She fights to contain the emotions that have gripped her body. "Come in, please. Cliff is in the den. That's pretty much the only place he goes, there and to bed. I have never seen him behave like this. He just sits in that chair, all day, or stands in front of the window, staring out at where the garage was."

"That bad, huh?" Warren stomps the snow from his boots and steps into the entryway.

"I keep telling him that he can replace the building and the things he lost in the explosion, but it's like he's trapped inside his own head." The quiver in her voice underscores the worry she has for her husband. "I was hoping that when he got home from the hospital, he might improve, but I think seeing where the fire took place has made him even worse. His physical injuries may have healed but clearly his mind is still hurting."

She closes the door behind Warren. "Anna says that when people suffer from a major trauma, like he did, they must recover at their own pace, and the worst thing I can do is try to force Cliff to talk about it, so mostly, I just let him be. But it's killing me that I can't find some way to help him."

"That's not like Cliff," Warren says. "Although I can understand why he's having such a hard time. The whole thing was pretty creepy. It would be hard on anyone's head."

"But the garage is only one thing. He's also worried about Carly and the girls. I wanted them to stay, but they've gone back to Halifax to be with friends. I understand that it was too hard for them to stay here. They are going through a lot with Leo's death, even though we still don't know what really happened with him. And then there's this house. Are *we* going to stay or not? I mean, someone did just die here and others could have died. It's a lot to take in."

"That Maggie Collins did quite a number on Cliff." Warren removes his heavy, uniform snow boots. "I would have gotten here earlier today, but I was on the phone all morning."

"Any news on the investigation?"

"It's like pulling teeth from a horse, but I have a little news." Warren slips out of his heavy RCMP winter coat and places it on a bench near the door. "That's why I need to talk to Cliff. Maybe the information I have will bring him around some."

"I hope so." Julie leads Warren toward the den. "I'm really worried about him, Warren. I have never seen Cliff in a state like this."

"If I know Cliff, he thinks he failed everyone and he feels responsible, in some way," Warren says. "He needs to understand that there was nothing he could do. That woman was bat-shit crazy and hell-bent on hurting someone. For some reason, she focused her delusions on Cliff and he ended up in her crosshairs. It's clear she blamed him for all her problems."

"And he almost died because of it."

Warren nods.

"I should just be thankful. It could have been so much worse." Julie struggles to keep her tears under control. "The fire investigators told me that he was lucky you pulled him outside before the garage exploded. He would have died, but for you."

Warren shakes his head. "That's just the thing, Julie. I didn't pull him out of the garage. I found him lying face down, unconscious, in a pile of snow. I don't know who pulled him out of the fire, but it wasn't me."

"He says he remembers someone pulling him out and after that everything else is a blank, until he woke up in the hospital the next day. We assumed it was you."

"Was it someone or some*thing*?"

"What do you mean?"

"I really don't know." Warren pauses. "While I didn't see anyone around the garage when I got there, I did see a bunch of crows. There were nine."

Julie is shocked. "You've kept this to yourself for a whole week? Why?"

"Cliff was having such a difficult time that I didn't want to make it worse for him." He grimaces. "But do you think I should tell him about the crows now? I know he gets worked up when the crows are around and I'm not sure how he will react to think they may have been involved."

She nods. "I think you should. He'll be mad if you keep it from him any longer."

"Okay," Warren agrees. "I better get in there. I know he saw me come up the walkway because I saw him through the window, so he's probably wondering what happened to me."

~

Inside the den, Warren finds Cliff still standing in front of the large picture window. This gives him an unobscured view of the charred remains of the garage, the building that was once his sanctuary. The contrasting black and white of the burned wood and the clean, fresh layer of snow that fell the previous night, are a stark reminder of his brush with death just one week ago.

"Hey, Cliff." Warren tries to remain chipper. He takes a seat on the corner of the sofa that's closest to the window. "How are you feeling?"

Cliff says nothing. Back to his friend, he stares quietly at the ruins.

"I have some information on the investigation, if you are up for it. Why don't you come and sit down so we can talk about it?"

Cliff sighs but remains staring out the window.

"Okay, then. I guess I will do the talking and you can just listen." Warren shrugs. "That woman covered her tracks very well. It's like this Maggie Collins was a ghost. There's hardly a trace of her anywhere, but we have been digging and we've made a little head way."

"How could she disappear for all these years?" Cliff's voice is but a whisper.

"We know it can be done." Warren hates to see his friend in this condition. He's never seen Cliff looking so distraught, so vulnerable. "You know, Cliff, none of this is your fault."

Cliff remains quiet, back still turned to him.

Warren takes a deep breath. He is determined to break through. "Remember that red Kia that I found abandoned out on the highway on New Year's Eve?"

It's ever so slight, but he sees Cliff nod and he'll take the non-verbal cue as a sign to continue.

"It's looking more and more like this Ms. Collins drove it here. Sergeant Earl Boone says the Houston PD has launched an investigation, and he believes that she may have been hiding out in their city for years."

"Why Texas?"

"Could be just because it's a long way from this town," Warren suggests. "No one ever thought of looking for her in Texas. Why would they? And if Josh Goodwin was fully paying her way, she could just lay low."

Cliff takes a deep breath and slowly exhales.

"Sergeant Boone thinks that maybe Ms. Collins was responsible for some of the unsolved robberies and break-ins that took place down there over the years. There's also an unsolved homicide that they're thinking she may be connected to. He's looking into that."

Silence fills the room and Warren understands why Julie is worried about her husband. "Are you okay Cliff? I'm worried about you, my friend. Is there anything I can do for you?"

He sees Cliff shake his head. "Anything else?"

"The ME has completed the autopsy on the woman's body."

"And?"

Warren swallows. "Her body was literally torn apart from the blast. They still aren't sure how the fire started, though. Did she start it on purpose or was it an accident?"

Warren had hoped Cliff might have some information on that, but instead Cliff has a different idea. "So the gas fumes didn't kill her?"

"She was wearing a mask. Not an expensive one, but it was good enough to do the job."

When Cliff doesn't respond, Warren continues. "Wonder where she would have gotten something like that? It would be a strange thing to carry around with you unless you were planning on dumping gallons of gasoline around someone's garage, but I figured that was a spur-of-the-moment thing to get your attention."

"She probably found it in the garage. There were some four-ply disposable ones on my workbench."

"Well, then that explains it." Warren welcomes the information. "Mystery solved."

Awkward silence fills the room again until Cliff speaks. "Anything else?"

"Not yet, but this investigation is far from over." Warren is reluctant to bring up the crows. but he feels it's important to talk about everything related to the case, so he rolls with it. "There is one more thing that I want to talk to you about."

"What's that?"

"Have you remembered anything about how you got out of the garage that night?"

Cliff shakes his head. "I saw the flames and then..." He pauses and stares out the window.

"And then what?"

"Next thing I knew, I was in the hospital."

"I might have an idea." Warren hesitates.

Cliff finally turns to face his friend. "Tell me."

Warren tries to stifle his surprise, but his loud gasp betrays his true feelings. While Cliff is usually a physically imposing man, now he's a shell of his former self. He has lost considerable weight. His complexion is pale and his eyes, with dark circles around them, are sunken and lifeless, as if he hasn't slept in several days.

Warren clears his throat. His voice cracks as he speaks. "Is it possible that the crows could have gotten you out of the garage somehow? I did notice that your sweater was ripped around the shoulders and the more I think about it, it's like something with sharp claws—or talons—had grabbed you and pulled you out. Does that sound far-fetched?"

Cliff glares at him. Warren shudders. He wonders if the idea that the crows could have pulled his friend from the burning garage before it exploded has caused him to snap.

"I counted nine crows hanging around the garage—like they were watching over you—when I got there. You were already outside, in the snow." Warren studies his friend's reaction. "But I have no idea if it means anything. These birds are a mystery to me."

~

Samantha takes a seat on the sofa and smiles at Cliff, who is sitting across from her in a plush armchair. She hasn't seen him since New Year's Eve. If she is taken aback by his appearance, she doesn't show it.

She smiles. "I'm glad Julie suggested I come over. I have been worried about you, my friend."

Cliff smiles. She can tell it's forced.

"We would have come to visit you in the hospital, but, other than your doctors and the police, only family members were allowed." Samantha feels the need to explain her absence. "How are you feeling?"

Cliff stares at her, almost through her. After an extended pause, he sighs. "Lucky to be alive."

Samantha studies her friend, a man she has known for many years. She is not used to seeing him being so aloof or looking so vulnerable. With his stature, Cliff has always been an imposing physical presence in any room, but today he's looking withdrawn, and she can sense that he feels insecure. "I must admit, Cliff, this whole thing with Maggie Collins coming back to town has just about blown my mind wide open. Can you really believe that she did all of this just to get money from Alex? Warren says she blamed you for driving her out of town. What kind of warped mind does that?"

"That's the theory, I guess."

"Well, she didn't deserve anything from Alex, and you were just doing your job all those years ago," Samantha answers, sharply. "Are we sure she's dead?"

Cliff nods.

She shakes her head. "I thought she had died years ago."

"Something saved me from the fire, you know."

"Something?" Samantha eyes her friend. "Why something and not someone?"

"There was no one else there, and by the time Warren got to the garage, I was already lying outside."

"But let me guess." Samantha hesitates. "He saw crows"

Cliff nods. "Nine, to be exact."

"Nine crows for a kiss."

"As in the *kiss of death*?"

"Perhaps." Samantha nods. "We know death followed Maggie Collins. Like I've always told you, Cliff, the crows often deal in riddles. But the idea that it was the kiss of death does seem to fit. It's a good thing there wasn't more death."

"Leo died that night," Cliff says.

"Yes. Sorry for your loss."

"It's no loss to me."

"Has the medical examiner made an official ruling on his cause of death?" Samantha asks.

"Maybe an accidental hanging. I've heard he was into some kind of perverted sexual shit. Or maybe it was even murder. It still isn't clear."

"Do you think Maggie had something to do with his death?"

Cliff shakes his head. "I don't see how, but I wouldn't rule anything out."

Samantha shivers. "It's kind of fitting, in a way, that Maggie Collins came back to this town and died here."

"How?"

"Well, remember when she first came to town? Death came with her, and so did the crows."

"There was that one crow in particular. It seemed to follow her everywhere and it did whatever she wanted."

"And now, she's dead." Samantha nods. "Kind of completes the circle."

"Do you think the crows could have saved me?

"I think it's possible. You did tell me that nine crows had been watching you all that day."

"I did."

"Then yes, I think it's possible. Their actions often defy logic, but they usually come down on the side of good and righteousness."

"I have never considered myself to be a righteous person." Cliff shakes his head. "I am anything but religious."

"Nor am I," Samantha points out. "But no matter what you believe in, God doesn't give us what we can't handle. I think he helps us handle what we are given."

She sees Cliff squint in her direction. "By way of the *crows*?"

"You will have to decide that for yourself, Cliff," she says. "But remember, they do move in mysterious ways."

Epilogue

Where nine crows have previously watched over this flock, ten have taken their place.

From their perches amongst the stately oak trees, where the early leaves of spring are just starting to emerge, the ten black birds watch the funeral proceedings. Their twenty pellet-like eyes blinking in unison, the crows feel the pain these humans are suffering for they, too, have lost loved ones. But they also accept that death is inevitable.

Remaining silent and still, as if frozen in time and space, the crows watch dozens of mourners gather around the open grave, weeping for the departed and waiting for the minister to speak.

"Do you see them?" Alex asks Oliver, who is standing next to him, protecting him and offering him comfort.

"Who?" Oliver whispers, as the service begins.

"Them. Up there." Alex motions toward the trees. "The crows."

Oliver nods.

"There are ten of them."

"I didn't count them."

"Shush," Samantha whispers, leaning close to her son. She throws Oliver a severe look.

Alex glances at her sheepishly. "Sorry, Mom."

He moves closer to Oliver and leans in. He lowers his voice to a light whisper. "Do you know what the appearance of ten crows means?"

Oliver shakes his head.

"It's *ten crows for a time of joyous bliss*," Alex says, quickly looking to his mother to make sure she isn't listening.

"What could that mean?"

"I'm not sure, but I guess we will soon find out."

Oliver glances around at the family and friends who have gathered on this sombre occasion to say farewell to someone they all love.

"A time of joyous bliss?" He considers the verse. "Well, my young friend, I think we could all use some of that right now."

Acknowledgements

I want to start by sending a huge shout-out to my loyal and enthusiastic fans. This series would not be possible without you, so thank you for being supportive throughout this extraordinary journey.

As you can imagine, creating a book is a major undertaking, and while the writing often takes years and is usually done in isolation, there are always numerous people who play key roles in completing the process. It's appropriate, then, to acknowledge a few of those people who helped along the way.

As I've done with previous books, I must extend my deepest and undying gratitude to publisher Brenda J. Thompson and my extraordinarily-talented editor, Andrew Wetmore, for their continued belief in me. They are the driving force behind Moose House Publications, and who knows where these books would be without their support. This has been an incredible journey. Thank you for your guidance throughout the process.

I also wish to extend my gratitude to graphic artist Rebekah Wetmore for the amazing cover design. Capturing the essence of an entire book in one image is no easy assignment, but she delivered a cover so compelling that it is simply stunning. Thank you, Rebekah. You do amazing work.

Another person I must acknowledge is my very talented photographer friend, Amy Grant. Thank you, Amy, for going above and beyond to make me look good.

A heart-felt thank-you goes to the booksellers and bookstore owners for their unwavering support over the years. Those of us who dare to think we can make it as writers would flounder without the support of such outlets. You are a vital piece of the equation, so I applaud you.

I've saved my last and most heart-felt thank-you for my most important supporters, my family, especially my wife, Nancy. She has been my rock through the many years I've been chasing this dream of becoming a published author. She is always the first one to give an insightful word of advice and a gentle criticism when it is needed, and to pick me up when

I'm sad or frustrated. To say I could not have done it without her is an understatement. There are not enough words to say how much I appreciate her.

Stay tuned for *Ten Crows for a Time of Joyous Bliss*, coming soon!

About the author

Vernon Oickle was born and raised in Liverpool, Nova Scotia, where he continues to reside with his wife, Nancy, and their family. Growing up in a small town in rural Nova Scotia, Vernon had always wanted to pursue a career as a newspaper reporter.

After completing high school in 1979, he attended Lethbridge Community College in Alberta. He graduated in 1982 with an honours diploma in Journalism and returned to Liverpool, where he worked at the local weekly newspaper, *The Advance*, for 13 years before becoming the editor of the *Bridgewater Bulletin*. His community newspaper career spanned 33 years.

Vernon is an award-winning journalist and editor, and is the author of 46 books, many of which collect and preserve the heritage and culture of Atlantic Canada. His best-selling books include *Ghost Stories of the Maritimes*, *Ghost Stories of Nova Scotia*, *More Ghost Stories of Nova Scotia*, the *Nova Scotia Outstanding Outhouse Reader*, *South Shore Facts and Folklore*, *Strange Nova Scotia*, *The Bluenosers' Book of Slang*, *Red Sky at Night*, *Forerunners: Harbingers of Death in Nova Scotia* and *Grandma's Home Remedies*.

He also writes fiction in the popular "Crow" series, based on the old Maritime poem *One Crow Sorrow*. In 2024, the seventh book in the series, *Seven Crows for a Secret Yet to be Told*, won an International Impact Book Award, taking first place in the Historical Mystery/Thriller category.

In addition to his long list of newspaper awards, in 2012 Vernon received the Queen Elizabeth II Diamond Jubilee Medal, recognizing his contributions to his community, province and country; and in 2015 he received a Distinguished Alumni Award (Community Leader) from Lethbridge College. He was inducted into the Atlantic Journalism Awards Hall of Fame in the spring of 2020.

As a testimony to his outstanding career, in 2014 the South Queens Middle School in his hometown, Liverpool, announced the creation of the Vernon Oickle Writer's Award, to be given annually to a student who excels in the art of writing, either fiction or non-fiction.